FRIENDS F

Devapriya Roy is the author
*Handbook* (2011) and *The Weight Loss Club* (2013).

In 2015, she published *The Heat and Dust Project*, co-written with Saurav Jha, a travel-memoir based on their journeys around India on a very very tight budget, which debuted at no.1 on the *Hindustan Times*–AC Nielsen list. Over 2016 and 2017, she collaborated with the artist Priya Kuriyan to create *Indira* (2018), the acclaimed graphic biography of Indira Gandhi.

An alumna of Presidency College and Jawaharlal Nehru University, she lives in Delhi with her husband, writer Saurav Jha, and often pines for College Street, Calcutta.

**From the readers of *The Romantics of College Street***

'… [I am] going through the roughest patch in my career just before retirement. And I take great joy in admitting that the brightest spot in my Sunday mornings right now is going through the next chapter of *The Romantics of College Street*. It features very high in my delightful reads category… The subtle and wry wit and humour was exhilarating. Only P.G. Wodehouse and Jerome K. Jerome have made me laugh so much…' —Chandraboli Sen

'I look forward to reading *The Romantics of College Street* every Sunday. I'm so addicted to it that if I don't get time on Sunday, I catch up later (sometimes during working hours by sneaking into the office library)… I admire the manner in which incidents crop up, the exploration of the characters' psychology and their varied nuances…' —Lahari Mahalanabish (Chatterji)

'… I wrote this mail to thank you for creating such an amazing array of characters – be it Pixie, Nimki, Hem, Duma, Aaduri, or Lata, Ronny of course. They will always have a special place in that nook of my mind, where I keep the fictional characters I cherish the most. The novel has unknowingly become a comfort zone for me! … P.S—It will be great if we can have the novel in a book form, you know, because I am already missing them very much ☺. —Meghna Nath

'The characters are so believable and lovable. I like the descriptions of the college life and look forward to experiencing it myself later this year. The plot is wonderful and the cliffhangers that you sprinkle along the way (Lata's marriage to Arjoe) make the story more exciting. Also, the overall simple and lucid style of the story is a plus. I can definitely get a feel of Calcutta in the '90s. If this series comes out as a book, you can bet that I will buy it!' —Subhadip Mukherjee

'[I have found] your narration to be compact yet lucid. The way you interweave pun and sarcasm is quite commendable…[It has been] a long time [since] I came across the work of a fellow Bengali that makes me look forward to the next installment with eager anticipation.' —Saurav Basu

'I think you are just mind-blowing. You give me a moment of freshness every day, even if it's 35 degrees outside. [The] stories bring a Ruskin Bond flavour to the streets of Calcutta.' —Pranay Aich Roy

# FRIENDS

## *FROM COLLEGE*

## DEVAPRIYA ROY

First published by Tranquebar, an imprint of Westland Publications Private Limited in 2019

1st Floor, A Block, East Wing, Plot No. 40, SP Infocity, Dr MGR Salai, Perungudi, Kandanchavadi, Chennai 600096

Westland, the Westland logo, Tranquebar and the Tranquebar logo are the trademarks of Westland Publications Private Limited, or its affiliates.

ISBN: 9789388754071

10 9 8 7 6 5 4 3 2 1

This is a work of fiction. Names, characters, organisations, places, events and incidents are either products of the author's imagination or used fictitiously.

Typeset by SÜRYA

Printed at Thomson Press (India) Ltd

MIX
Paper
FSC  FSC® C010615

*this book is dedicated to my cousin Shivangi Bose*
*whose spur-of-the-moment-wedding*
*is the stuff of family legend*
*and*
*to her partner-in-adventure, Varun Verencar, as a*
*comprehensive(ish) guide to understanding the mad Bengalis*
*he has embroiled himself with.*

# PART ONE

# 1

# Helen of Troy

Everyone says you'll get used to the weather, *of course you'll get used to the weather*, thought Lata Ghosh, but you never do.

London, sliding greyly past her window, was predictably rainy, chilly, giving off its signature wet winter scent: drizzle on stone and beer and smoke (and this at eleven o'clock in the morning!). She wiped the fogged-up window with her palm, imagined the November wind outside, and London instantly became greyer, smokier, trees collapsing into each other as the water drummed down, now hard.

Even though there was a fair bit of time to her flight, Lata Ghosh was Ubering her way to Heathrow from the client's office in the suburbs – a fat amount even for successful management consultants like herself – since she couldn't bear the thought of reaching the airport with bedraggled hair or a fussy umbrella, heaven forbid a mac smelling of the Underground.

If there was one thing Lata had learnt from her mother, Manjulika, it was that when you travelled, you put your best self forward. Life – that everyday thing of running out of milk and forgetting to pay bills on time and unremitting grocery shopping and crying inconsolably some afternoons – that thing could well be lived in fits and starts, bursts of planning and good housekeeping mixed indiscriminately with unironed clothes, unwashed hair or unmade beds. Manjulika made allowances for Lata's life in London, she was not unreasonable, but travel was something else. A superior state to mere living, Manjulika contended. Stepping out of your own small life into the vast cosmos, into history *and* geography? You'd better be dressed for the occasion.

(Manjulika Ghosh taught history and geography in middle school. She also only wore the finest Dhakai saris on her annual journey to London, where, unlike the other passengers who emerged from Heathrow looking like crushed paper towels, she glided out like Aparna Sen on set.)

Lata craned her neck and caught the driver's mirror. Her shoulder-length hair, coloured freshly at Martha's yesterday – at a price which would give Manjulika a heart attack – was, luckily, still salon-fresh. She saw a gently brown, heart-shaped face, the café au lait complexion as blemish-free as it was on her fifteenth birthday, the legendary bee-stung lips creamed lightly with Chanel's velvet allure, L'amoureuse #47, her signature colour. Lata smiled at her own reflection, tentatively testing its effect with her new hair but, mid-smile, her chestnut eyes behind the oversized Chanel spectacles accidentally caught the driver's.

It was awkward.

*Smilus interruptus,* Lata quipped to herself, and quickly looked away to hide her amusement.

The poor cabbie, though, promptly found himself blubbering mildly, as men were wont to when Charulata Ghosh – for that was her original Tagorific name – flashed them a smile, however unintended. She had that kind of beauty.

'Nasty weather, innit?' he said first and then, buoyed by her agreement, took a couple of wrong turns, despite what the GPS was saying, blushed deeply at his own inadequacies, and eventually sputtered to silence. Lata looked impassively out of the window.

After a childhood and early youth spent as a geek in an all-girls' school, when Charulata Ghosh (it would be years later, in London, that she dropped the Charu formally, much to her mother's chagrin) first stepped into Presidency College in 1997, around two decades ago, at the ripe old age of eighteen, she was gobsmacked by her strange ability to make boys do ridiculous things. Within three weeks of college, she had received five heart-wrenching proposals, three sets of complete notes and photocopies from outgoing third-year toppers – not just those pursuing Economics, which was her discipline, but from Mathematics and Statistics, merely her pass courses – and two letters written in what could be either a lurid red ink or blood. Freak-magnet, her classmates began to mutter. (Most of the girls agreed, in private, that they *just* couldn't understand the secret of her SA. She was of medium height and build and boobage. Good in studies. Cotton kurta-jeans. *Where* was the mysterious SA located?)

But the myth took on a life of its own.

Boys from various departments, and even from colleges as far down south as Ashutosh, would lurk outside the department library where Lata was often found, and her classmates were regularly sought out and bribed with chicken samosas at Pramod-da's canteen to make introductions.

The rumours reached professors.

One day in end-November, several months into her first year, renowned economist K.D. Sen, who headed the department, bestowed upon Lata the cruel moniker, Helen of Troy, when she failed to answer a simple question in his Microeconomics seminar. It was shortened to HOT and institutionalised by her classmates even before the two-hour lecture ended.

Later that afternoon, Ronny Banerjee found Helen of Troy weeping on the canteen roof. The twin discovery of her beauty and stupidity had confounded no one more than her, especially since she'd been an ace student with ugly braces all her life. Ronny fished out a large blue checkered handkerchief from his pocket and told her, 'Don't mind these old men, Charu. At least he's given you a daak naam. Helen of Troy is memorable. It's better to be memorable than nothing. No?' After all these months of classes, K.D. Sen still didn't know of Ronny's existence.

'I'm sure you'll get the highest in Micro,' he predicted (correctly), flopping down next to her and fishing out his fancy camera from his bag. He always carried the damn thing around. 'Look through the lens. There's a couple kissing in the Math department.'

Charulata Ghosh wiped her eyes and nose, stretched out her arms for his camera, and allowed the beginning of their friendship to unfold on that sun-dappled, damp-handkerchiefed, canteen-roofish note.

Ronny Banerjee; Shomiron.

Prominent chin dimple, goofy smile and acute obsession with books (never *any* that had to do with the syllabus), Ronny had scraped through exams without caring a whit for marks.

As the years rolled by, though, it became clear that K.D. Sen had been wrong in his assessment. It was Ronny – and not any of his favourites who had aced Math and Micro or gone to DSE or IIM or Cornell – who emerged as the most remarkable face of the Class of '97. After dabbling for a decade or so in advertising, Ronny moved back to his parents' flat in Salt Lake and began to make documentaries. A prize here, a magazine article there, a fellowship sometimes. That sort of thing. Then came the films.

Ronny's first feature film, a wordless story about the end of a marriage, was nominated for something somewhere – Lata had forgotten exactly what. Silver or Golden Lion? Bear? His second, an adaptation of a children's classic, had run to full houses in Calcutta for fifty weeks. Awards and encomiums, Cannes and Venice.

Almost spitefully, to prove that not everybody had to leave Calcutta to follow their dreams, Manjulika followed and reported on Ronny's victories with relish. Venkatesh had apparently signed a three-film deal with him; Bollywood was sending feelers; Vidya Balan had expressed an interest in working with him...'Humph,' Lata remembered reacting to her mother at that point, eyes firmly on her laptop, scanning through the balance statement of a company they were advising on restructuring. 'Let's not get ahead of ourselves, Ma.'

*However*, Manjulika had continued, without registering Lata's input, Ronny was staying put in Calcutta.

'Here we go,' the cabbie said, parking outside the terminal.

He unloaded her suitcases reverentially and lined them up by height, three matching cloud-like confections in ivory, as Lata gathered her bags and wits. The rain had stopped. The sidewalks glistened in the pale, washed out sunlight that had appeared in a half-hearted, Johnny Come Lately way, trying to rally and give her a gracious goodbye home. And in that half-shadow of sun and cloud, half annoyed at the salty rush of memories, Charulata 'Helen of Troy' Ghosh thought, as she walked into Terminal 2 on her pointy stilettos, of the two warring men she was leaving behind in London, who had both messaged her in a half-hearted, too-little-too-late sort of way in the last two hours and whom she would not reply to, not any more, and wondered idly whether her train-wreck of a love life made her the second-most remarkable Class of '97 alumna, after all.

# 2

# The Relive Box

'May I sit here?'

Lata Ghosh looked up from her book. The owner of the voice was a South Asian child-person in an orange coat and cap, clutching a white owl with one hand and a sparkly bubblegum pink backpack in the other (at which point her ensemble totally fell apart, thought Lata, with an involuntary half-shudder). Terminal 2 at Heathrow was thickly crowded with returnee South Asians and their noisy offspring.

'Of course,' Lata said, moving her bag to the floor. 'But shouldn't you remain with your...umm, adults?'

The little girl flicked her bangs from her forehead. 'My parents, you mean? No thanks. They are trying to feed my brother and I'd rather not have that goo on my new coat.'

'Well, alright then.' Lata shrugged. 'As long as you don't miss your flight.'

The child, by now, had sat the owl next to herself and her backpack next to the owl. She crossed her legs daintily.

'Where's your...adult?' she asked.

Lata looked up from her book again and bit her lip. 'Umm...I *am* my own adult?' (Mostly, Lata hated the American habit of casting regular replies as questions – 'Where do you study?' 'Harvard?' – but, for the first time, she discovered its utility.)

Her interlocutor fixed a piercing gaze upon her. After a beat, probably deciding that Lata was old enough to be her own adult, she got busy with her backpack, giving Lata the perfect window to offer a well-then-happy-journey-have-a-good-life sort of nod, and return to T.C. Boyle's *The Relive Box*. It was another of those travel rituals that could be traced to Manjulika. You bought a new book to read on a journey – and mind you, no potboiler or whodunit either. A worthy book. To accompany your worthy self.

Lata tried to focus on the beautifully composed lines but soon found her attention wavering. Was it the smell of coffee wafting in from Caffe Nero's? The surprisingly robust sibilants of Gujarati from a bunch of stockbrokers across the aisle? The sight of a large sniffer dog licking a baby's toes much to the delight of its hippie parents?

The girl in the orange coat had a scrapbook out and a bunch of colouring pencils on her lap. But it seemed her attention was wavering too.

'Wait!' she cried suddenly, poking Lata's arm in mounting hysteria. 'Is that…?' Her eyes widened into saucers, her fingers pointing to Lata's open-mouthed bag on the floor, inside which glistened an almost-magical, silver-black pool. 'An iPhone X?'

Lata smiled, 'That's right. You have a good eye, kid.'

'But it only released *yesterday*. My dad said there was a waiting list.'

'I have my sources.'

Now the child allowed herself to be impressed. 'Hi.' She stuck her hand out. 'I'm Payal. But you can call me Pixie. You are?'

'I'm Charulata. But you can call me Lata.' Lata grabbed her bag, a sudden affection welling up in her. 'And yes, Payal – or should I say Pixie? – you can have it. *For now*.'

Pixie Das Biswas was used to driving hard if nuanced negotiations with her own adults over the uses of their devices and the sharing of their passwords – and, even then, her success rate hovered at fifty per cent. She was so overwhelmed by the impossible generosity of Lata, a complete stranger-adult she *nearly* did not sit next to, she nearly would not have met in this life, that Pixie found herself hopping impulsively off her seat and giving Lata a hug.

In the process, her colour pencils clattered all over the tiles.

As Lata and Pixie crawled on all fours, scooping up the pencils and giggling uncontrollably at the ridiculousness of it all, Lata saw – through the legs of the Gujarati stockbrokers and the baby's stroller-wheels and the open-toed sandals of the hippie parents – a medley of moments flashing before her eyes. Parallel lives her other, un-train-wrecked selves were leading elsewhere in the world: the house with a garden and a three-car garage in Connecticut, with Aarjoe and his dogs; the flat in Bandra, with Joy and his instruments, smelling deliciously of sex, cigarettes, and fish cooking in coconut milk; the apartment in London with Ari, their shared books and records and so many plants. But in all the homes, in all her other avatars – consultant, food blogger, hedge fund manager – she suddenly saw this version of herself, rolling on the floor with Pixie (a Pixie with better dress sense, naturally) gathering colour pencils from nooks and crannies, and laughing as though it were the most hilarious thing on earth. It caught her off guard. A sudden, hot liquid seemed to course through her arteries and veins, scalding her palms and the bottom of her feet.

'Where's the phone?' the flesh-and-blood Pixie demanded.

'Since when did I become so conventional?' Lata asked herself, scowling. *This* is what Calcutta did to her. Unravelled the well-knitted being she was busy preserving through the year – and she hadn't even landed. She crammed the hot stuff back into her heart or uterus or wherever the hell it had originated from, lifted her palm, and flashed Pixie the phone from three feet away.

'Thank god,' said Pixie.

Forty minutes later, when Pixie's parents came to look for her, pushing her brother in a stroller and trailing several bags and suitcases, Lata and Pixie were sending animojis to themselves.

'Pixie,' Nisha called. And then louder, 'PIXIE!'

'Oh, hi,' Lata smiled, getting up with a bright smile. Pixie ignored them.

'It's time for us to go, Pix,' Nisha nudged.

'Is that an iPhone X?' asked her husband.

Lata suppressed a smile.

'Ei, wait wait,' the dad said next. 'Aren't you Helen of Troy? I am Bappa. Bappaditya Das Biswas? Statistics? I was two years junior to you and Ronny-da, Aaduri and the whole gang? Chomchom was in my batch, remember? He is in California now, coding for Facebook. Nisha, this is Charulata Ghosh. Are you still Ghosh? She came first class first in Economics.'

Lata peered at Bappa Das Biswas. Behind the solidness of his paunch, and the sophistication of his horn-rimmed glasses and receding hairline, she tried to find familiar wisps from the past, an airy strand or two – and indeed, something stirred, a faint trace of a memory, leaves falling from a tree in slow motion.

'Didn't you sing?'

Bappa smiled bashfully.

And then it came to her, as vivid as though it were from a week ago. A young Bappa, a head full of curly hair, lustily singing '*Esho shyamolo shundoro*' outside the canteen in August, as clouds roiled in the sky and a rain-breeze quickened the air. The others in their group had smirked and packed up their CAT question papers, ready to leave, but she and Ronny had walked up and joined the little clot of people around the singer.

'This is my wife, Nisha,' Bappa was rambling on. 'Our son, Posto.'

'And…' Nisha added, 'it appears you have already met our daughter, Pixie. Where…?'

'She is going to Calcutta, like us.' Pixie piped up. 'But unlike us, Lata is not moving back permanently.'

'Chhee,' said Bappa. 'Lata Pishi. Where are your manners?'

'What do you do?' Nisha asked Lata. 'Where do you live? Are you travelling alone?'

'She is a management person, she's travelling alone,' Pixie said impatiently. 'Will you please give me my ticket now? Then I can check in with Lata *Pishi* and get a seat next to her. Wait,' Pixie narrowed her eyes again and addressed Lata. 'You're not flying business class, are you?'

Everyone laughed.

'Let's head that way,' Bappa said. 'Meeting you after so many years, Lata-di, it makes me so nostalgic. Nisha, I can't tell you what a cult following she had in college.'

Pixie collected her owl and her bubblegum pink bag, all the while carefully holding onto Lata's phone, and followed her dad. If she said she didn't want birthday presents for ten years, might he upgrade her ticket so she could sit with Lata, who, let's face it, was probably flying business?

'Your hair is such a lovely colour,' Nisha sighed, as she fell in step beside Lata, who was now briskly pushing her trolley with the suitcases stacked like an elaborate leather hatbox.

'A lot of it's gone grey, Nisha,' Lata confided softly, 'underneath that golden honey brown.'

# 3

## Ronny Banerjee, Flâneur

Halfway through the reading, Ronny Banerjee finally accepted what the acid puddling in his stomach since lunch was trying to tell him: the story was shit.

*Shit.*

Inside Pragya's drawing room, the six or seven people who'd assembled this morning around ten – an unearthly hour for Tollywood – sat scattered on the plush sofas and the mahogany divan, all sleepy eyes and polite expressions, unmoving, seemingly absorbed in the narrative as Pragya read, her soft voice rising and falling to the hum of the air-conditioner. 'And then, Mondira rose up in a fury and swept off the bed...'

Pragya made an arresting picture though, Ronny had to admit, as she sat on the ottoman. If her ramrod straight back drew attention to how statuesque she was, how much like her mother, with the broad shoulders and yoga-regular arms, the angle at which her knees were splayed and the way the pages scattered in front of her on the purple velvet softened the forbidding quality of their family beauty. Her lack of self-consciousness was what had made her so ideal for the part. But was that enough? Could character compensate for story?

'Srijon walked through the streets, hunting for something, a few tangible remnants of the past, perhaps?'

Pragya read; the audience listened; Ronny sighed in his corner, flexed his toes and looked about his person.

It seemed the afternoon had paused; in this house, a true testament to the pleasures of the Bengali bhadralok, with its wide verandas and select art and bookcases, it would be afternoon forever. Outside, Calcutta's post-lunch hush had enveloped the neighbourhood, the shuttered shops, and the darkened bedrooms where mothers and children were napping after schoolday. Inside, the white marble dazzled where the sunlight fell; the lacy curtains fluttered in the breeze as delicately as the harmonious clinks that emerged from Pragya's kitchen.

Pragya read; the audience listened; Ronny cursed silently.

At some point, a tea-trolley was wheeled in by Shaarani Sen, looking regal in a black Kashmiri caftan with red embroidery.

Pragya's mother, the legendary if neurotic Shaarani Sen, appeared so rarely before Pragya's colleagues that this tea ceremony became the climax of the reading. The heroine might be stranded and the hero walking through the streets of Calcutta depressed beyond belief – but nobody cared any more, if they ever had.

The acid now found its way to the back of Ronny's throat.

Almost in panic, he stood up and stretched his arms. 'Good work, guys,' he said, keeping his voice even. 'Thanks. Shall we break for tea? *Aami ektu ghure aaschhi tawbe?* I'll be back. Naa naa, no tea for me, complicates the acidity. Please carry on.' He bowed to Ms Sen, waved briefly at Pragya and slipped on his moccasins. Pragya looked somewhat put out. But then Pragya was Pragya – too well bred to ask questions – and without waiting to hear any comments from the audience, who were already gushing in the slightly dizzy manner people fell into before Shaarani Sen, Ronny stepped out into the garden.

The budgies in their gigantic enclosures were chattering in unison, much like the actors within. It was still quite hot. The gardener was dragging his hose behind him, and Debu, the cook, plucking curry leaves in a basket, muttered under his breath. Neither quite approved of Ronny and looked away pointedly as he walked past.

'Ronny-da, wait. *Wait!*'

Bobby had followed him out of the screen door, barefoot, and now hopped on the burning walkway from one foot to the other.

'Are you going to buy cigarettes? I'll get you a pack, baba,' she said, ineffectually. 'Wait a second. Ronny-da!'

But Ronny flashed past the bougainvillea and hibiscus, and by the time Bobby returned in her slippers, he had vanished into New Alipore, leaving the red wrought-iron gate open behind him. 'Fuck,' said Bobby, willing herself to come up with excuses on behalf of her boss. 'Should have quit when I had the chance.'

Ronny Banerjee did not have quite the celebrity yet that people would stop him and ask for autographs. It's not that he wasn't recognised – he was regularly in the papers and had a big following on social media – but the most common fallout of recognition was that when people *did* recognise him, they usually asked him about his star, Judhajit (Still his real hair? Actually so fair or was it make-up? Weight training or diet?); otherwise they told him the story of their life at a breakneck speed, hopeful of its potential for the silver screen.

And therefore, celebrity status notwithstanding, whenever Ronny found himself wavering and panicking – oftener than you might think – worrying or over-thinking, he slipped right back into his college-day habit of walking the streets of Calcutta, long and hard, grinding the footpath and crushing the gravel underfoot, almost wearing through his shoes in the span of one long day, a pair of dark glasses perched on his nose as a sort of joke. In his Presidency days, he would carry a camera around, and these days he had his iPhone, but in essence the process was the same: there was the thing he knew in his heart; there was the thing he found himself committed to (world, parents, girlfriends, teachers, bosses, friends, yada yada yada). And the quarrel between the two played out fiercely in his head as he walked through the avenues and by-lanes of Calcutta, threading through throngs of people, each one of whom had their own compelling private quarrels playing out in their heads. His own private quarrelling rose to a crescendo and then, suddenly, the collectiveness of it all calmed him down in a rush.

Then the mad walking simmered into a quiet art form of its own.

Ronny loitered in street corners, sampling shingaras; photographed decrepit shopkeepers proudly plying their nearly forgotten trades, who frowned at him suspiciously as he lurked in their radii; played football with boys who wondered *why* he looked so familiar; slipped in and out of the gates of Presidency College at night – the security guards were all fans of Judhajit, the star of his films. All the while, his ears were tuned to the secret life of the city that coursed underneath the roads and railway tracks.

After all, you were a true Calcuttan only if you were an animal of its streets. It was on the streets, in a sort of communal individualism, that life in the city flowed. The places where you were known, the houses, the offices, the para clubs and the community centres – there was way too much politics and noise inside. It was, paradoxically, in the buses, the parks, the markets, the streets and the metro stations where, among strangers, despite the heat and din and crowds, that you found a sort of peace.

New Alipore was not one of Ronny's favourite paras, not by a long shot. And perhaps for this reason, his panic did not abate even after fifteen minutes of circling the lanes with their quiet, once-stately houses. By the time he got to the middle of Majerhat flyover, having hurried to avoid the new-age yogurt boutiques and nitrogen ice-cream parlours on Nalini Ranjan Avenue and hoping to walk to the congested galis of Mominpur and Khidderpur where he had a couple of low-life friends who always cheered him up, late afternoon had begun to stain into dusk.

The traffic roared at him now. An un-November heat clung to his body as he walked hotly ahead, and eventually, bang in the middle of Majerhaat Bridge, rivulets of sweat pooling below his nose and running down his cheeks, Ronny felt the circumstances of his life congealing into an appropriate – but rather inopportune – metaphor. He was hemmed in from all sides.

There was the matter of money. The constant, corrosive worry about money. (He didn't have any savings or health insurance, and all the investments he had made in his advertising days had lapsed.) There was the matter of his parents, they were not getting any younger. There was the matter of the contract for *Shomoy* that he had signed in a bout of euphoria, the fineprint of which included an iron-clad time frame for delivery. And he was pushing forty. Yes, on balance, he had had a small spot of fame. Only thing nobody told you: fame didn't pay for anything. Travels, yes, and fancy hotels – but every minute had to be accounted for.

When he had outlined all this to Pragya last night, she had laughed her merry, tinkly laugh: 'Pushing forty is gynaecologist-speak, silly. Not meant for artists!'

He had hidden his face on her flat, flat stomach, but failed to find any comfort.

At Majerhaat, the lights changed; the traffic stalled; a goods train whistled below the bridge. The orange in the sky lit the buildings behind Ronny with a sort of heartbreaking lucidity.

'Forty,' Pragya had said, running her fingers through his hair, 'is for artists to come into their own.'

Except, Ronny was quite *quite* sure he hadn't been within sniffing distance of Art (or art) in the last two years, and now, with his so-called magnum opus, he was going further and further away, so much further that all he could see were the wasted years behind.

In front, everything was blurry.

# 4

# Cow-Dust Hour

Around the time National Award-winning filmmaker Ronny Banerjee was teetering on Majerhaat Bridge, suspended between his contract and his artistic principles, to the background symphony of rush-hour traffic and goods trains, metal clanking on metal, and consequently missing his assistant Bobby Bansal's increasingly hysterical phone calls, his former batchmate and frenemy Aaduri Bagchi – she hadn't been called Aditi in a whole decade – was sitting at her desk, in her office in central-tending-towards-north Calcutta, basking in the quiet hum that fell upon the newsroom when most meetings of the day were done and the madness over page layouts was yet to commence.

Well, basking for about a minute and a half, to be honest. For the first time in that whole month, it seemed, she could hear birds chirp, she could feel the air-conditioning freeze her ears, she could smell the lemon squash the peons were circulating. Aaduri looked out of the window and sighed. Her website, coffeehouse.in, had registered its millionth hit this afternoon; she could cut herself some slack.

It was cow-dust hour. Or what would have been cow-dust hour, Aaduri ruminated, beginning to clear her desk of random post-its and pencil stubs and days' worth of biscuit crumbs, if Calcutta had a significant cow population, and said cows were to return home from day-long wanderings at the appointed time. She pushed back her chair, kicked off her shoes and chuckled at the mental image of a thousand cows at dusk, crossing Park Street, their hooves kicking up clouds of dust through which Oxford Bookstore and Trincas looked sepia, as though viewed through the Rise filter on Instagram.

Wait, was there a meme lurking behind this image?

At that as-yet-uncomposed meme and a renewed wave of mirth at the irony of it all – a few months ago she hadn't known a meme from a mashup – her green eyes crinkled and vanished for an instant; her bob vibrated ever so slightly. (If the interns who sat around Aaduri in a phalanx of sorts observed that hair-bobbing or eye-vanishing – they wouldn't hear the laugh, naturally, since their earphones were plugged into individual play lists through the damn day – they were not surprised. Part of Aaduri's charm as a boss was how much she lived in her own head.)

Till a couple of months back, cow-dust hour used to be Aaduri's designated time to open the post and disburse books for review. She would sit by the book-mountain in the middle of the newsroom, on her purple yoga mat (she hated yoga but swore by the mats), brandish her mother-of-pearl paper knife and slice through the brown packages sent by publishers, reading a page or two when the book looked promising. She would interrupt that pleasurable task often (the interruptions heightening the joy of it all) to walk up to colleagues, catch up on Calcutta gossip, stand by the window with her cup of coffee and admire the pink light which softened the worn-out surfaces of the roads, the trees, the buildings.

Today, though, despite the million hits and counting (she'd just refreshed the stats page and it was 1,009, 258 views exactly) Aaduri couldn't afford to dawdle by the window or catch up with people. She would have to leave early to get through her list of errands, and then make her way to Bagbazar. Everything was set for the next day's edition. The cover story the entertainment supplement would publish tomorrow would be broken by the website at 6 a.m. All on auto-pilot. Just that the traffic would be ghastly near New Market but there was no way of avoiding it since Madam would need her fix from Nizam's...

At Nizam's she was reminded.

Fuck.

Aaduri fished out her phone from her capacious tote. Helen of Troy had WhatsApp-called thirteen times several hours ago, followed by a slew of messages:

*blast from past in heathrow – tell you soon*

Two hours later:

*toblerones got + beggared by duty-free perfume for you, Ma and Mashi.*

Then:

*where the hell are you? why aren't checking your phone? what kind of emergencies do book editors have? genuinely curious to know...*

A good hour-and-three-quarters after:

*boarded.*

*maybe you are busy organising MB. I am off alcohol, so DON'T tempt me with any. It's a cleanse thing. I have company so shall survive this stupid flight. DW, it's not some man. Off men too. It's a cleanse thing.*

Two minutes later:

*also, no G.*

One minute after that:

*okay, wait, G. blast from past stressful. bye. see you at the other end.*

Aaduri smiled. Lata had crossed the English Channel by now, she supposed, gadding about with some man or the other. Aaduri was never convinced about her cleanses. Either kind.

*Come soon you foolish creature*, she typed, *you will have your mutton biriyani. may not be able to score G since no longer friends with delinquents. And while reminding you of stuff, please to note I am the editor of a website now. We are called to save the world every five seconds.*

A great fondness welled up in her heart as she pressed the white arrow – Aaduri never realised just how acutely she missed Lata until Lata was about to reach Calcutta – though the message now, naturally, would only get delivered in Dum Dum.

~

'Aaduri-ji,' a familiar voice purred, 'you are dodging my calls.'

'Yes,' Aaduri replied shortly, putting away her phone and resolutely refusing to look up. 'I am damn busy. Shoo.' She picked up a sheaf of printouts. 'I have to figure out before I leave, which of these Sourav Ganguly memes we will start circulating tomorrow.'

'Sir is asking you to come to his office, Aaduri-ji, if possible. There is a crisis with Friday Favourite Scoop.'

Aaduri did not want to panic already. 'What?' she said carefully. 'I thought *everything* was settled with the break-up story. Where is Sumona?'

Sumona was the cinema editor and mostly responsible for Friday Favourite Scoop.

'Hanging out at the Feluda set for an exclusive,' Hem replied. 'We've got her on the phone though.'

Aaduri's chair screeched and her long black skirt with flowers embroidered at the edge fluttered around her ankles as she flounced out of the newsroom and down the corridor. Hem followed her like a puppy on leash. 'Palash and Tinni have got back together. They tweeted their make-up kiss forty-five minutes ago and it's gone viral, so *we* can't run our how-Palash-and-Tinni-are-giving-us-break-up-goals' story. Which means *you* can't run that break-up-goals story. What we do have as a back-up is an exclusive interview with

Ronny Banerjee.' He directed his words at Aaduri's dancing ponytail. 'But it was for later and Sumona is not sure we can run it. She says she is waiting for some confirmation from his assistant – that Bobby person? – who, it seems, can't reach Ronny. Sir is flipping out.'

'First,' Aaduri said, straightening her red tunic, 'you must know, Hem Shankar Tiwari, I disapprove of Ronny Banerjee. Always have. Phony Banerjee, I used to call him in college. With his camera and collapsible tripod and chao questions. And now you're saying our millionth page view story will be *his*?'

They'd reached the end of the corridor where a few benches from Hastings' time were arrayed outside a massive Burma teak door, behind which, within a colonial-era, wood-panelled, book-lined office sat Aaduri and Hem's super-boss. One of the seniormost editors in the company (and the country), he simply went by 'Sir'. Even the board of directors called him that. The owners were terrified of him. Aaduri took off her cat-eye glasses and wiped them with the edge of her tunic. Sir couldn't abide smudged glasses – apparently, clouded eyes meant copy errors.

Hem took advantage of that moment of thaw and asked, 'Aaduri-ji, please enlighten me, what is a chao question?'

After placing her spectacles back on her nose, Aaduri fixed her green-eyes-flecked-with-gold on Hem, debating whether or not to bring him into the fold. His face had an openness that she liked, a youthfulness undestroyed by Calcutta weather and politics, and although his routine interruptions were insufferable and his ears unnecessarily large, his smile was authentic.

Aaduri decided to educate him.

'Here's a chao question for you: In which Indian city are many things forbidden?'

As Hem opened and closed his mouth several times like a goldfish, Aaduri pushed the gigantic door to Sir's room and marched in.

# 5

# Our Lady-Witch of Ghosh Mansion

Lata's eyes popped open to a soft but persistent *shoop shoop shoop* travelling up to her window from the inner courtyard of Ghosh Mansion.

Raju. The rhythmic swish of his broom was as familiar to her ears as the gentle, whistling snores emanating from the bundle next to her.

In all her years of sleeping over at Lata's, Aaduri had never been affected by the morning orchestra: Raju's obsessive sweeping, Nimki's multiple clatters from the makeshift kitchen outside their room, the shrill exclamations of the fishmonger who, for several decades, had arrived with fresh fish and tall stories every morning (though, according to Boro Jethu, he was now far wealthier than the Ghoshes and reserved his freshest fish for some online company). Aaduri would resolutely sleep through *everything* except the tuneless guitar twangs that wafted in from her asshole-cousin Goopy's room across the courtyard. That is, Lata corrected herself, when Goopy was here in Calcutta and fancied himself a musician and was still an asshole – it was believed he had redeemed himself marginally since.

*Shoop shoop shoop.*

Lata closed her eyes. The bedroom, with its four-poster bed, carved almirah and barely any room to walk around, disappeared. Instead, Raju swam up to the front of her consciousness, methodically sweeping the oblong space downstairs in his technicolour shorts, casting lovelorn glances at the marbled maiden who towered over the inner courtyard with her broken wings and silent eyes. At ten, Lata had christened her Dayanara: Guardian Goddess of Ghosh Mansion.

The name caught on like wildfire, albeit with a Goopy-like modification. Within days, the maiden began to be referred to as Munni's 'Dayni'. (In the contested territory of Ghosh Mansion, Charulata was, naturally, not Lata but Munni, only and forever.) Boro Jethu even wrote a short story about 'Our Lady-Witch of Ghosh Mansion' in the season-special publication of the Bagbazar Sarbojanin Puja Committee.

But Dayanara?

Dayanara was beautiful. Curvy, clothed in fabric scraps and foreign flowers, her large eyes overshadowed by a mysterious yet gentle smile.

Lata had loved Dayanara with such tenderness between the ages of ten and twelve, reporting her mother's small treacheries to her silent best friend so faithfully that, at one point, Manjulika began to get a tiny bit resentful of Dayni. But the battle was short-lived. When Lata was thirteen, out of nowhere, her father died. That October, along with the amateur philately, the old harmonium, French lessons and the sense of financial well-being, Lata and Dayanara's friendship too was cast away in time.

*Shoop shoop shoop.*

Lata realised it would be impossible to sleep any more. She reached for her phone and – god, her neck hurt! – realised it was still on London time. She clicked on WhatsApp.

Oh wait, what was the Wi-Fi password?

*Home: the place where your devices are auto-synced.* That's something Ari used to say.

Lata put away the phone with a shudder. What was happening to her? *Ari?* She was quoting Ari and his cruel-ass one-liners in the context of her own relationship to her ancestral house?

She was in Bagbazar. There was no need for Wi-Fi. Kakimoni would crash into the room, bearing the world's news, soon enough. Until then, though, maybe she should meditate. Why on earth did she feel hungover? She hadn't had any alcohol. Oh, maybe *that's* why. Travelling from Heathrow to Dum Dum without a single finger of wine and Pixie's exhausting parents – it was enough to make a person light-headed.

*Shoop shoop shoop.*

A series of clangs now sounded from the kitchen – Nimki must have arrived – and soon Lata felt the thrum of the washing machine. Nimki was a clean freak and ran the washing machine every single day, often twice, electricity be damned. It had been Lata's gift to them the last time she'd come to Calcutta, and Nimki considered the Bosch to be her personal slave, to order about as she liked. Soon, she would brew tea and the whistling kettle would be heard sirening away. Lata poked Aaduri tentatively – but Aaduri, uncaring of crashing utensils and rising voices, swatted her hand away.

'What time did she get in?' Lata heard Nimki ask.

'Past one-thirty,' Manjulika replied. Lata could imagine her at the kitchen table, reading *The Telegraph*, a solitary toast with its thrifty layer of marmalade by her side.

'Uff, so late at night they ate all this haabijaabi? This dalda-laden nonsense?'

Nimki must be surveying the remains of their 'dinner': mutton biriyani from Nizam's, paired with Manjulika's pineapple raita. Lata was grateful that Aaduri hadn't been able to score the weed after all, Nimki had the nose of a sniffer dog.

'You know their rituals,' Manjulika replied soothingly. 'But both said they want to eat Nimki Didi's maachh-bhaat this afternoon.'

The clatters subsided. The utensils breathed a sigh of relief.

'I am going downstairs to choose the fish for the curry,' Nimki announced. 'Also prawns. The girls like prawn pakoras. Give me some cash.'

Sitting up in bed, Lata scrabbled around for her spectacles. A little sunlight fluted in through the green shutters – this room got a real dose of sun only in the afternoon – and a smell of eggs frying wafted in from Goopy's side of the house. It must be seven-thirty. Time for Boro Jethu's breakfast. Her olfactory system started to boot up. There, now, the burnt-toast smell right on cue. Boro Jethi's bread had to be scalded at the edges. And now they were spooning guava jelly out of the jar. How Lata loathed that home-made guava jelly, Boro Jethi's family recipe, jars of which were pressed upon her at every arrival and departure.

*Shoop-shoop-shoop.*

*Shoop-shoop-shoop.*

*Shoop-shoop-thud-crackle-crackle.*

The sweeping was done for the day.

Raju would now shove the accumulated dust and yellowing leaves and twigs into a polythene bag. He would sprint up and down the various flights of staircases in the various wings of the house and its annexes, visit all fourteen kitchens that functioned, collect yesterday's trash, and then, with his bicycle bell trilling merrily, he would leave.

For decades, Raju's sweeping had worked better than any alarm clock ever. In school and college, Lata would try her best to drown out the unwelcome shoop-shoop-shooping but it was like some kind of default programming in her body that could never be overwritten. *That's home, Ari.* She told him off in her head. But what do *you* know about home-love?

Lata threw open the windows and squatted on the floor over her suitcases.

Meanwhile, Aaduri's phone began to emit odd grunts and animal screeches on the nightstand. A sort of roar – but it didn't seem to be from any animal spectrum she recognised. Lata peered at the screen. 'Who's *Avoid*?' she asked Aaduri, handing her the phone. Aaduri sat up and barked a hello into it. Lata went back to her suitcases.

'I have had no time to check my messages, Hem,' Aaduri muttered into the phone. 'I am on leave. Is there an emergency? Can I not take a single day off without getting a call at an unearthly hour? Not all of us went to Saraswati Shishu Mandir where we sang Vande Mataram at the crack of dawn…'

'Who're you being so brutal to?' Lata wondered aloud.

Aaduri just shushed her airily.

'What do you mean Bobby Bansal is mad? Who cares about Bobby effing Bansal? Tell Sumona to tell Phony that he should be happy we broke the story. The website reaches all these NRBs, scattered around the world in their IT burrows and university libraries, and by the time the damn movie is out, we would have outmatched all the other websites.'

For the next few seconds, she listened. Soon her expression changed from annoyance to disdain.

'You're not getting it, Hem. The answer would be "Riyadh" if it were a literal question. Or "Vatican City". It's not. Also, if you remember, I asked which *Indian* city. The first trick in chao is to listen carefully to the question. Bye.' Aaduri put away her phone.

'What is that ringtone you have?' Lata asked, finally extracting a small package from one of her suitcases and zipping everything up again.

'It's only for this one colleague. It's a raptor.'

Lata looked blank.

'A velociraptor? Didn't you see *Jurassic World*?' Aaduri asked. 'Uff, you've become so boring, Lata Ghosh.'

Before Lata could retort, the bedroom door was pushed open. 'You girls are up?' asked Manjulika.

# 6

## Tea for Three

'You girls are up!' Manjulika repeated, sweeping in with a large tea tray, wearing a blue gingham nightie and a matching kimono. Lata never understood how her mother could be so festive in the mornings. 'That's good. If you don't get up now, your cycle will never get corrected, Munni. Aaduri, no, don't slide back into bed. It's nearly eight!'

Manjulika placed the tea tray on the little table Lata had used to study in bed right through school and college, and settled down to chat. Lata winced. She ran her tongue over her furry teeth. Was she ready for this?

She nibbled some shortbread that was sitting prettily beside the tea. 'Which one is this, Ma?' she asked finally. 'The Marks and Spencer's box? Or Meg Rivers?'

'This is from a local bakery, Munni,' Manjulika twinkled. 'I haven't opened the M&S biscuits yet. I thought we should decide what we want to gift people first. Chhoto Mami loves that thing, what is it called, it's on the tip of my tongue…?'

'The biscotti,' Lata supplied.

'And Kakimoni likes the Tim Tams. Although we get Tim Tams in Montu's shop now. What do you girls want for breakfast? Nimki's scrambled eggs with cheese? Or shall I make you omelette with microgreens?'

Aaduri, who'd been scrolling through her messages, promptly replied. 'I don't feel like microgreens so early in the morning, Mashi.'

Lata suppressed a laugh.

'And speaking of eggs,' Manjulika said, fishing a newspaper cutting out of her pocket, along with her glasses, 'I was just reading this article about how career women like you two are getting their eggs frozen. There's an offer from a clinic. See?' She flapped the thing in their faces. 'Bring a friend, the ad says!'

'That's *so* gross, Mashi!'

Lata said softly, her voice on edge, 'Ma, please can you relax?'

'I am very relaxed,' Manjulika trilled. 'I am *chill*. I am not saying anything out of the ordinary, baba.' She sipped her tea delicately. 'It's a global trend. Freeze your eggs now. On the *off chance* you want kids later.'

'Ma!' The angry flicker in Lata's voice was now dangerously red. 'I'm too jet-lagged for this conversation. I've been here less than twelve hours.'

Aaduri put away her phone and began to slurp the tea. 'I have missed this tea, Mashi. Your secret source for tea leaves is The Best.'

Nobody was distracted by this red herring.

'Munni, don't always react like this. I know that girls can't "have it all" *all* the time. So I am saying – not just me, that woman, what's her name, Anne Marie Slaughter is also saying – this is a good way to keep your options open.'

Aaduri's phone began that unholy cacophony again.

'Sorry, Mashi,' she told Manjulika, 'it's the office. Hem,' she said, shortly. 'No, *it's not Ahmedabad*. You have to break down the name of the city. I have told you everything now. Gotta run. Bye.'

By then, the room had become strangely airless. In the specific aftermath of mother and daughter catching up in person after a year, the forced optimism of one and the sulky exhaustion of the other collided mid-air, and a heaviness settled upon the bed. Aaduri had an acute sense of déjà vu.

Lata fell back onto the mattress and covered her face with the crook of her elbow. The exhaustion of last year, things staggering to a stop after the final break-up with Ari (after which she went through the excruciating block-unblock-block-unblock saga for months). The annoying clients, the terrible Tinder dates, the daily commute, the wetness of weekends that followed the terrible Tinder dates. The long journey from Heathrow to Dum Dum. Everything seemed to rise around her like a river in flood. She was sinking.

Meanwhile, Manjulika had coolly refilled her own cup and Aaduri's.

'Mashi,' Aaduri asked, innocent interest animating her face, 'since when have you been reading Anne Marie Slaughter?'

'Since I joined this feminist book club in Hedo.'

Lata uncovered her face for a second just so she could see Aaduri's expression. (Ms Bagchi did mock-seriousness better than most.)

'As a geo-political scholar, that Anne Marie Slaughter has pretty weird views on India. Only saying,' Aaduri replied mildly, grabbing a shortbread. 'Plus, I think it's very upper-class and white, her position on this whole women-can't-have-it-all thing.'

Lata sat up in excitement and said, 'And why hasn't your feminist book club taught you to question this very premise?

That "having it all" for Slaughter simply means career plus bourgeoisie lifestyle plus kids. Why can't "all" be something much bigger? Like the destruction of capitalism?'

'That might be interesting,' said Aaduri, picking up another shortbread. 'But where would you, Lata Ghosh, *shop* if capitalism were destroyed?'

'Oh shut up, you two. Always trying to get on my nerves about my life choices. Have I given either of you a hard time about *your* none-too-sensible life choices?'

Aaduri smirked and sipped tea. Manjulika, now slightly penitent, followed suit. Both looked at Lata, tentatively trying to work out the terms of thaw that might be required. Much of the drama in Lata's life had been enacted upon this bed, a fair bit of weeping and thrashing about, with Aaduri and Manjulika alternately scolding and consoling her, interrupting each other's 'I-told-you-so' with kinder admonitions.

Probably sensing the onset of something, Nimki entered the room, brandishing a ladle. 'Why are you not letting them sleep?' she bellowed at Manjulika. 'Just because you took leave today?' She walked over to Lata's side of the bed and gave her a hug.

'Naa, Nimki Didi,' Lata's voice came out slightly leaky. 'I can't sleep anymore. Will you make me a cup of *your* tea? I don't like this at all. Ma has tinkered with the proportions, I think. It's plain weird.'

Everyone breathed a sigh of relief. Revenge had been slight, after all.

Puffing up, Nimki said, 'Yes, I know. Her mind is going these days. Changing your grandmother's recipes of our tried-and-tested dishes. Adding nasty things like soya milk to mango shake – chhee! – or putting gojuri instead of kishmish in the kheer.'

'Goji berry,' Manjulika clarified. 'It's a superfood. I'm trying to improve my memory, baba. Nimki, you go and make your Mamoni's tea now.'

Nimki looked meaningfully at Lata. 'Mamoni, there are many things I have to tell you. When you are a little rested.'

'Oh, Nimki Didi,' Lata called out. 'Give this packet to Raju when he comes up. Momo had asked me for a watch the last time.'

'No, no,' Nimki said, 'that won't do now. Since that last time, much water has flowed down the Ganga. Momo has a wife and two children.'

'Raju's son, Momo? The boy who was given his name because he didn't eat anything *but* momos? He has a wife and children? Plural?' Lata repeated.

'If you came every year and stayed updated, it wouldn't be quite such a shock,' Aaduri commented smugly. Nimki high-fived her and left the room.

'Ma,' Lata said finally, sighing, as she lay her head on Manjulika's lap. 'So much has changed. Give me more news.'

'Well,' Manjulika said, gently beginning to run her fingers through Lata's honey-brown hair. 'Lots has happened in the Ghosh family. You would know if you checked your Facebook *ever*. Molly is getting married any day now. Kaku will be going to the groom's house later tonight to fix the date. Pandit Moshai has given two-three options for December but the girl and boy have their own ideas.'

'Wait. Our Molly? Who is she marrying?'

'This Marwari boy. Aditya Jaiswal. Kakimoni is trying to be very open-minded about it.'

'But she is a baby!'

'She is as old as you were when you married Arjoe!'

'We all know how that went,' Lata commented darkly.

'Piyal is having a baby,' Manjulika continued, without missing a beat. 'Boro Jethu has bought a new Baleno. Jethi is learning to drive it. It's automatic, baba, don't look so impressed. Goopy just came out of the cupboard.'

'Closet, Mashi. *Closet*,' Aaduri giggled.

'Same difference,' said Manjulika. 'We are all trying to be very open-minded about it.'

'I knew it,' Aaduri sighed. 'Otherwise how could he have resisted my charms?'

'And lots has happened *outside* the Ghosh family also,' Manjulika continued. 'Ronny Banerjee has cast Pragya Paramita Sen in his magnum opus. Shaarani Sen's daughter. Girl seems marginally more intelligent than the mother. Has a liberal arts degree from some American college and a nice face. Not beautiful or anything. It is there in today's papers. You must have known about it, Aaduri?'

# 7

# Pixie Meets Josh

'Pixie!' Her father's voice rang out. 'Come and see who's here.'

Pixie Das Biswas, nine-going-on-nineteen, threw an exasperated look at her grandfather and muttered, 'What do I care? It's not like it'll be Lata.' She clapped the iPad shut.

'Carefully, shonamoni,' her grandfather mumbled. This generation was far too casual with expensive things, Dr Das Biswas felt. But he could never bring himself to say the words out loud to Pixie. After all, it wasn't exactly the child's fault. Her parents were just as bad. Bappa was always throwing his fancy phone on the bed, and Nisha's slender silver laptop was flung about like a paperback.

'Lata Ghosh,' Pixie said, cutting into his thoughts, 'is the only person in Calcutta I like other than you, Dadu. Don't get me wrong. I love a lot of people in Calcutta. Thammi, Pishi, Babun Dada, etc., etc. But *like* and *love* are different things.'

Dadu patted her hand in gentle agreement, although he wasn't sure he quite understood the sophisticated semantics of like and love. Pixie sighed theatrically, left the bed, and peeped into the corridor from behind the curtains. A hum of conversation punctuated by crystal splashes of laughter echoed from the drawing room. She could visualise the setting easily.

Her father must be ensconced in the egg-yolk yellow wingback chair he'd ordered online from London, talking about chelo kebabs or the old job in London or the new job in Jamshedpur. Her grandmother must be fluttering about him, slipping in trivia about London, which she had visited several times in the last three years and which she loved talking about knowledgeably. Pixie's mother, Nisha, preferred to sit on the window ledge, so she could both tower over the conversation – correcting her mother-in-law on the finer points of London geography – and escape discreetly when Posto needed to be fed. The guests must be all squished together on the leather three-seater recliner-sofa – also ordered online by her father from London – which, in Pixie's opinion, clashed horribly with the wingback.

Her father called out again. 'Pixieeee! Where?'

In Calcutta, much to Pixie's anxiety, her dad became someone else. Simultaneously regressing into the past (constantly talking about two thousand years ago) and jumping into the future: where he seemed exactly like all the boring uncles they met in the city, whose faces merged into a generic uncle-face. Like a whirlwind, Bappa rushed about in Calcutta: favourite bookstore to favourite school-friend's mother's house to favourite car mechanic's garage to favourite something-or-the-other. It was exhausting. And the more her dad rushed about – favourite singer's live concert, favourite fish fry place – the tighter her mother's smile became. And the tighter her mother's smile, the colder Pixie's grandmother's kitchen. Pixie did not understand adults. They were so obtuse.

'Nisha quit when Posto was born,' Bappa was telling someone. 'Now I think she is ready to go back to work.'

'I'm not sure I will find something suitable in Jamshedpur, though,' Nisha added coldly.

An unfamiliar female voice began to say something, but Pixie's grandmother got there first. 'Of course you'll get a job in Jamshedpur, Bouma, it's a city. But it would be better if you stayed on in Calcutta with the kids. Get a good job here. Babu can come and go.'

At this point, Pixie decided to make a rapid entrance. Between her dad's insane whirlwinding and her mother's moods, the last thing she wanted was a public fight. Her mother could manage Calcutta for about a week with good humour. Today was Day Eight. And while Pixie agreed with her grandmother's well-meaning suggestion and would much rather stay on in the city with Dadu, she knew what Nisha thought of that idea: suicide or homicide.

'Hello, Pixie,' they all chorused. A beautifully wrapped present was thrust at her.

They were, predictably, an uncle and aunty – exact same type she'd been meeting all week, the aunty in a dress-like kurta paired with tights, and the Uncle in an open-necked Burberry shirt – Pixie knew it was Burberry because her dad had the exact same thing – and their son, a boy Pixie reckoned was somewhat taller than her, in a US Army T-shirt. He was sitting stiffly between his parents, frowning into his lap. Posto was crawling around his feet, using his knees to stand up. The boy had a semi-interesting dog tattoo on his hand.

'Hello,' Pixie said in his general direction. The boy frowned deeper into his lap.

'Pixie,' her mother gushed, her voice which was icy five seconds ago all sunshine-and-brownies now. (God, adults!) 'Meet Josh. He is only a year older than you. Josh lives in Jamshedpur too. Now say hello to Tilottama Aunty and Vikramjit Uncle.'

'You and Josh better become friends quickly,' Tilottama Aunty said, her long silver earrings tinkling, 'You will see *a lot* of each other over at Jampot.'

'What's Jampot?' asked Pixie.

'Jamshedpur is affectionately called Jampot,' the aunty clarified.

'Oh,' said Pixie, 'I actually thought of a pot of jam.'

Everyone laughed. 'You can see she takes after me,' Bappa said proudly.

'The real name of Jamshedpur is Kalimati,' Josh offered sullenly, and then sank deeper into his frown.

'Very good, Josh,' Bappa said, encouragingly.

'Tea?' Pixie's grandmother stood up now. Nisha swung Posto up into her lap and told everyone, 'It's time for Posto to have his tea too. Just excuse me for a bit.'

The drawing room lightened.

The uncle and aunty – wait, what were their names again? – leaned back a little, and started speaking to Bappa in Bengali. In her years with Bappa, Nisha had learnt to speak Bengali fairly well, but Bappa's friends tried gamely, at least when not drunk, to keep the conversation to a mix of Hindi and English, with a smattering of Bengali, when she was around. Pixie knew what the subject would be: Calcutta. *How changed, how good, how bad, blah blah blah.* And Didi. *Whose didi?* Pixie had always wondered, until her grandfather enlightened her.

'Do you want to see a bird's nest with eggs in it?' Pixie walked up to Josh and asked.

Josh jumped up immediately.

'It's in our balcony,' she said. 'There's a mother pigeon sitting on the eggs. She's not too friendly but doesn't mind me. After that, if you come up to the terrace, I can show you Sourav Ganguly's house.'

Pixie's grandparents lived in Behala, and as Bappa had never tired of telling his British friends, just a stone's throw from Sourav Ganguly's house. On Ganguly's wedding day,

Bappa's friends had had a snooping party on the terrace, food and all.

'Why do you have an accent like Sherlock?' Josh asked, after the nest had been admired from a safe distance. They stood next to each other in the balcony, as the evening light faded from the sky and the cricket game in the alley grew boisterous.

'I lived in London for four years. I didn't really want to move back,' Pixie replied. 'Your parents allow you to watch *Sherlock*?'

'Oh, I don't depend on my parents. I hang out a lot with my mother's students. They let me watch anything.'

Josh's stock immediately went up in Pixie's eyes. She had been prepared to pity him.

'Have you been to London?' she asked.

'Twice,' Josh said. 'But I don't like big cities much. Jampot is nice, it's an appropriately sized city.'

The conversation reached a lull. A certain transaction of power had been achieved swiftly and silently by Josh. Pixie wanted to withdraw her kindness, make him unsee the bird's nest.

'Your brother is cute,' Josh said, finally.

At that cutting blow, Pixie said coldly, 'Excuse me a second.'

Back in the drawing room, Pixie opened the fridge and started glugging cold water directly from a bottle. She loathed Josh. She couldn't bear the fact that they would be expected to become chaddi buddies in Jampot, *yuck*. The adults were yammering on in the background.

'Ronny Banerjee, the filmmaker, is going to be the keynote speaker,' Vikramjit was saying. 'And I can see it's going to end up as a sort of a reunion party. Remember Aaduri Bagchi? I am in touch with her on social media, she's been promoting that website these days – coffeehouse.in? I asked her if she would come. She didn't say no. Maybe we can invite Lata Ghosh too? How long is she staying in India?'

'She didn't have a return ticket yet,' Pixie supplied, walking up to her dad's chair.

Bappa smiled. 'Our Pixie is in love with Lata-di.'

At that, Vikramjit Uncle extended his palm and swatted her cheek playfully. 'Get in line, Pixie,' he said.

# 8

## Sumonagate

Privately, Bobby Bansal was convinced that Ronny-da's interview with Sumona Munshi, cinema editor of only the most popular film supplement published in eastern India, was a fine piece of publicity for their project. The interview was signature Ronny-on-good-days – warm, funny, modest, full of praise for the work of his contemporaries, full of hope about the future, and full of jokes about casting Shaarani Sen's daughter – the same Shaarani Sen he had worshipped for decades as a student of Indian cinema. It had gone viral. There were thousands of comments on the website from Bongs around the world. Even now, a week or so later, stories were appearing daily – all speculative, of course, since the entire team had been instructed to maintain a studied silence.

If fans were thrilled, the producers were *elated*. Orchids had been sent to Ronny's house; an arrangement of pink roses for Pragya had followed; and then, in a thoughtful gesture – the youngest scion of the Maheshwari family was nothing if not solicitous – lilies for Ronny's mother and Shaarani Sen. Pragya was pleased. (Her annoying American cousin could no longer phussphuss in her ear that Bobby didn't care to organise publicity for her. It was really Ronny who'd wanted Pragya to remain outside the limelight until the film had been shot, so that the audiences first saw her as Mondira, a heroine of almost Ray-esque complexity, and the idea had Pragya's full support. But Mimi-the-cousin was being a bitch.) And the Tollywood grapevine was now buzzing round the clock. Ronny Banerjee: no longer an outsider. Shaarani Sen was cinema royalty, after all. She could have launched her daughter in Bombay – she still had old friends and contacts. But no, she had trusted Ronny.

As for the fallout of the Friday Favourite Scoop – for which Bobby had to ring Sumona in Ronny's presence and say things, which, ten minutes later, she furiously retracted from the bathroom – Bobby *did* understand why Ronny-da was so mad. The day of the interview, Sumona had come to chat with him exclusively about his favourite books! They were running a series on book-loving celebrities in the literary pages, and all of Calcutta knew what a great bibliophile Ronny was. He spent hours browsing in College Street, he ordered books on eBay, he never missed a single issue of *Desh*, Bengal's premier literary journal.

That morning, Ronny-da had thrown open his library to Sumona and her photographers. He'd shown her the well-thumbed Agatha Christies and the read-so-often-that-the-pages-were crumbling-at-touch Saradindu omnibus; he'd taken out the rare first editions of Jibananada Das he had bought with the (meagre) money he had made from his first film (before the awards, that is); he'd authorised the photographers to rummage through dusty bookshelves and stage startlingly beautiful shots; and, finally, he'd allowed them into his bedroom where his books on cinema were stacked in staggering piles.

Bobby had gently interrupted the conversation several times once Sumona's time was up – she'd been generously given a two-hour slot, from half past ten to half past twelve. Under Ronny-da's nose, Bobby had checked her watch again and again, faked urgent phone calls, and then finally thrown up her hands in despair and cancelled whatever else had been scheduled that day. It was a lazy Sunday, after all. Ronny-da sounded so relaxed and happy. Tea had kept coming, too, with different kinds of baklava. And around two, luchi and mangsho had appeared from Mashima's kitchen. (Luchi and chhaanaar dalna for Bobby.)

Ronny Banerjee had just returned, baklava-laden, from jury duty at the Sharjah Film Festival, and he'd been in high spirits after spending a whole week watching fantastic cinema. 'You know,' he'd told Sumona, during lunch, 'I read somewhere that Tolstoy used to say – now don't quote me on this, it might well be an apocryphal story – when he read great books, the tips of his fingers began to itch. He would want to write immediately. After this intense week, my fingers are itching too. *All* I want to do is start shooting! Like, tomorrow, if I could.'

Sumona had steered the conversation to what it was that he was going to shoot next. And Ronny had finally opened up about *Shomoy*, an idea that had been with him for nearly a decade, vaguely based on the story of his grandparents. He also let out that Pragya was going to be Mondira.

Much later, after she'd finally wound up the recording and Instagrammed pictures of the 'unforgettable adda', Sumona had said she would transcribe the *Shomoy* part of the conversation and keep it ready. They'd run it *when* he was ready to announce the film. 'Any day now,' Ronny had said, still buoyant from his travels, still sanguine about his script.

Bobby's phone buzzed. It was Ronny-da. *5 minutes. Urgent call. Sorry! You want to come up and get a cuppa? I've got some nice Darjeeling tea.*

*No time no time!* Bobby typed rapidly, her fingers like lightning on the keypad. *Rush hour! Taratari esho. Taj Bengal = far away.*

For the last ten minutes, Bobby had been sitting snugly inside her red Nano, parked under the krishnachuda tree that reached right up to Ronny's balcony two floors up, answering her emails, sorting out Ronny's calendar and generally reflecting on things. Her own home was a madhouse these days. Between shopping and a conference of aunts, not a moment of peace. Only delicious besan-ki-chakkis thrown at her along with the ubiquitous 'When will *you* settle down, beta?'

Ah, yes.

*Give Ronny-da his card*, she quickly typed a reminder to herself.

There was literally nothing left for her to do. She'd even replied to WhatsApp messages from her eager intern, Hindol. Bobby stepped out of the car without the phone and stretched her arms luxuriously. It was November weather in Calcutta: the air almost velvet with longing. Darkness fell in a swift swoop these days. Dusk had contracted to a half-hour. By the time she'd got here to Salt Lake, to Ronny's quiet block, the windows were lit up in every house.

#SumonaGate, as Bobby had taken to calling the interview – let the record reflect they had *not* consented! – had caught Ronny-da in a dark phase. He was consumed with doubts about the story. The idea was too dear to him for anything less than perfection. He retreated into a cave, glowered in his bedroom, read old Asterix comics and did not answer the phone. Finally, Bobby recommended he decamp to the hills with his backpack and sort the damn mess out in his head. She had booked his favourite little guest house, run by one of her cousins who loved his films, got him a hefty discount, and ensured that not a soul disturbed him there. She'd printed out the rough script – the one Pragya had read from and everyone else seemed to love – and got it bound so pages didn't go missing. 'Whatever you need to fix, Ronny-da,' she'd said, handing him the bound script and a printout of his ticket outside the station, 'fix, please. Not that it *needs* any fixing. Also, I am going to need you back in exactly a week. I promised you'll accept the award from the Chief Minister in person.'

And here we are, thought Bobby, walking up and down the footpath outside Ronny's house, nine days later.

'Should I requisition the Merc?' Bobby had messaged Ronny, when she'd called to remind him about the award.

(In the hills, she'd only badgered him that once. Well, maybe twice.) On occasions, she'd borrow her brother's chauffeur-driven car. 'Of course not,' Ronny had replied promptly. 'RK is our mascot.'

Ronny had christened the red Nano 'Raktakarabi' after she'd driven him to Judhajit's house in it with that first script – she was then an unpaid intern. Judhajit had loved the idea so much that he'd signed up on the spot to be a part of their as-yet-unfunded-project. The rest, as they say, was history.

And herstory?

Bobby spotted her boss at the doorway of his house, speaking on the phone, smiling at her, managing a mass of papers in his hand that were threatening to fly out, and as she ran to RK, jumped in and turned the ignition, she smartly quipped to the imaginary interviewers in her own head: '*Her* story was that a summer internship consumed her life.'

# PART TWO

# 9

# Coffee Sprungli

The newspapers were full of Ronny's 'Young Bengali Gem' award, the first floor of Ghosh Mansion was teeming with Manjulika's students who had come over for some reason (and who either had bad mohawks or bad taste in clothes or both), and the family WhatsApp group was abuzz with Marwari-Bengali wedding jokes. Lata's head was ready to explode. Even Kakimoni's part of the house, her refuge once upon a time, was no longer a peaceable place.

Just so no one could accuse her of being a churlish divorcée, Lata would drag herself there every morning and ask if she could help with something wedding-y. But apparently there was nothing specific for her to do – Molly was executing everything online – except admire Kakimoni's daily shopping, which included bizarre items like matching His'n'Her umbrellas from Mohendralal Dutt & Sons, several beautiful peach-coloured mosquito nets, and pressure cookers and tiffin carriers in multiple sizes. Every time Lata tried to intervene – Molly would be leaving for Berlin exactly a week after the wedding, and the tiffin carriers or the peach mosquito net, while stunning, would *never* be used – Kakimoni shushed her.

Eventually, after Kakimoni put away the precious trousseau, Lata would shuffle back to her room, climb into bed again and read one of her battered childhood books. Nimki served her meals in bed. The day would be spent in dribs and drabs. A cup of tea now, a glass of orange juice then, a head massage sometimes, until a half-hour before Manjulika's return from school. Then, a sudden burst of energy would invigorate them both. Lata would shower and get dressed, Nimki would turn the TV off. A respectable front would be cobbled together. In the evening, Manjulika would ask her, 'So what are your plans, Munni?'

'I am not sure, Ma,' Lata would reply. 'I've told the office my cousin is getting married. I might need to extend my break.'

Later, Lata would stay awake in bed, staring at the ceiling, where a few luminous stars stuck in sappier times still attempted feebly to throw their dwindling gleam upon the room and its familiar corners. Lata did not feel sad, no. The feeling that suffused her at night was a sort of emptiness that felt bluish-grey and dense. But it wasn't sadness, not at all. By eleven-thirty, the rickshaw-pullers who slept in the outer courtyard at night – and mid-winter moved into the covered verandas that ran around the courtyard – would get busy pitching their communal mosquito nets and discussing the events of the day. The rolling sounds of their Bhojpuri would provide a soothing hum. And Lata would finally fall asleep.

Ten days of this. *Just* this. Contrary to the elaborate plans hatched during dull hours at work, Lata and Aaduri had barely scratched the surface of their long list of things-to-do. They hadn't gone to Gariahat, New Market, Calcutta

Club – where Aaduri had just become a member – or even New Town, Rajarhat, which Lata had a tourist's curiosity about. Aaduri's website was like a colicky newborn that needed constant attention. And Lata had no energy to follow up with Bappa or Nisha, who had been messaging every other day, telling her how eager Pixie was to accompany her to College Street. (It was entirely possible that during the long plane ride Lata might have made a promise of that sort to Pixie, and her lack of initiative on the matter now made her suffer mild stabs of guilt.)

Ten days, Lata said to herself, pausing by Dayanara, on the way to her room from Kakimoni's. In their wing, Manjulika's students would be lurking every which way. She couldn't bear the thought of chatting pleasantly with them.

*Flurys at 12. You'd better turn up.*

She sent the words into space – before lassitude consumed her again – and hurried up the stairs.

Lata had just managed to secure a table when she spotted Aaduri at the entrance. Aaduri was trailed by a handsome-ish man. Mid-thirties? 'Helen of Troy,' she said, dumping her bag on the extra chair, 'this is my colleague, Hem. He's just leaving.'

'Hello, Hem,' Lata said. 'I imagine you have to deal with her rudeness day in and day out so I need not apologise on her behalf. Do sit.'

'No, no,' mumbled Hem, continuing to stand at attention (good posture, Lata noted). 'I was going to Oxford

Bookstore. Since Aaduri-ji was coming here, I offered to drop her.'

'You may as well have a cup of tea. It's a tad early for lunch,' Lata said, glaring at Aaduri.

With bad grace, Aaduri relented, removed her bags and motioned for Hem to sit.

The corners of Hem's eyes crinkled rather cutely as he smiled. 'How's your vacation been thus far?' he asked. That slight accent of formality in his English was almost charming.

'Thanks to my friend's new world-conquering job, quite dull. Where are you from originally, Hem?'

'Gorakhpur,' he replied. 'But then I studied in Allahabad mostly.'

'Ah,' said Lata. 'I believe there are many Bengalis in Allahabad?'

'Yes. Some of my close friends, in fact. That's why I understand Bengali. When I visited them at home, they would speak to me in chaste Hindi and to their parents in a horrible Bengali. The first Hindi magazine, *Saraswati*, was published by a Bengali, in fact. Chintamani Ghosh. My grandfather wrote for *Saraswati*.'

Aaduri now said, sounding irritated, 'You never told me you understand Bengali *or* that your grandfather was a writer.'

Hem neither smirked nor said but-you-never-asked. He just smiled.

Lata, meanwhile, turned to face the waiter who had mysteriously surfaced at her elbow. 'Coffee Sprungli for Madam. Hem, what will you have?'

'Darjeeling tea, if that's what you're having?'

'Fine. One Coffee Sprungli, a pot of Darjeeling tea, three mutton patties? Hem?'

'I'm not vegetarian,' Hem clarified.

'Don't worry, Dada,' Lata told the waiter, 'I know the rules. We'll order lunch in a bit. This is just an appetiser. Onek din pawre elaam toh…'

'When Aaduri and I used to come here, Hem,' Lata turned to him again, 'the mutton patty was fourteen rupees.'

'Humph,' said Aaduri. 'You're getting it all mixed up. You *rarely* came with me to Flurys in college. It was always with Ronny.'

Lata smiled. 'That's true.'

'Is that why you dislike Mr Banerjee so much?' Hem asked, with a straight face. 'Because Lata-ji would come here with him and not you?'

Lata chuckled.

'Don't get too clever with me, Hem Shankar Tiwari. Just because you have finally managed to answer a chao question or two doesn't mean you can start getting ideas above your station or ask me why I dislike X or Y. I have my reasons.'

Lata said, 'You know, I finally watched both his films. On Epic. Have you seen them, Hem?'

His face lit up. 'Of course. I loved both. But the wordless one: it's *exceptional*.'

The mutton patties arrived.

Lata said, 'So, Hem, you are now a master of the chao?'

'Not master,' Hem said modestly, 'but I am trying. Took me days to guess that Ban-galore answer. Aaduriji was very strict. Did not tell me even when I begged for the answer.

I kept awake at night, googling names of cities randomly at work. Sir was quite disappointed in me for two days. But then I got it. In which Indian city are many things forbidden? *Ban. Galore.* So elegant.'

'Okay,' said Lata, biting into her patty. 'Since you are Ronny's fan, let me ask you a chao question he invented on our second formal date. It was, in fact, here in Flurys. Over one mutton patty, halved. At the time Flurys had plain white walls with pictures of old Calcutta on them.'

Aaduri rolled her eyes. *NRIs and their never-ending nostalgia.*

'Which Indian city should you visit if things are not going your way?'

Hem closed his eyes in concentration.

Aaduri got up. 'I'll come from the restroom in a minute. Do. Not. Touch. My. Coffee. Sprungli.'

'What is this mystifying Sprungli?' Hem opened his eyes.

'You'll see,' Aaduri smiled. 'And Hem, don't go by the bluster. Aaduri and Ronny go back a long time. Their mothers were best friends. Both only children, they grew up like siblings. And even now Ronny never forgets to call her on her birthday...'

'When *is* her birthday?' Hem asked.

'It's actually next week. The first of December.'

'Hmm, Sagittarius,' Hem murmured.

'When is your birthday?' Lata asked.

'First April,' he replied. Lata tried to compose her features into an appropriate well-what-can-one-do expression. Then she caught sight of Hem's eyes, the corners crinkled, and threw back her head in laughter.

'Much bonding, I see,' Aaduri commented drily, sitting down.

The tall glass of chilled Coffee Sprungli arrived, its fifty-shades-of-brown bringing a smile to Aaduri's lips.

'You needn't stare,' Aaduri told Hem, kindly. 'Here,' she extended the glass, 'have a sip.'

Hem Shankar Tiwari blushed beetroot.

# 10

# That Man in the Cape

Around two-thirty, when the plates had been cleared away – though the bewitching aroma of Tuna Melt lingered in the air still – Aaduri started to genuinely panic about her colicky baby. Lata and Hem were matily sharing their second rum ball and going on and on about the time Aaduri had started a poetry magazine in college – that is, Lata was going on and on, Hem nodding along enthusiastically.

'Excuse me,' Aaduri touched Hem's shoulder. 'Done? Once my website has caught up with ScoopWhoop, I can relax and have long lunches, Hem. Chop chop.'

'What's ScoopWhoop?' asked Lata, claiming the last of the rum ball.

'Try to keep up, Luts. ScoopWhoop is the BuzzFeed of India,' Aaduri replied, now waving manically at the waiter.

'The what of what?'

'I shall parse pop culture for you one of these days. When I have some time. Meanwhile, what are your plans?'

'You sound just like Manjulika Ghosh,' Lata huffed, slipping her card into the waiter's hands. '*What are your*

*plans? What do you intend to do with the rest of your life?*
That's *all* she asks.'

The waiter returned the card to Lata. 'No need,' he said,
frowning. 'Sir has paid.'

Lata and Aaduri turned to Hem. 'I know my
presumption poses complications,' he said immediately.
'But this is the first time I am meeting you, Charulata-ji. It's
our Ganga-Jamuni tehzeeb to partake food together.'

Hem left a hundred on the table.

'What nonsense,' said Lata, crossing over to them and
linking her arm through Hem's. If Hem was surprised,
he did not show it. 'Who said I'd be offended? I am the
first to appreciate gallantry in men.' The doorway tinkled.
Lata and Hem marched out of Flurys into the sunlit
pavement. Aaduri paused for a second inside, eyes on her
phone. Having dispensed several messages to her interns,
she followed in Lata and Hem's direction. 'We should have
split the bill,' she grumbled. 'But at least Hem's *gallantry* has
saved us valuable time.'

Park Street was awash in a pleasant, post-lunch glow.
Three yellow cabs were parked across the street, the drivers
passing around a newspaper animatedly. Hipsters from
neighbouring colleges walked past them, rapt in their
friendship bubbles, glass orbs that kept the rest of the world
at bay. Aaduri softened. 'What are your plans *for the rest of
the day*?' she asked Lata. 'That's what I meant.'

Lata said, 'I have a date at five.'

'With?'

Lata smiled mysteriously and indicated her lips were
sealed. 'Aren't you late? Go, go, go,' she waved Aaduri away.
'A great pleasure it was, Mr Tiwari.' Lata shook Hem's hand.

'Ms Ghosh,' Hem said warmly. 'Till we meet again.'

'What *date*?' Aaduri asked again, but her words remained curled up as a question-mark in the air and hovered outside Flurys, to be demolished by the next person who walked out through the magic doorway.

Lata about-turned and strode away, towards Magnolia, and then, past, in the direction of the metro station.

Aaduri trotted alongside Hem down Middleton Row, to where they'd parked. 'It's not a date with Mr Banerjee, that I can say,' he supplied.

Aaduri narrowed her eyes. 'How would *you* know that?'

'He's gone to Giridih to scout for locations.'

'Stalk him much, Hem?'

'*We* ran that story today. I read everything we publish, Aaduri-ji. That's my job as copyeditor. I am very well informed. If I took the UPSC – I can't any more because of age – I would surely top.'

❧

'There she is!' cried Pixie, exhaling in relief. (Though she had kept her doubts to herself, she had been half afraid something would come up and – through no fault of her own – Lata Ghosh would be forced to cancel the plan.) '*Oi toh*. Can't you see her, Baba? Lata is wearing a dusky pink shirt. She's sitting under the photograph of that man in the cape.'

'Pixie, that's young Rabindranath! As Hamlet! *Man in the cape!* I really have to do something about your education.'

Father and daughter made their way towards Lata, who was absorbed in a book.

'Hello,' Pixie said softly, tugging at the edge of her shirt. Lata looked up and her face broke into that signature, melt-the-heart-of-a-stone-god smile. Pixie hugged her. In that smoky place, to Pixie, Lata smelt like a fresh new bar of soap.

'Sit, Bappa,' Lata said, gently mussing Pixie's hair. 'Where's Nisha?'

'I just came to drop Pixie off, actually,' Bappa smiled. Nisha is with Tilottama-di – remember her? – at Quest Mall. We will come and pick you up around seven? Dinner? Vikramjit-da and Tilottama-di are very keen to catch up with you. I told you they are both professors at the Indian Management Institute in Jamshedpur?'

Lata nodded vaguely. 'I didn't know there were dinner plans. Sure, I'll tell Ma.'

Pixie had, meanwhile, occupied the chair across from Lata and was looking around the cavernous room. Coffee House looked cheerier than it had in the past, Lata noted. Cleaner too. The walls had been painted, there was art on the walls, even the floor seemed to have been swept.

'Why do you want to come back here then, Bappa? Pixie and I can take a cab. Just send me the location on the phone.'

Pixie nodded vigorously. She, for one, would definitely prefer to cab it to dinner directly with Lata Ghosh than be trapped next to Posto in their car.

'That'll be great,' Bappa said. 'Given the traffic…I'll text you the place then?'

'Sounds good.'

'Byeeee…' Pixie sang at her Dad's retreating back.

They were now alone. A sudden, inexplicable shyness descended on Pixie. She fiddled with the salt-and-pepper shakers on the table and swung her legs. She had chosen for herself a flouncy Fabindia skirt in earth-red tones and a black halter T-shirt. Lata noticed the sudden fidgeting but didn't say anything.

'Shall we eat chicken pakoras, Pixie? I love their pakoras. To be honest, I should say *loved*. Haven't had them in years!'

'TBH,' Pixie said. She took in the look of bafflement on Lata's face and explained, 'Instead of "to be honest", you can just say TBH.'

'Thank you, Pixie,' Lata laughed. 'I shall be saving precious minutes of my life with that. TBH, I can add it all up and find time to go to a gym!'

'Baba says gyms are overrated. Mummy says he shouldn't really speak of things he doesn't know. Because he's never, in his life, stepped inside a gym.'

'My mother wants me to join one. There's a new gym next door. Years ago, when I *desperately* wanted to join a gym, she said flat out there was no need, and I needed fattening up and not thinning down.'

'Parents,' Pixie summed up sagely.

'So. Good trip so far?'

'The worst.'

Lata raised her eyebrows. 'Would you like to unpack that a little for me?' she said, trying, for the second time that day, to attract the attention of a passing waiter. But as everyone knows, the staff at Coffee House were far snootier than their counterparts at Flurys. They glided, liveried and turbanned, white trimmed with green, and did not cast even a glance at Helen of Troy. Lata shrugged. Some things never changed in the city. And that was just as it should be.

'We had a really late lunch, I'm not hungry. You know we are moving to Jamshedpur, right?'

'Yes, of course,' Lata replied, attempting to summon up a few of the million details Bappa had laid out before her in Heathrow, about his new job with the Tata group and the hundred noble – if somewhat theoretical – notions about raising children in a rooted way.

'Jamshedpur is called Jampot. And, in Jampot, my parents will have these new best friends. Vikramjit Uncle – who TBH may have been in love with you – '

Lata narrowed her eyes, trying to remember this Vikramjit.

'And Tilottama Aunty, who seems nice. But they have a son. *Josh*. I *hate* him.'

'Hmm,' said Lata. 'The plot darkens. How about we ditch these waiters for now, Pixie, and take this critical matter outside. Let's walk among the bookshops. It's the best place to talk about annoying boys. Trust me.'

There was no one else in the cosmos Pixie trusted more in that instant.

As twilight cast its purple net upon the neighbourhood, Lata and Pixie stepped out of the dimly lit entrance to Coffee House, onto Bankim Chatterjee Street. A couple of hand-pulled rickshaws piled high with stacks of paper went past, bells ringing, presumably on the way to a local press. Book-buyers and booksellers argued loudly. Pixie got distracted by a dog, and Lata rooted around for change for a couple of sassy urchins. Then, turning right, they joined the throng of people sailing up and down College Street, walking hand-in-hand and talking seriously about life and friends and parents and cities, often stopping to browse in the glorious world of books that winked at them from all directions.

# 11

## Fresh Catch

*Lata: imagine that suddenly your phone, the one you've been using for years, breaks.*

*Aaduri: How? I thought this wasn't that kind of a date?*

*Lata: let's not get distracted. you buy a new phone and transfer your SIM card.*

*Aaduri: And data card.*

*Lata: will you pl let me finish?*

*Aaduri: Go on.*

*Lata: you switch it on and scan the photographs and contacts and find something super-strange. everything is mixed up. things on your phone memory are gone. there's all this stuff from the SIM memory you clean forgot about because your old phone had dumped them at the bottom of some pit. there are pictures of a party from four years ago — a party full of people you aren't friends with any more. haven't seen in forever. but there it is. all the details…what you wore, what you ate, who you slept with. snapshots of business cards of plumbers. from a former neighbourhood. pictures of pubs visited on holiday. once. but along with that there's nimki posing in her new apron yesterday or you and hem at lunch* today.

*Aaduri: And? I assume all this is leading somewhere...*

*Lata: there's an elegant point if you let me get to it. in the restaurant, with these people who were in college around our time, i am having a new-phone moment. i have these vivid memories which had apparently been filed away in my subconscious (unconscious?) surfacing. for example,* [or- E.g.] *i remember tilottama wore a white dhakai with golden dots at our freshers'. if i close my eyes, i see it. i'd thought that was the height of sophistication, that white dhakai. that level of detail. then there's a blank of two decades. it's all very weird.*

*Aaduri: That's a long message to type from a bathroom stall.*

*Lata: not bathroom. i came out of the restaurant to call ma, and now am standing outside a gaming arcade. no idea where the restaurant is. you see what i mean?*

*Aaduri: I do, actually. So who's there in addition to Pixie?*

*Lata: pixie's adults+vikramjit and tilottama. they are lovely people, warm, smart, etc., etc. Just.*

*Aaduri: Slightly smug? Your favourite phrase these days. Smug. STOP BEING NEGATIVE. You've been whining all week that you're bored witless. Now you're out and about but doing exactly what you do every evening from Bagbazar. Badgering me at work. Go back. Mingle. Eat. Whatevs.*

*Lata: shall i come over to your place tonight? then I'll tell ma not to worry and go to bed?*

*Aaduri: Cool. Come to the office after dinner, we'll get back together.*

Saturday evening at Calcutta's hep new mall. It was full and noisy and so bouncy with young people having determined fun that when Lata looked up from her phone after messaging Manjulika, she felt disoriented for a full minute. Overdressed xennials and underdressed millennials flashed past her at great speed, jabbering, eating on the go, taking selfies, balancing their countless shopping bags.

Lata sighed. She really had overcompensated today for the torpor of the last week, hadn't she? Old Calcutta, older Calcutta, and then the new-noveau-new. Her feet ached, her hair felt frizzy, and the idea of making small talk for the next few hours with these lovely people felt like a chore she hadn't quite signed up for. But now that she'd spent so much time typing out the (frankly ludicrous) messages to Aaduri, Lata gave up the idea of popping into the restroom to freshen her lips and made her tentative way back to the seafood restaurant Tilo had selected for dinner.

Fresh Catch occupied nearly a thousand square feet at one end of the food court, its lighting and décor part-izakaya, part-Italian, the hostesses discreet and perfectly groomed, the menu peppered with just the right words to woo her specific demographic: polenta, tempura, organic, Ottolenghi, blue-fin. The restaurant was full of them, Lata's ilk, the true children of globalisation. The successful, upper-middle-class-now-tending-to-rich, well-travelled, well-spoken, multiple-home-owning former yuppies who had learnt to ask intelligent questions about the provenance of their fish, as they savoured, almost hysterically, the horrified joy of blowing 15k over dinner on a weekend.

Lata's mood turned. She didn't feel like sushi. (She had a feeling that Vikramjit was waiting to hold forth on the subject.) Perhaps she would revolt and have something from the last page of the menu? A dramatic divergence from the cultivated setting – fish tacos and peanut-butter ice-cream? – presumably designed for the offspring of the paying demographic. *That's* what she wanted.

Lata had had occasion to peruse the menu at leisure since she and Pixie were the first to reach the Riviera. They were, in fact, sitting in companionable silence, gazing at the lights on the riverfront, when the rest of their party arrived, gushing, laden with bags full of beautiful things and eyes shining with the small pleasures of a day well spent. Shopping, conversation, eating well, and the prospect of more of the same. After the first bit of catching up and convivial laughter, Lata had excused herself to go speak to Ma.

Their table was at the far end of the restaurant – how many tables had she commandeered in all today? – and with an apologetic smile, 'Yes, all sorted with Ma', Lata slid into her place next to Pixie and accepted her part in this mediocre, set-piece moment from a clichéd script. A sip or two of her Chablis, which had arrived flinty and ice-cold in her absence, and Lata finally felt fortified if not ready to shine.

Nisha and Tilo were discussing schools in Jamshedpur – and the possibility of scoring a Christian nanny (Christian nannies were The Best, though getting one now, mid-season, was not going to be easy). Vikramjit and Bappa tried to draw Lata into a conversation about old times – K.D. Sen, Milieu, and chicken samosas from the canteen. But one way or the other, everyone ended up talking about the corporate sector. After several years with PWC, first Tilo and then Vik had gone back to school and acquired PhDs. They'd returned to India to teach – and administer – at the renowned B-school in Jampot, the city Tilo had grown up in, and it was the sort of transition they liked to champion. Teaching was so rewarding. Returning to India was so rewarding. It had made all the difference to Josh. So on and so forth.

'Where's Josh?' Lata wanted to ask, but it was likely that Pixie might consider even the question a betrayal. She smiled liberally instead and agreed with everything and wondered if the food would ever arrive. Then her attention wandered and from her seat opposite him, Lata observed Vik's hair while he descanted and his wife made faces. His hair was woven with silver, adding gravitas. Now she remembered: it was the winter of 1997, before Ronny.

The third-years, Vik and Tilo among them – they weren't a couple yet – were all going into their study breaks, leading to the Part Two finals and the end of college. Vik had handed her his second-year notes with studied nonchalance. 'Helen of Troy, I believe you've topped KD's test? There you go. I worked hard, and I was waiting to gift them to someone worthy.' She had been flattered, bought him a chicken roll in gratitude – she used to earn quite a bit of pocket money from tuitions – and he had accompanied her in the metro to Rabindra Sarobar where she was going to meet Aaduri. They'd laughed a lot. Separated from the general arrogance of his topper-group, Vik could be charming in a Bengali over-achiever sort of way – guitar, football, academics, philately. She was certain he would ask for her number, and she wondered what she would say to that, she couldn't possibly say no. She liked him well enough, though there was a faint trace of vanity underneath the layer of charm. But then suddenly Lata had remembered that Aaduri had planned to meet her at Kalighat, not Sarorbar, and so, in a rush, she had disembarked. No numbers were exchanged.

'There he is,' Tilo said tartly, looking to the entrance. 'My missing son, the apple of my eye. His radar is tuned to food.' At least ten different kinds of starters had arrived, three or four waiters descending upon the table in a well-choreographed performance. Glasses were refilled. Appetites were unsheathed.

Pixie glanced up from the book she was reading – they had bought thirty books between them, most of which were for Pixie – and turned to Josh, who was now seated next to his father: 'So you *are* here. I thought you were indisposed.'

Everyone laughed.

'I was browsing in the Starmark downstairs,' Josh replied.

'Meet my BFF, Lata Ghosh,' Pixie said. 'She is a management consultant. We went book-shopping in College Street. What did *you* do today?'

'Hello Josh,' Lata interrupted. 'We bought you a few books too.'

'Are any of the books about birds?' Josh asked, cocking his head. 'I own a pair of plum-heads and I am researching parakeets these days.'

# 12

# Optimus Prime and Max

'If we are going to be accurate,' said Vikramjit to the table, expansively, 'it is Josh who is owned by the pair of plum-headed parakeets. Not the other way round.'

Pixie raised her eyebrows. The adults sniggered. Plates piled high with crabmeat dumplings and beer-battered bekti, lemon-infused scallops and smoked salmon involtini, steamed mussels with tarragon and god-knows-what-what-with-caviar were passed around in a hectic way. Good food should not be allowed to get cold, they all kept saying, speaking over each other, urging the children to help themselves, allowing themselves to finally let their hair down.

Lata's generation had grown up in socialist India and still marvelled at the new plenitude of their lives, often wonder about their American or European counterparts, who pecked at beautiful plates with little splashes of food and dribbles of leaves on them, people who'd relinquished – for reasons of health, environment or some such – the natural diets of their ancestors for vegan fetishes. It is true that they themselves were ever-petrified that this golden glow over their lives might vanish someday – and so they made more investments than they could keep track of – but as long as that day was not today, there was briny Gujarat oyster and scampi bruschetta. Plenty of it.

Lata stretched her slim, shapely hand out in the direction of the handsome young waiter for the prawn cocktails that came floating their way in delicate martini glasses. She smiled at him, murmured thanks. He rushed to the bar to get her a fresh glass of Chablis.

Napkins unfolded, cutlery clinked, drinks spilt. A pleasant lull in the conversation.

'I can't believe, Josh,' Pixie said in an accusing voice, raising her neck from her burrow next to Lata, crab cake in each hand, 'that you would keep birds in a cage. My Dadu says it's very cruel.'

Josh replied witheringly, 'They don't live in a cage. They live in a vintage aviary. We bought it online.' He looked quickly at his parents and they nodded gamely in confirmation.

'Expensive affair, I tell you,' Tilo said. 'Etsy. But since it was going to be in the garden – and our garden is the crown jewel of the house – we decided not to scrimp.'

'Wait, Pixie, I'll show you a picture of the birds,' said Vik. 'Once we have eaten.'

'They fly about the house and garden freely,' Josh said, 'during the day.' Now taking a gigantic bite of a fish fry, he added, somewhat kindly, 'When you visit us, if they like you, they might perch on your shoulders. But you have to be careful. They like to nibble on people's ears.'

As Pixie digested this, Lata turned to Nisha. 'When are you guys moving to Jamshedpur?'

'Bappa leaves on Sunday and joins work on Monday. We'll reach by the end of next week. I have an appointment with a paediatrician for Posto in Calcutta. While we stay in the guest house, we are supposed to get the bungalow renovated.'

'Oh, those bungalows are beautiful,' Vik added. 'You can grow flowers out front and vegetables at the back.'

'Maybe we should add a gardener to our list of staff?' Bappa asked Nisha, in all earnestness.

'Oh, I'll send you a couple of references,' Tilo said. 'I have a battery of gardeners at the institute.'

'What are their names?' Pixie now asked Josh, curiosity having got the better of her.

'My original plum-head is Optimus Prime. Not *Octopus* Prime as my classmates keep saying. Optimus. It's from the *Transformers*?'

'I know,' said Pixie. 'The leader of the Autobots. I've seen the movies.'

'Optimus Prime is a girl. And the new addition is Max.'

'Max is a boy?'

'Yes,' said Josh. 'Max is going to be her mate.'

'Lata,' said Tilo, 'you will be coming to Jamshedpur during our pre-Christmas festival, right? Bappa's told you?'

'He did mention it. Around the twentieth of December? But I'm not sure what I'll do…'

'Oh, you don't have to do much,' said Vik. 'It's a two-day workshop series we organise for the first-years. You can simply speak to them about what management consultants do. Anecdotally. And I did have a chat with Aaduri. She is going to talk about the transition from print to digital media and basically do a spot of Aaduri-style plainspeak. Ronny Banerjee – the filmmaker? – he's agreed to give the keynote address. He is brilliant. He was in your class, remember him?'

Bappa, who knew more about Lata and Ronny than Vik, quickly interrupted, 'And we'll book you at the club.

So, after your session you are free to wander about town, play tennis, swim, relax…'

'Spend time with Pixie,' Pixie declared.

'And Optimus Prime and Max,' added Josh, shyly.

Tilo and Vik exchanged a meaningful glance. Vik said, 'Charulata Ghosh, you are the first person in the universe our son has invited on a playdate with his parrots. Clearly, you can't say no.'

'It's an idea, certainly,' Lata laughed. 'I'll think about it. I mean, I have so much of leave due that my boss has practically ordered me to stay on till the New Year. And the wedding stuff is going to be well over by the twentieth. It depends on my mum, though. Let me ask her. I was planning to deal with all her routine check-ups and stuff after the wedding, once her school session is over.'

'She still teaches?' Vik asked politely.

'Only because the school won't let her retire,' Lata smiled. 'It keeps her busy.'

The plates were cleared away. Everyone said how full they were but insisted on ordering a spot of main course anyway. And Josh, after effecting a nifty exchange with his mother, found himself next to Pixie. The books were discussed. Photos of Optimus and Max admired. And Lata observed, with amusement, the tentative thaw between the formerly warring parties.

'Why did you get the new bird?' Pixie asked. 'Didn't Optimus feel bad?'

'No, no,' said Josh. 'Parrots are social creatures. I go to school during the day. There's no one to chat with her. I realised she was developing anxiety. She banged herself against the aviary and ended up injuring her chest. Her feathers were falling off. I spoke about her on parrot forums online, and everyone said that she needed a friend, a mate. The vet also agreed. So we got Max. It was a little awkward in the beginning. But now they're bonding.'

❧

Dinner ended at around eleven. At least for Lata, because that was when her Uber appeared. By then the adults too had bonded better – though probably not as well as Op and Max – and conversation was warmer, less stilted, less about jobs and holidays. Though at their age, Lata realised, while navigating her way through the emptied corridors of the mall, the terms of (renewed) friendship were not as simple as they had been once.

In the cab, as she made her way to Aaduri's office, that cold, empty feeling entered her heart again, the one she fought each night from her childhood bed. 'Uff, your hair is falling,' Nimki would tell her every day. 'Why don't you make her your special oil,' she ordered Manjulika, 'Mamoni's hair is thinning out.'

The last thing she wanted was to be the sort of person who cried in a cab.

The newspaper office was blazing with lights, a luminescent hub in a dark street. Lata had messaged Aaduri from the cab. At the entrance, she saw Hem waiting for her.

'Twice in a day, Ms Ghosh,' Hem said, stubbing out his cigarette and checking his watch. It still *was* the same day. 'Please come in.'

For a second, Lata saw something in his eyes, a shade of surprise-turning-into-worry as her tear-tracked face came into the light, but he didn't say anything. They got a visitor's card made for her at the reception and he ushered her into the conference room upstairs. 'I'm afraid you won't be allowed into the newsroom. Aaduri-ji is just coming. We had a crisis.'

'What?' Lata asked, her voice still thick and damp.

'The site crashed. IT is working on it. Coffee?' Hem said, stepping out. He doubled back immediately though. 'It's Lucknow, isn't it?'

Lata looked confused for a moment. Then she smiled. 'Correct! Luck. Now. You have mastered the chao. In fact, Mr Tiwari, I may as well go there since nothing seems to be going my way.'

# 13

## House of Dreams

'If we were in college now,' Ronny Banerjee mused aloud to his assistant, Bobby Bansal, as they cruised along an unfamiliar road lined with sal trees, 'instead of inventing chao questions, I imagine I'd be creating memes.'

'With due respect, Ronny-da,' Bobby looked up from her phone and her ever-mobile hands stilled in the air for a second, 'good memes aren't that easy to create.'

It was a sunny, late November day in Ranchi, a city Bobby was visiting for the first time, and whose scented air and piquant evening breeze had already softened her hard-nosed Calcutta attitudes somewhat.

When Ronny had announced last week that he was going to Giridih in connection with *Shomoy* but did not want the entourage to trail him, Pragya had inveigled Bobby into accompanying her to Ranchi instead, the pit-stop where Shaarani Sen's family had maintained a house for generations and where, apparently, they would work on her diction. (Bobby, despite her Marwari roots, had studied Bengali in school for twelve years while Pragya had read Spanish.) Bobby agreed to the plan chiefly because Pragya's superbitch cousin Mimi and her American boyfriend Clay (what kind of a moronic name was *Clay* anyway?) had dropped out of the trip.

The lessons though, it must be said, were going badly.

Till date, they had met thrice, between nine and eleven – after Pragya's orange juice and yoga sessions – and ended up merely trading confessions.

Bobby had told Pragya that her real name was Bansuri Bansal, entirely her mother's doing, and that after her Hindustani Classical teacher had taken to calling her 'Besuri' Bansal, she'd chucked the name alongside the music lessons. From then on, she was Bobby; for a bit in the middle, Basketball Bobby. As an honorary Bong, it didn't take long for the daak naam to become the bhalo naam.

Pragya had, in turn, confessed how she didn't understand many of the words Ronny peppered his conversations with – auteur, for instance, or tasavvuf – but nodded along anyway. To that, Bobby had said, 'Pragya Paramita Sen, I've been assisting Ronny-da for five years now. I still don't have the foggiest what an auteur is – or does.' Other things had come up after that. Giggling, they'd explored the sal forest adjoining the estate in the evenings and become sort-of friendly over the lazy days as they waited, for different reasons, of course, to hear from Ronny.

Swapnapuri, where Pragya had spent childhood holidays with her grandparents, was a ramshackle bungalow, set in the middle of a sprawling compound of tamarind, berry and cork trees, its gloomy rooms filled with old (creepy) hunting trophies and heavy furniture. Bobby, at least, was glad she'd checked herself into a cheerful hotel close by, rather than take Pragya up on her invitation to live in the house.

'As every self-respecting deputy must,' Ronny began, turning to Pragya, who was sitting next to Bobby in the SUV, 'Bobby underestimates me vastly. But, Pragya, didn't *you* say the two memes I'd generated last week for Instagram were funny?'

About an hour and a half ago, the girls had picked Ronny up from the station and after stopping at a café for breakfast, they were now on the way back to Swapnapuri, the day spooling out in front of them, sunlit, languid, almost holiday-like.

Pragya and Bobby exchanged a quick glance.

'Those two memes were *cute*,' Pragya replied finally, 'in a how-adorable-it-is-that-your-favourite-aunt-is-now-on-Facebook way.'

Ronny looked somewhat put out. 'But there were 4k likes.'

Bobby said, 'Yes, *precisely* because your fans love you and the memes were, as Pragya pointed out, adorable in that favourite aunt way.'

Ronny looked out of the window and airily waved away their words. His Ray-Ban caught the sun. A mysterious smile played around his lips.

Bobby peered at him suspiciously.

There was *something* going on. In fact, she knew this manner; it was what characterised the early days of his obsession with an idea, when he'd be calm and happy and ever-so-slightly aloof in his comportment. As though there was a whole world he was carrying inside his head, a miniature cosmos that was so perfect and complete, so promising, that he could be patient with the disappointments of *this* world, take everything in his stride, not lose his temper, show generosity even to the nincompoops he happened to encounter on a daily basis upon this plane.

Distracted, Bobby forgot what she'd been writing in the email and started reading from the top again.

Meanwhile, Pragya was patting Ronny's shoulder gently. 'I'll forward some really good memes to you. Ones with at least four or five levels. You'll learn.'

Ronny turned to them again, 'How many levels did my memes have?'

'One…' Bobby began.

'And a half?' Pragya finished.

Ronny made a face. 'Since you are so evolved, why don't you solve this chao question? If I ate my very favourite type of meat in this city, I'd get renewed life force.'

Pragya debated if she should pretend to think about the answer – she detested chao questions but did not want Ronny to think she was apathetic to them – or might she slink back into her cloud of music undetected? And leave the chao to Bobby, who was more likely to solve it in any case?

'How on earth did they know you were in Giridih?' Bobby asked, suddenly serious. She looked up from her phone, eyes flashing. 'I see it was reported.'

'*I* told Sumona,' Ronny said. 'I had a nice long chat with her a few days ago. Did I forget to tell you?'

Bobby threw her hands up in the air.

Ronny flashed her an apologetic smile. 'You'd been asking me to call her, Bobby.'

The car slowed to a halt outside Swapnapuri, and as the driver jumped out to open the gate, Bobby put away her phone grumpily. 'The answer to your ridiculous question is – but obviously – Ranchi. Raan. Chi. To be precise.'

'Wait, what?' Pragya looked mystified.

'His favourite kind of meat is raan,' Bobby explained. 'And renewed life force is chi. And here we are in Ranchi. It isn't very difficult, is it?'

'I agree it is a bit lame,' Ronny grinned.

Pragya looked at Bobby admiringly. 'You *will* have to coach me on chao.'

They'd rolled down the gravelled driveway to Swapnapuri's well-proportioned porch. Two cars were parked outside. 'Ooh, Mimi's here!' Pragya shrieked, and ran inside.

Bobby was irked.

'You should have told me you made nice with Sumona. Anyway. I take it things are finally resolved in your head? Since you are inventing chao questions again?'

'Oh yes,' said Ronny, 'I've made up my mind. Let's speak after lunch.'

'That sounds vaguely ominous,' Bobby replied. 'I'll go back to the hotel then.'

'What rubbish! Stay for lunch! Judhajit is here with Manali. And Bablu-da. I'd specifically requested Judhajit to bring him along. You must stay.'

'Ronny-da,' Bobby said firmly, trudging after him into the beautiful, crazy-china-inlaid sitting room with its hundred-year-old stuffed deer heads, 'Wait a moment.'

Ronny paused.

Bobby noticed the room had been aired this morning. The windows were half open and the slipcovers removed from the furniture. Through the gloom of the trees outside, a little sunlight filtered in and weakly gilded the ancient trophies of Pragya's dead ancestors. Beyond them, from the large dining room, there came a happy hum of sounds.

'What's going on? I am beginning to imagine dreadful scenarios, so you may as well come clean.'

'Fine,' Ronny replied. 'I'll tell you. Don't overreact, Bobby. I'm changing the script.'

'How much?' Bobby's voice was soft and small.

'Not that much,' Ronny replied, sitting down on the ancient sofa, looking away.

'Why have you invited Bablu-da?' Bobby walked up to the divan across from Ronny but did not sit.

'I'm going to ask him to play J.C. Bose.'

'*Who*?'

'Jagadish Chandra Bose. Acharya. You know how I kept focussing on the story inspired by my grandparents?

But something vital was missing. What *Shomoy* needs is the ballast of a larger narrative. I was just not able to see it at first. Instead of beginning our story in 1930, when Srijon Shekhar is married to the much younger Mondira, we will go further back in time. 1917. Presidency College. Srijon Shekhar is a brilliant young botanist who works in the new laboratory established by an eccentric professor, Jagadish Chandra Bose.'

Bobby sank onto the divan.

'There's more,' Ronny replied, now looking Bobby straight in the eye.

# 14

## Acharya and Abala

Less than a hundred kilometres from Ranchi, there still lurked in the surrounding forests of the Chhotanagpur Plateau, men and women who were at war with the Indian state. Their manifesto of revolution was designed to help – or hinder – ordinary members of the various local tribes (permutations and combinations were complex, nuanced and ever-changing), depending on which side of the fence one was on at any given time. Most people, however, had finally come to agree upon one thing: the adivasis were, indisputably, the original inhabitants of the land. The early waves of settlers, the ones who had arrived before the British, or at around the same time, and who now owned land and businesses in these parts, harped on *their* rights constantly. But for the first time in a century or more, their voices had an uncertain edge, a silvery weakness, even us they hotly debated the new 'All outsiders out!' battle cry of radicals wherever they went.

Swapnapuri, though, seemed entirely unaffected by the vocabulary of justice that had swept through the rest of the countryside. Conversations in its dark, cosy rooms had remained the same: Calcutta versus the Provinces. Menus too. (After all, who knew how to slow-cook country chicken or goat better than the tribals?) And as for the décor, the stuffed deer-heads had gone through various cycles of appreciation and revulsion to enter a new age of Instagram celebrity – #throwback – and, in any case, there were no budgets for major renovation work to be undertaken. Other than the addition of a few air-conditioners, the house had been kept precisely as it had been for the last five decades, by dedicated retainers from the time of Shaarani Sen's parents.

The cook, the gardener and assorted other staff were under the command of the redoubtable Montu-r Ma, a bossy, once-stunning Munda woman, who still lived in situ with her extended family, the highlight of which was the eponymous Montu, who was not her son but her grandson, and who cared for Shaarani Sen and her siblings dearly. If the old people of Sen's generation offended the young ones through a thoughtless comment or two – 'Arré, since when are *you people* on Facebook?' or 'If only *you people* had managed to export *haanriyaa...*' – the youngsters allowed them to slide in deference to shared history and a certainty that these encounters would not last more than a week or two at a time. Also, Montu knew his grandmother would not hesitate to slap him if he displayed any cheek.

The last few days had been more interesting than usual, however Montu might be averse to intoxicants, but his close friend Mutroo ran a thriving business supplying impoverished college students in Ranchi and so he had no trouble getting little casks of superior desi for Pragya Didi and her new friend. Montu had been sent by his grandmother to trail them when they went for a walk in the sal forests (Nani, forever suspicious of the criminals in the area, was worried that Pragya might get kidnapped), and Pragya Didi's new friend – with that weird boyish name, Bobby – had quickly become Montu's friend too, offering him smokes, taking songs from his pen drive, chatting with him about politics. She'd even promised to buy a life insurance policy from him.

Today, though, there was a great deal of coming and going – snooty people from Calcutta who looked straight through him – but also this famous actor, someone his grandmother loved and was cooking up a storm for. Montu didn't much care for Bengali cinema. Now if Pragya Didi became a big star and acted in some Bollywood films – that would be something.

Thinking his thoughts, and wondering what sort of a time frame might be enough for Pragya Didi to get a chance to work with Ranbir Kapoor, Montu sat under the jamun tree outside the porch, watching videos on YouTube, and waited for his grandmother to finish clearing up after lunch, paying no attention to the passionate voices spilling out from the half-open windows of the sitting room.

'So, what I am trying to say is,' Ronny was explaining ardently to the assembly, 'is that now we have a multi-layered narrative. There is Trina, the returning granddaughter, estranged from her American husband, who revisits the story of her grandmother, Mondira – and by extension, the story of her brilliant grandfather, Srijon Shekhar. But the tempestuous marriage of Mondira and Srijon is counterbalanced by the story of Acharya and Abala.'

'It's a *substantial* addition to the script,' Bobby said, her face thunderous.

The rest of the audience, sated by the exquisite lunch, wore contentment on their countenance. Judhajit, who was going to play Srijon Shekhar, looked mildly piqued. Pragya, Bobby realised, looking at her impassive face, had probably known about this 'Damn you, Pragya,' Bobby muttered in her head. 'You should have told me!'

Ronny ignored her. His eyes, radiant with a fundamentalist's zeal, were now fixed on Bablu-da. One of the best known thespians of Bengal, Madhusudan Manna was called Bablu-da by all and sundry. He used to joke that when his son was born, he lived in half horror that the baby would call him Bablu-da too. While he had done his share of memorable films – directed by Buddhadeb Dasgupta, Goutam Ghose, the late Rituparno and his current favourite, Srijit Mukherji – his first love had always been theatre and he chose his films carefully. No wonder, thought Bobby, that Ronny was wooing him with such care.

'Recently I've been reading about Acharya and Abala. Bablu-da, you would be the perfect J.C. Bose. And Bose has never been portrayed in Indian cinema – you'd be the first to essay this role.'

Bablu-da's face retained its mischievous gleam.

'Meanwhile: Abala Bose. One of those highly underrated Renaissance women of Bengal. Did you know, Bobby, that Abala was the first Indian woman to study medicine? Because the colleges in Calcutta refused her entry, she travelled all the way south. Unfortunately, she fell ill and never could finish her degree. The story of their marriage is fascinating. In the many years that Bose refused to take his salary from Presidency College – where he was doing path-breaking research, practically unsupported – he and Abala lived in serious poverty, something that must have stretched her patience and idealism thin…'

'Why did he refuse his salary?' Shaarani Sen asked.

'The British professors were paid double or triple what the Indians were paid. JCB wouldn't stand for such racial discrimination and refused his salary until the management took notice.'

Despite her views on the additions, Bobby was curious. 'Who do you have in mind for Abala Bose?'

'Well,' said Ronny, 'I have an extraordinary artiste in mind. But she has refused to act for the last twenty years. I am going to take my chances, though, and ask. 'Shaarani-di, will you consider it?'

A frisson of electricity energised the room.

Pragya looked up at her mother eagerly and said, 'Please, Mama. I would really like that.'

And in her head Bobby had to admit that this was a master stroke. If there was any way the producers could be urged to wait around while Ronny rewrote his masterpiece, it was the promise of this. Shaarani Sen's comeback.

But all Shaarani Sen said was, 'Let's continue with the narration, shall we?'

◥

Meanwhile, Mimi Dasgupta, Pragya Paramita's cousin and currently a newly minted graduate from a fancy liberal arts college in New England, sauntered out onto the porch, arm in arm with her 'partner' Clay. 'Montu-da,' said Mimi, her bright orange shorts a sunburst of colour against the faded pillars and browning grass. 'Didi said you can get us safe haanriya?'

Montu nodded. 'Today I can't, though. I'm busy. Maybe tomorrow.'

'That's fine,' said Mimi. Her oval, nut-brown face was framed by a shock of curly hair. Clay, on the other hand, was pale and blonde and deeply polite. He was learning Hindi in college – that's how invested he was in India (and Mimi, possibly) and practised it on unsuspecting Indians. Before coming to Jharkhand, he had been reading up about the Naxal movement.

Clay shot a meaningful glance at Mimi. She now sat next to Montu and asked chummily, 'Montu-da, are you a Maoist?'

Montu looked first at Mimi, and then at Clay. His light-brown eyes were dancing in amusement. He ran his fingers jauntily through his hair and slipped his phone back into his pocket. 'Would you like it if I were one?' he asked.

# 15

# Dessert a la Charulata

It was around twelve-thirty when Lata returned from New Market, her arms full of things, a film of sweat shimmering on her brow. Her hair was freshly blow-dried, her manner decisive. She took off her shoes in the corridor, pulled on Manjulika's apron from where it was drying on the clothesline at the end of the long veranda, handed Nimki her packages (Nimki had given her a detailed list, all things for the house, since apparently Manjulika always forgot what was necessary and brought home what was not), and popped straight into the kitchen. Nimki followed in her wake. But Lata did not mind her pottering about.

Humming 'Jolene, Jolene, Jolene, *Joleeeeeene*,' which had been circling in her head, Lata began to set out her precious ingredients on the counter: two oranges, a bottle of double cream, a jar of French marmalade, a slab of dark cooking chocolate, a hunk of white butter, a box of digestive biscuits, a small container of plain cream cheese. From the other bag, the one she'd forgotten on the dining table outside and doubled back to get, she took out a round springform pan and a pricey palette knife and placed them artfully next to the mise en scéne of ingredients. Lata took out her phone to take a photograph – she had joined Instagram a few days back and found she enjoyed its chatter-free aesthetics far more than Facebook – but in the end, she remained dissatisfied with the results. Not Insta-worthy. The kitchen was too cluttered with Nimki's spices and oils and condiments; the wall behind had darkened with soot; plus, the sunlight was too dim.

'What was the need to buy another cake tin?' Nimki was now at her side, giving off the feel of a little dark cloud of tantrums. 'We have thousands of these. Heart-shaped, clown-faced, diamond-like, star-cornered. You are throwing money like kholaamkuchi just because you can…'

'Ordinary cake tin won't do, Nimki-di. Not for this recipe. See, there's a lever on the side. It loosens the bottom like this' – Lata demonstrated – 'and the entire cake can be lifted out.'

'I know, I know,' said Nimki. 'All tricks for lazy cooks. That Kalojeere lady uses this on TV. I have seen.' Retreating to the furthest end of the kitchen, she now began to wash the heaped utensils noisily, all the while keeping an eye on Lata's movements.

'Who is the Kalojeere lady?'

'That good-looking, somewhat-chubby girl who cooks. Your Ma told me her name means kalojeere so I call her Kalojeere. Though she's fair. Have to give her that.'

'Ah, *Nigella*. Now don't you fat-shame her! Where did Ma keep the cake ornaments I brought this time?' Lata paused again, remembering the stunning hand-crafted flowers and edible gold paint she'd got from London.

'Must be in her almirah, under lock and key,' Nimki replied.

Lata twinkled. 'Is your mood *off*?' she asked Nimki.

It was what Nimki used to ask her when she returned from school, back in the day, when she had newly discovered moods.

'My mood is mostly *off*,' replied Nimki.

'Then I have just the job for you,' Lata smiled. She counted out digestive biscuits from the packet, sealed them in a clear plastic foodbag – also sourced from New Market – and handed Nimki the flour-coated marble rolling pin that was kept alongside the board in the kitchen.

'What?' Nimki asked.

'Just bang the biscuits to smithereens,' Lata smirked. 'Use all your moods.'

'What weird recipes you try out,' Nimki muttered suspiciously, but soon enough she'd taken to the task with keenness, and in five minutes the biscuits were the right texture of powdery brown.

Meanwhile, having set up the makeshift double boiler to melt chocolate, Lata cut the butter into little cubes and began to work them methodically into the biscuit-crumb base. *Nothing would faze her any more in life,* she had decided. The butter-and-powdered-biscuit concoction coated her fingertips lightly and the base began to come together in a cloud of cheery nuttiness. *She would be happy.*

Lata was still a little mortified by the memory of her stupidity that night at Aaduri's office, after the big dinner, when she'd been a pathetic blubbering idiot right in front of Hem – God bless him! – and after which she had been feverish and bright-eyed in Aaduri's tidy little flat, her all-over-the-place drama unsettling the orderly books and furniture. Aaduri had given her a severe talking to, apparently to cure her from falling prey to 'bourgeoisie ordinariness' every now and then. She had accepted Aaduri's admonitions with humility.

*She was fine, Lata was.*

*She was going to be okay, better than okay. She was going to be divine.*

Lata zested the oranges quietly, the fresh scent and fine sprays of juice filling the kitchen with an air of quiet joy. This was what growing up meant.

And now it was time to make the chocolate ganache.

It was a success.

At night, after they'd eaten the dinner Aaduri's parents had sent from Calcutta Club, and polished off half the Dessert a la Charulata, and drunk large helpings of mulled wine that Hem had helped make earlier in the evening, Aaduri and Lata finally went to bed.

Aaduri had a beautiful king-sized bed with matching table lamps on either side, where Lata had discarded her glasses, her earrings, her phone.

'Good birthday,' Aaduri said contentedly, gently patting her stomach.

'It was,' Lata agreed. 'Appropriate too. Quiet. Just us.'

'You invited Hem,' Aaduri pointed out. 'So not just us.'

'He's become one of us, Aadu,' Lata said. 'Somewhere down the line, that happened.'

'Ha!' Aaduri half sat up in indignation, 'You didn't know him from Adam a few days ago.'

Lata drew up the dohar and covered herself up to her chin. The nights had become cool.

'That's not my fault, is it? You've been working with him for two years and you didn't know what a nice guy he was.'

'Enh.'

'What enh? He's a nice guy. Not everyone has to be complicated and white-haired and writerly.'

'Shut up,' Aaduri muttered.

'How is he? The Professor?'

'Back in Boston. Back with the wife. He sent me a box of books, actually. They're in the office.'

Lata had never really liked Aaduri's ex, the Professor. A famous social psychologist, twenty years older than Aaduri and a redoubtable intellect, Aaduri had met him at a lit fest a few years ago. But there was something about him that Lata never could put her finger on: a smoothness that discomfited her, a vague sense that he was too at home in this complicated arrangement. But in his presence – he had elected to teach a semester at Jadavpur University every year for nearly a decade – Aaduri would blossom in such a way that Lata would have no way of hinting, 'But he's oooold, Aadu.' However, something had happened last winter, Lata still didn't know the details. The Professor had not renewed his JU commitments and Aaduri had stopped speaking of him altogether.

'Ari called to wish me,' Aaduri said.

Lata turned to face the wall. 'Good for him,' she said. 'Never remembered your birthday in all the years we were together!'

'Well, he confessed as much. He faked a grown-up and pleasant and having-moved-on voice. Though below that I think I could discern pain. Otherwise, why is he calling *me*? He's never really liked me. And that's not even the weirdest thing,' Aaduri chuckled, her low, soft voice sounding almost gravelly. 'Among your former lovers, there were two others who wished me. Joy left me a message on Facebook. But then, he does every year, so that's okay.'

'What's his wife like?' Lata asked.

'Odd,' Aaduri replied immediately, 'but his type.'

'And the other former lover was Ronny, I presume.'

'Nope,' replied Aaduri.

Lata turned to face her.

Aaduri hoisted herself up on her elbow. 'Not Ronny. He must have forgotten. His mother called, though.'

'How is she?' Lata asked. 'I always liked Mashima. When I was young, if I had known anything about anything, I would have married Ronny simply on the strength of that mother of his.'

'She is okay, getting old. His dad has a whole bunch of health issues. Anyway. Guess who called to wish me.'

Even if Lata had an inkling, she didn't say anything.

'Aarjoe. Apparently, he is coming to India. And Molly, whom he met somewhere in Europe, has invited him to the wedding. He's not sure if he should attend, though. Would you mind, Luts, if he came?'

Lata buried her head in the pillow and did not offer any reply.

# PART THREE

# 16

## Liaison Officers

The days leading up to Molly's sangeet felt hectic and endless all at once.

But of course there was going to be a sangeet. That's the way things were done now, even if you came from one of those hundred-and-fifty-year-old houses in Bagbazar. It was fine. The days were sunlit; the skies an exquisite cerulean. Calcuttans were basking in the mellow weather, dreaming of nolen gur – the diehards refused to eat it round the year, even though a few shops did sell the sweets even in the peak of summer, but waited for the right season to come – and everyone was arguing considerably less on street corners or in buses.

At Ghosh Mansion, a choreographer had been pounding the inner courtyard every afternoon, trying, under Dayanara's bitter gaze, to coax the bride's relatives into some manner of Bollywood synchronicity. There was still a spot of pointless wrangling happening about venues, though Lata thought the Ghoshes had left their battles for too late if victory had indeed been an object of desire.

The wedding and the reception, scheduled one after the other on the same evening, were going to be at the Oberoi. The bride and groom had paid for it themselves and consequently brooked no discussion. An ashirbad-cum-engagement ceremony was going to precede the wedding by two days, in the old dancing hall at Ghosh Mansion. According to Boro Jethu, the family gods were likely annoyed that the wedding had been summarily outsourced to a hotel. As it is, Poush Maash had been missed by a whisker. Kaku's response on the subject of household deities and their opinions – he would not dream of disagreeing with Molly – had been cruel but accurate: not one of the weddings conducted in the last two decades, under the benign eyes of the family gods, had been particularly successful. So maybe it was alright to go with the times and be happy with the ashirbad-cum-engagement. Manjulika and Nimki had both taken great offence to Kaku's statement – though Lata reminded them of its inherent truth – and were now threatening to boycott the wedding.

The Jaiswals, meanwhile, had won the bid to host the sangeet, along with dinner, the day after the ashirbad-cum-engagement. Boro Jethu, after conducting intensive research into Marwari wedding rituals on the internet, tried to offer his input or muddy the waters, depending on your perspective. If the Jaiswals wanted, they could host a post-wedding vadhu pravesh party – but why claim the sangeet? Shouldn't that be at Ghosh Mansion?

'Jethumoni, let's get this straight right now,' Molly told him on FaceTime. 'Jaiswals are *not* Marwaris. AJ's family is from Uttar Pradesh. Why don't you forget all that and tell me what kind of Bailey's I should get you from Duty Free?'

After Molly's arrival, Ghosh Mansion was engulfed in an unseasonal Pujo fever. Or what, thought Lata, as strings of lights were hauled up one by one under Boro Jethu's loud supervision, and fish fillets and sweets were ordered in larger and larger numbers, she remembered of her girlhood Pujos: a sense of waiting in the pit of one's stomach, intense peer pressure about clothes, and a vague panic that in the heady days that lay ahead, something momentous might turn her life upside down altogether (or the worse fear that something momentous might *not*).

Lata accompanied Molly on shopping expeditions – though the clothes Molly would wear at the different ceremonies had already been sourced from a global supply chain (Banarasis from Benares, shipped to a Bengalideshi–Nigerian designer in Queens, who ordered the rest of the fabrics online from Turkey, and had the outfits delivered to Calcutta). For herself and Ma, Lata bought saris from her favourite boutique in Hindustan Park: soft pinks, crushed oranges, dull golds and pista greens. Nimki chose a turquoise Kanjeevaram for herself from the College Street market. Lata also visited her mother's ophthalmologist, Aaduri's dentist, got her hair done, found a masseuse online. One day, Manjulika took leave from school, and mother and daughter went to their locker in Hati Bagan and brought home a small selection of family jewellery, wrapped in red mulmul and resplendent with memories.

Lata had always felt considerable affection for this youngest cousin, who still looked like a miniature version of herself, despite the pageboy haircut she now sported. This time round, though, Lata and Molly quickly found their roles reversed. Molly affected the acute certainty of the young. All of life lay in front of her, full of enormous possibilities; paradoxically, this made her worldly wise and emotionally savvy. Lata set aside her management consultant avatar, the richness of her many accomplishments and experiences, the depth added to her laugh by so many failures, and allowed herself to become an ingenue again, lectured to by Molly, laughing fondly as Molly's dark eyes flashed and her hair shimmered with knowledge of the world. Molly had eventually drawn Lata into the dark web of wedding conspiracies: *AJ's mother knows* this *but can't know* that, *my mother knows* that *but cannot-for-the-life-of-me know* this, *neither of our mothers know we live together in Berlin so you have to make sure the German contingent does not slip up.* The days passed in a heady blur.

And then, four days before the sangeet, after a protracted meltdown involving AJ's mother, Boro Jethu, the designated fishmonger (whose orders were cancelled since the ashirbad-cum-engagement had to be declared vegetarian in honour of the groom's ninety-two-year-old great-grandfather who was coming all the way from Rae Bareilly) and one of the Germans who'd found a single hair in her soup, Molly called Lata in a panic. 'Didibhai, we are appointing two liaison officers. You from the Ghosh side, and AJ's cousin to represent the Jaiswals. Will you go and meet her once, please? So that a basic level of communication is established between the families and the messages are from one sensible sister to another? Please? Everything will fall apart otherwise. Purohit Moshai has been insulting their Pandit-ji, it appears. Boro Jethu is behaving extremely weirdly. And the cousin is really nice. She's from your college, I think.'

'It's fine, Mollykins,' Lata had laughed. 'I think I can deal with people from other colleges too.'

That afternoon, Lata messaged the cousin and the two of them fixed to meet up in a café in South Calcutta which apparently made great cinnamon buns. 'I know you're visiting for a few days and I would have come to GM myself,' the cousin had written. 'I love its courtyards. But I'm having some trouble at work. Damage control type. So, if it's okay with you, I'd rather meet in the south? I might have to run in an hour. Besides, the café is lovely.'

Lata reached early and found a table in the corner. The place was fussy and cute, like an English tearoom. She thought she'd deal with her overflowing inbox in the meantime. Suddenly a fly was buzzing at her nose and as she looked up, she felt something in her eye.

Oh dear, her right eye stung.

*Crap.*

Lata rubbed her eyes vigorously, the sting in the right one became worse, and as her eyes watered stupidly and she scrabbled around in her bag for something that might help – but what? – there was a sudden darkening by her side.

'Charulata Ghosh.' A voice, fervently familiar in its timbre, if unfamiliar in gravitas, stated. 'It appears you still need this.'

A monogrammed kerchief was handed to her, with a brief bow.

'Ronny Banerjee,' said Lata, looking up and not seeing anything as her eyes were now leaking preposterously. 'I never should have worn these dumb contacts. I think one of them is out. Can you spot it?'

And so, when Bobby Bansal, having parked her car and surreptitiously checked her emails, entered the café and breathed in the warm cinnamon scent, she saw her boss, Ronny, and Molly's cousin, Lata – whom she vaguely recognised from Facebook – craning at the table with its glass top, their heads bent forward, an intimacy framing them in a strange youthful shot.

Bobby paused in the distance.

# 17

## Character

'That's the house?' Pixie asked her parents. 'But it looks so *dilapidated*.'

The parents ignored Pixie. For once her father did not ask admiringly where she'd learnt the word dilapidated. Instead, continuing to argue under their breath, Bappa and Nisha stomped towards the gate. That is, to the gap in the wall where there should have been a gate if the house weren't so rundown.

Pixie sat sullenly in the car with Ram Singh, the sixty-something, luxuriantly moustachioed chauffeur who had been assigned to them when they first arrived. Over the week, Pixie had decided that he was in fact her favourite person in Jampot. He reminded her a little of

Dadu – incidentally, nobody was telling her when Dadu would come to visit them in this godforsaken place – and it helped that RS was the only one around here who told her anything approximating the truth. When RS had driven them back the first time from her new school, her parents had gushed endlessly about how lucky she was to get admitted to a proper convent. Ram Singh had looked at her and said in his stoic fashion, 'Good school. Good teachers. But very strict. Too many tests.'

It had barely been a week. But Pixie had already appeared for three – three! – practice tests. And other than the English essay, where she'd used words like *astringent* and *radical*, she was quite certain she had performed *abysmally*. Ugh.

TBH, Pixie was quite underwhelmed by this new life.

Lata Ghosh had told her fifty hundred times to not compare her new life with her old (they both knew she meant 'London') life and she was trying, she really was. But it wasn't easy. For one, the new school was full of insufferable goody-goodies who flaunted the nuances of Hindi grammar or multiplications with fractions – neither of which had been part of her curriculum in London – and who seemed to have all arranged themselves into little, *impermeable* cliques, long before Pixie arrived on the scene.

For another, Pixie was yet to find a bookshop where she could browse at leisure. (It's true that Lata had promised to send her a few books to compensate for the lack of bookstores. But how long could that be sustained? What about when Lata returned to London or found a new friend or – God forbid! – had a baby or something? Pixie was stuck here for the long run.)

And worst of all, her brother Posto, who was never-ever taken seriously in London, had emerged as quite the star in Jampot. People were randomly stopping by to compliment his curls or his gurgles or his dimples. They didn't see how prone to drooling he was, or how he was yet to articulate his first clear words. Pixie didn't want to brag, but by the time she was Posto's age, she had spoken her first, grammatically correct, sentence.

'The house will be renovated by the company, Baby,' Ram Singh finally spoke up from the wheel, curtailing Pixie's list. 'Then it will become a beautiful home. Maybe you should choose your room and tell your parents what colours you want on the walls? Otherwise they'll make all the decisions on your behalf.'

Pixie sighed and got out of the car. Ram Singh walked with her to the gate-shaped hole in the wall, and Pixie saw, past the long driveway which led to the bungalow with its wraparound veranda on the left, a deliciously overgrown garden. The bright sunlight – Pixie had to admit that one category where Jamshedpur clearly scored over London was the weather – became almost greenish as it passed through the tangle of trees and vines and fell on the grass, which was ankle high. 'That's a mango tree,' RS pointed out, walking towards the garden. Pixie followed. 'And look, by the boundary wall at the back, there's a row of neem trees.'

Pixie looked in the direction of RS's outstretched hand, but somewhere, somehow, her gaze drifted.

'Who is that?' Pixie asked.

Then, before RS could say anything, she began to sprint in the direction of the mango tree.

A few kilometres away from Bappa and Nisha's new house, Vikramjit Sen, distinguished professor of Strategic Management, walked into his wife the dean's office. It was one of the nicer offices on campus, with a view of the lake and a sense of low hills in the distance. She had also 'curated' the furniture and curtains with the same kind of fastidiousness she brought to their home, giving it a part-art gallery, part-Irish pub vibe. It was exhausting, Vik didn't know how she did it.

Meanwhile, Tilottama Chaudhuri, the dean his wife, sat at her desk in a huddle with a bunch of younger colleagues. She waved at Vik wordlessly and, while he sat himself on the sofa at the far end of her room and picked up a journal that was lying on the coffee table, Tilo returned, serious-faced, to her cabinet meeting.

They all wore intense expressions and, Vik noted, at least three people were feverishly taking notes. For all the apparent bonhomie and only first-names and elaborate teas at home that Tilo insisted upon, she ran a tight ship and people were petrified of her. Vik was too, actually, though he wouldn't admit it. In her powder-blue shift dress and power jewellery – sourced mostly from Jaypore, the site she'd instructed him to buy her gifts from – Tilo, with her hair piled artfully on top of her head, was a commanding presence. Vik ran his hand through his silver-edged hair and wondered exactly when he had come to dislike her so.

After ten minutes, the state secrets were put away and the others shuffled out of the room, having exchanged banalities with Vik. Finally, when the room had emptied out, Tilo walked up to him and collapsed on the sofa opposite with her bottle of Evian. Vik still didn't know how she'd managed to find a vendor in Jamshedpur who kept her stocked in Evian.

'So Ronny's assistant has finally replied. She says he cannot send a copy of the keynote address in advance because he is not an academic and won't be reading out from a typed text. Her tone was a bit rude if you ask me. So much for printing it out and circulating it at the venue.'

'I think an extempore address will be much more interesting, Tilo,' Vik said mildly. 'And I think the students will learn a great deal. We keep talking about our "rounded-person model" and highlighting "art awareness in adult life", but unless they actually hear artists and real rounded-persons being themselves, how will they learn?'

Tilo arched her eyebrows. It was her code for if-I-deigned-to-respond-I-would-destroy-this-argument-but-let's-just-let-it-go. Tilo prided herself on being a true rounded-person. She was a mother, a professional, a volunteer, a wife, a social conscience, a good dresser, a hobbyist, a dedicated meditator, a great cook, and a sensitive daughter and daughter-in-law. She was quite certain that it added up to greater roundedness than what that Ronny Banerjee, with his two films and a documentary or two, had achieved. Anyway.

'Lata Ghosh emailed her confirmation in the afternoon,' Tilo continued. 'Aaduri, I spoke to a few days ago. She's going to bring one of her colleagues.'

'And the Stanford duo?'

'You mean, the Staaanforrrd duo. They're going to be here. In fact, they're bringing their kids too. So we have to book connecting rooms for them at the guest house. And

I do think all the guests should be at the guest house on campus. It doesn't look nice if our friends are in Beldih Club.'

'I have to be off now if I am to pick Josh up in time,' Vik said, standing up. 'You coming?'

'I'll see you guys at home,' Tilo replied, returning to her table and switching on her laptop again. 'I have this paper to finish.'

Eventually, Pixie found her parents perched on a window ledge in one of the rooms overlooking the tangled garden. Her mother was weeping, and her father was patting her shoulders gently. 'Moving continents is not easy, Nisha. It'll all fall into place. Don't worry.'

'Bbut llook aat tthe sstate oof tthis hhouse,' Nisha blubbered.

'They'll fix it. Until then we'll stay in the guest house. For as long as it takes. There, at least, you don't have to worry about food and stuff. And we've got a good nanny for Posto. Pixie's in school. Let's count our blessings.'

'Ii'm sso ttired,' she said, resting her head on Bappa's shoulder.

Pixie walked up to them and said in a honeyed voice, 'I'm sorry I said the house is dilapidated, Mama. But it has *character*. And the garden is great. Also, look who I found.'

Nisha raised her head from Bappa's shoulder and, smiling despite their worries, the parents turned to her.

Pixie had an angelic expression on her face and a white puppy in her arms. The puppy mirrored her expression.

# 18

# I Shall Spout Joy Goswami
# Night and Day

In dating circles, there has always been a theory that every romantic relationship has a 'reacher' and a 'settler'. Like all self-respecting theories, it has, naturally, been debunked often. Yet it persists. Whether because of some ingrained truth contained in its folds, or simply because it sounds clever and cynical, we will never know for certain. But, yes, it persists.

If the autumn of 1997 was one long hot memorable Calcutta day, then in the brief dramatic dusk of said day – the sky streaked rashly with pink and orange – had someone sat Ronny Banerjee down, say by the quadrangle or the lovers' lane in Presidency College, and outlined to him this school of thought, Ronny would have been the first to admit that as far as Charulata Ghosh was concerned, he was the undisputed 'reacher'. *However*, he would quickly go on to clarify, what he and Charulata Ghosh *had* could not be called a romantic relationship. Not by a long shot.

'It can't even be called a *friendship*,' Aaduri Bagchi, the most likely candidate to have sat him down and sold him this theory – she kept up with global dating trends even though she had sworn off prem altogether – would have said to that. 'What *Luts and I* have is friendship. What *you* have for Luts: it's byaatha, nothing more, nothing less.'

Byaatha. As ubiquitous as prem in the vocabulary of Bengal, but far subtler in implication. Prem was robust, a cat with nine lives, you might 'fall' into it just as you fell into conversations about Godard or Derrida – prem-e pawra – but you could also, with varying degrees of agency or casualness, *do* prem, prem kawraa.

Byaatha was a different continent.

It hearkened to the sort of languid longing that Hindustani poets celebrated in Urdu poetry, that first prick of intense if sweet suffering, often unrequited, signalling the commencement of something momentous.

Byaatha was also where our story really began, and to quote Aaduri Bagchi, it was two hundred or more years ago.

Meanwhile, in the tearoom in that quiet South Calcutta neighbourhood, with its fine china and famous cinnamon buns, the lost lens was not found. After her eyes had stopped watering and Ronny's handkerchief had been put to good use mopping up her face, Lata reached two fingers into the other eye – Ronny winced perceptibly – and matter-of-factly extracted the other. 'So much for my vanity,' she said, and shucked the lone lens into a little white lens case that had emerged from her bag. 'And now I'll be squinting until I get home. I should have stuck to the glasses instead of trying to get lenses for the wedding!'

'Whose wedding?' Ronny asked casually, carefully concealing the sudden irrational panic that gripped him – a feeling that was so far out there and so very ridiculous that he was embarrassed even in the act of careful concealment.

'Oh, I thought you knew,' Lata replied, her eyes finally focussed on his face. They were no longer watering. Even so, they seemed different somehow, Ronny thought.

'Molly, my cousin. Do you remember her?'

It was as though a weight had lifted. 'Of course I remember Molly, she was my carrom partner for years! In fact, I ran into her once or twice when she was studying at JU. I used to take a few classes for the film studies department in those days.'

'Ah,' said Lata.

'Am I talking too much?' Ronny asked himself.

'So. Our Molly is marrying your Bobby's cousin, AJ.'

'Oh! I have in fact been invited to this wedding. Posh one. Taj?'

'Oberoi,' Lata corrected him. 'And Bobby and I have been designated liaison officers.'

Ronny looked appropriately perplexed.

Lata smiled. Somewhere, a violin concerto started up and the hearts of stone gods melted. (Again.) Ronny sat up straighter. Lata tucked her hair behind an ear as she explained: 'You know the Ghoshes and their propensity to wreck stuff? *My* job is to ensure that nothing unseemly happens, and the wedding doesn't get ruined in any way whatsoever by the esteemed elders of our extended clan.'

'Boro Jethu?' It was now Ronny's turn to smile.

Lata remembered in that instant her twentieth birthday party when Ronny and Aaduri and the rest of the gang had been invited by Manjulika to lunch, and when, outside the formal dining room downstairs, Boro Jethu had announced loudly to Jethi – well within everybody's earshot: '*That's* the boy, the one with the hangdog expression. Saw him? Comes and goes all the time. Can't expect Manjulika to run a tight ship. I presume all this photography, filmmaking nonsense will pass, and he'll take the WBCS exam like his father. But good she's found someone at least. I was always afraid she would fall into the "oti boro sundari" trap.'

That day, Lata now remembered, she had worn a pair of ripped jeans. It was the global rage that season and she had saved up for months for it, even though Manjulika kept telling her it would be cheaper to buy a regular pair and rip it herself. She remembered the hot flush that had passed through her as Boro Jethu's booming voice entered the room, bouncing off its dusty corners. (Manjulika and Nimki were in the kitchen.) They were all Bengalis there, that afternoon, and everyone knew the proverb – the greatest beauty doesn't find a husband, the finest homemaker never gets her house – and even though they were all radicals, believing neither in the institution of marriage nor in the art of homemaking, Boro Jethu's tone had lodged somewhere, reopening a wound she had forgotten.

But before her eyes could fill with tears, Aaduri had linked her arm with Ronny and hummed their new favourite Chandrabindoo song, '*Jodi bawlo hyaan, BCS-e boshe jaabo aami*...If you say yes, I shall take the BCS exams right away...'

Ronny joined her immediately, adding the gentle baritone of his beautiful singing voice to Aaduri's. The two of them swayed their way to Lata: '*Jodi bawlo naa, aaoraabo Joy Goswami*...If you say no, I shall spout Joy Goswami night and day.'

And somehow, the afternoon was salvaged, redirected towards its original agenda: food, long, pointless, never-ending conversations that provided such energy and joy, music. Ronny forced them to see his documentary on a middle-class travel group's journey to Sikkim (it had been rather funny). They'd listened to the mix-tape Aaduri had made for Lata. They'd argued about college politics.

Lata could see them now, curled up on her four-poster bed, twenty-year-olds all, limbs tangled, flyaway hair, fashionable clothes. At twenty, they'd been sure they would live forever, they'd climb the highest mountains and dive into the deepest oceans – maybe simultaneously – and save lives and make art and find love and be happy. Oh, future happiness. They never questioned its reliable presence. It was right ahead, waiting, like a well-known monument on a traveller's path.

'Boro Jethu, by the way, is now the custodian of liberal values. Ever since Goopy came out,' Lata smiled.

'Goopy wasn't a half-bad guitarist,' Ronny reminisced. 'Even though his choice of music was a tad derivative.'

And then Bobby appeared. She had taken charge of ordering tea after she'd introduced herself at the unwitting reunion party – and while in the queue she'd added up the details she knew, about Lata and Ronny individually, working out how it all sat with his body language – and now she arrived at their table with a very large tray: pot of tea, milk and sugar on the side, a tidy three-tier stand with little cakes and sandwiches. Both Ronny and Lata stood up to help, but it was unnecessary. With single-minded efficiency, Bobby apportioned the tea into the dainty porcelain cups on the table – asking Lata how much milk, how much sugar – one sandwich, a piece of cake, leaving them nothing to do to stave off the awkwardness.

For all his spying on the comings and goings of 'that boy', Boro Jethu had never guessed that Ronny and Lata weren't a couple, not exactly, not until the night of her twentieth birthday.

Ronny greatly preferred email to the phone. For one, Lata and Manjulika did not have an extension up in their quarters so he had to depend on the largesse of the eccentric Ghoshes to even get her to the phone. For another, his poetic soul soared with the written word, typing out long quotations and chatty missives almost daily. Every evening, Lata would go over to Kakimoni's, where Kaku had a desktop with VSNL dial-up internet and check her inbox.

The night of her twentieth birthday party, his email was brief.

'Should I spout Joy Goswami night and day?'

Hers had been briefer.

'Not just yet.'

# 19

# Roaring Twenties

It took exactly five minutes for the tea to turn cold in the flowery porcelain cups and a further five to discuss the liaison-officering. Bobby had, in anticipation of this meeting, created an Excel sheet about the various functions leading up to the wedding, marking up dates, times, important phone numbers, even going on to anticipate possible hiccups. Lata, feeling weirdly naked without spectacles or lenses, squinted at the sudden multiplication of screens in front of her, trying hard to pay attention but feeling somehow hollow and vague inside, as though there were a faint ringing in her ears.

The plates and cups were cleared away. Bobby stood up and dusted off crumbs from her clothes. Following suit, Ronny and Lata stood up and filed out of the tearoom behind her, rather like obedient students.

'I guess I will speak to you tomorrow and see you at the ashirbad?' Bobby said. She added, slightly apologetically, 'Really have to run. I've had to park two streets away, sighhh, and we must get to this meeting by five-forty-five… Ronny-da?'

Ronny was looking away. Into the traffic that flowed past in a constant stream of colour and sound. At the buildings across the street, where men stood in balconies and sleepy women in daytime saris or nighties picked laundry off nylon lines that had been strung across the grilles.

'Where are you going?' Ronny asked Lata.

'I should go home,' Lata replied. 'There are wedding things to do.'

'Bobby,' Ronny said, measuring out his words carefully, 'I think you should meet them by yourself. I might lose my temper – and that's going to make things worse. I have to go towards the north anyway. So I'll head in that direction with Lata. You don't mind, do you?'

Bobby's jaw stiffened.

'Well then,' she said, her lips pursed. She turned to Lata. 'Tell Molly not to worry. Bye.'

In a flash, she had turned. As she crossed the road, her flying mass of hair caught the parting sun. Soon, Bobby had disappeared into the traffic and, in a while, the lingering traces of her displeasure began to dissipate too.

'She is quite dazzling, really,' Lata smiled. 'You are lucky to have someone like that looking out for you.' She rested her palms on the iron railing that separated the pavement from the street.

Unconsciously, Ronny mirrored her pose. But it was only for a moment or two. Then he leaned forward and gently rested his elbows on the warm metal.

The silence swelled between them. It was not quite a companionable silence, the kind that sat between some married couples, or many young children with iPads and their loving grandparents. But neither was it loaded with the weight of the past. It was breezy, quiescent, almost like the dusk that was waiting in the wings of the yet-blue sky. The years that had gone by gently collapsed into one long absence and then, as the minutes ticked and the scent of the city went to their heads, into one long season. So that, almost counter-intuitively, now that *that* season was over with this chance meeting, they could become more like their old selves. The men in the shirtsleeves withdrew from the balconies across and returned with cups of tea; their wives had disappeared with the armloads of clean dry laundry that smelt of flowers.

'Manjulika Ghosh will be happy to see you,' Lata said finally. 'She has been following your career closely.'

*And your love life*, she was going to add. But then she didn't. Let Manjulika Ghosh do the asking. Lata was not going to bring up Pragya Paramita Sen.

(Unless, of course, Ronny said something about

relationships in general and she felt the need to respond in a casual, don't-give-a-tiny-rat's-arse kind of way.)

'You're being very *extra*,' she could hear Aaduri in her head. 'Calm down.'

'I don't understand this usage. What is "extra"?' Lata had asked Aaduri.

'It's what *your* generation calls OTT. Over the top.'

'Oh, and suddenly you're a different generation?' Lata had commented drily.

'Yes. My target readership and I are one now. It's a kind of communing. *We* use OTT to mean Internet TV.'

'Let me call a cab,' Ronny said.

'We really should get one,' Lata agreed.

But neither of them pulled out their phones. They continued to stand by the railing, unmoving, until the streetlights began to glow, the traffic became a flow of streaming light, and the crowd at the tearoom reached such proportions that people congealed around them, noisy young people, full of young-people problems they needed to discuss loudly. The years that had collapsed began to right themselves. And when a few phones flashed in their faces – Lata realised Ronny had been recognised – they walked ahead quickly. Eventually, a cab was found.

❧

'Do you still read as much? In the early days in England, I used to think of you when I went to bookstores.'

'Not as much as I used to,' Ronny confessed. 'I read a lot of things online these days. Twitter's great. If you follow the right people, there are all these fascinating links that show up.'

'Twitter is vile, and people are nasty, and nobody actually reads anything anyone shares!'

Ronny looked at her. Her eyes were dancing with mirth. 'I thought you lived with the guy who ran Twitter in the UK?'

'Stalking me, have you?'

'Only sometimes, when I am down and out and miserable. And then I go to Facebook and see everyone through their shiny filters.'

'Well, then you shouldn't have been so high-minded and pursued *Art*. Like the rest of us, you should have sold out, left Calcutta and put your Economics degree to good use. But then again, who would have made *those* films? Don't flatter yourself. I'm not saying there's a dearth of good filmmakers. But others would have made other films. How would some of *my* secrets have been immortalised?'

'You've seen them?'

'On Epic. I'll have you know I liked the children's one much better. The other one, I found her – what was her name? – quite irritating.'

'Labanya.'

'Labanya. I did see that she was a lot like me. Or a particular version of me from a particular time.'

'You-ish, let's say.' Ronny half-smiled. 'But not you.'

'Though I did run away to Goa when I was fifteen and hung out with hippies on the beach. Like Labanya.'

'And you did walk home from Presidency because you spent all your money buying that fat *Vogue* book but didn't want to borrow ten bucks from me.'

'We'd fought, my friend. I was *storming off.* You don't ruin that by coming back for ten bucks. Unless it's a sitcom, and I do not like sitcoms. I thought you portrayed *that* bit rather well. College Street, in memories. You made changes, though. The collector's edition *Vogue* became a first edition Tolstoy. Why? *Vogue* too déclassé for your Labanya? And Labanya walked to Gariahat!'

'Not very dramatic, walking to Bagbazar from College Street.'

'Hey!' Lata protested, still smiling.

'So,' said Ronny, 'this thing with the Twitter guy is…?'

'And that's my phone,' Lata said, waving her hands to explain the sudden music that had filled the cab. 'Hey, Molly. I'm on my way. Calm down, sweetie, calm down.' She put her phone away after further commiserations.

'What's happened?'

'Not sure. I couldn't hear her through the sobbing. But I presume it's something highly minor. Wedding nerves.'

And then, Ronny's phone rang. It was Pragya. 'Sure,' Ronny spoke into the mouthpiece. 'Yes, that's great. Sure.' The conversation went on for a while in this vein. Lata pretended to look out of the window, then began to give directions to the cabbie.

By the time the cab drew to a halt in front of Ghosh Mansion and Ronny had to wind up the conversation with Pragya, he realised this whole detour was a bad idea. He had promised to have dinner with Pragya at home tonight – her mother was still in Ranchi – and what was he thinking, sending Bobby off to such an important meeting by herself at such short notice?

Lata was the first to alight.

'*Aiye aiye*,' said Boro Jethu, who had been lurking on the porch. '*Aapkaa swagat hai.*'

'If you are practising your Hindi for the Jaiswals, then maybe you should practise the *next* few lines,' Lata twinkled. 'After the *aaiye aaiye* bit.'

'Ronny Banerjee,' Boro Jethu now declared.

Ronny was looking up at Ghosh Mansion, glittering with tiny golden lights. The last time he'd been here, it had looked exactly the same. (In fact, the Ghoshes had probably used the same damn decorator.) It was the night before Lata's wedding to Aarjoe.

# 20
# The Lights of Ghosh Mansion

'Ronny Banerjee,' Boro Jethu repeated. He had come down the stoop to meet Ronny midway, and now, in the light of the hundred thousand toony bulbs winking, Ronny could see how much he'd aged. The skin below his chin hung in loose folds; his eyebrows were white; his eyes seemed cloudy in the dim red-gold light.

Ronny's legs were wobbly. A skein of forgotten despair, mixed with the peculiar smell of Bagbazar evenings, had begun to pulse in his blood in the cab, even before he'd entered the gates of Ghosh Mansion, and now he smiled bravely at Boro Jethu, patted his hands in what he hoped was a grown-up, I-did-not-think-we-would-meet-again-but-I-hold-nothing-against-you way, and followed Lata inside.

After the dazzling display of lights outside, he stumbled in the dark corridor, stubbing his toe in the process. 'The bulb is fused, I think,' Ronny heard Lata in the distance. 'Wait there.'

Ronny paused in the gloom of the hallway, Lata's ancestors glaring at him from the walls on either side. He closed his eyes. The layout of the entire ground floor flashed in his brain as though it were only yesterday that he had obsessed about the old house and its architecture, hunted out the original blueprint of the layout from the archives, photographed its denizens in the pristine morning light of autumn, smoked up in the warren of inter-connected terraces upstairs as evenings fell swiftly in winter, and discovered nooks and crannies that not even Lata – who had spent her whole life there – had known. The library, a few feet down the corridor, was his favourite place, all cool marble and Burma teak wall-to-wall bookshelves.

Once upon a time, the Ghoshes, who had acquired immense wealth in the early twentieth century through a wondrous legal talent, chiefly representing Bengal's landed aristocracy whose favourite pastime was fighting cases against their own brothers and cousins and uncles and granduncles (on fewer but by no means rare instances with their fathers and sons) had used the library to meet posh clients. A large wooden screen had been acquired from Kashmir to provide a sense of zenana-like privacy for the occasional lady client. By Lata's time, though, the men, none of whom had completed law degrees, had all been reduced to the other side of the karmic fence – and were fighting various cases, chiefly with each other but also against random encroachers and tenants in their still-considerable property holdings in the now-Communist Bengal. The library was a mere shadow of itself.

The original fabric on the chairs and the chaises had frayed to the point of falling apart and nobody had dusted the bookshelves since the night of India's independence. However, the large mahogany tables were still in great demand. An uncle played bridge with his set, a grandaunt taught needlework to neighbourhood girls once a week. The various school-going children of the family were allotted slots for their myriad tuitions. For example, Molly did Sanskrit with Pandit Trivedi between four-thirty and six in the evening, while Goopy's guitar guru came past nine-thirty at night. Kakimoni maintained the roster. And through her good offices, Lata knew when the library was available.

On the afternoons that Ronny and Lata studied there for the Part II exams, sunbeams would slant in through the skylights, dot the marbled tables in strangely shifting patterns – the windows were mostly shuttered on the ground floor – and fall on Lata's hair. The familiar sounds of the household would come to a pause during a small window between three-thirty and four-fifteen, between the last child returning from school and Pandit Trivedi appearing a quarter of an hour before time. It was what they called the magic hour. In fact, the sounds of the entire neighbourhood, the whole city, the cosmos for crying out loud, would fall away from the library during magic hour, and a perfect spring would descend.

Afterwards, Ronny and Lata would kick off their slippers and sit on the veranda, dangling their legs into the courtyard, laughing to their endless supply of private jokes, as Molly dolefully parroted 'narah, narau, naraah' in the background.

'You are a filmmaker now,' Boro Jethu said from behind. Ronny started.

'I still hesitate before calling myself a *filmmaker*,' Ronny replied, turning halfway to face him. 'Sounds too grown-up.'

'Hmm,' said Boro Jethu, '*modest*. So tell me, young Bengali gem, have you seen *La Règle du Jeu*?'

'I have,' Ronny replied with a straight face. 'Though a long time ago.'

'And *The Throne of Blood*?'

'Ah, Boro Jethu, of course. How could I not have seen Kurosawa's adaptation of *Macbeth*?'

'Is the fuse out?' Lata's voice, dulcet to the accompanying bass of her heels clip-clopping on the marble, preceded her. She passed them by, looking annoyed. 'Barun-da? Tulsi?' she called, stepping out again.

'What about *La Jetée*?' There was a hint of desperation in Boro Jethu's voice.

'No,' replied Ronny, though he had, in fact, seen *La Jetée* several times over the last two decades, loved it, hated it, then loved it again, and he had even written an impassioned post on an online French cinema forum, defending its aesthetics.

'No?' Boro Jethu's cloudy eyes lit up with joy. 'Really?'

Suppressing his smile, Ronny replied, 'I am afraid not. Let me note down the name.'

'L-A J-E-T-É-E...'

As Boro Jethu came closer and peered suspiciously at his phone, Ronny felt that familiar old-people scent – the semi-sweet smell of decay, as though somewhere deep inside his body, something had gone off – crawl into his nostrils, and he felt he wasn't able to breathe. 'The grave e, baba, é,' BoroJethu wagged his finger. 'Check in Symbols.'

Lata reappeared. 'Okay, so I have sent Barun to fetch the electrician,' she said. 'I think we'd better go up and meet Ma. Jethu, given how dark it is, maybe you should go upstairs too? Let's walk you up first.'

'Absolutely no need,' Jethu puffed out his chest. 'I know every inch of this house, Charulata Ghosh, and I have been sleepwalking for decades. Have I ever stumbled anywhere? All this stumbling and falling and spraining ankles is your Jethi.'

He marched ahead and climbed down into the courtyard. That was the shortcut to his part of the house. Lata and Ronny and the light on their phones followed in his wake.

'Where did you see *La Jetée*?' Ronny asked.

'When I was visiting my son in USA, there was a film appreciation week on campus. Jethi and I had nothing to do, nothing at all, so we attended every screening. Very educative. You know my son Goopy?'

'Yes, yes,' Ronny murmured.

'He came nineteenth in Madhyamik,' Boro Jethu announced, panting. 'Did you know that, Ronny?'

Lata rolled her eyes. Everybody in Bagbazar knew Goopy's rank in Madhyamik.

Upstairs, the wide veranda that opened into the various bedrooms and ante-rooms was dark too. Lata went ahead and flipped on a switch. Thankfully there was electricity in this wing and a small pool of light lit up a couple of armchairs. Boro Jethu collapsed into one.

'Come, sit, Young Gem,' he said.

Ronny and Lata exchanged a glance. 'Don't look at her. What does she know? Come, come,' he said.

'Let me go check on Molly,' Lata said, resigned, and Ronny surreptitiously looked at his phone.

'It's a disaster, Didibhai,' Molly wailed, when Lata walked into Kakimoni's bedroom. Kakimoni was putting finishing touches to the trousseau – beautiful trays that had been packed with Molly's tawtto, her trousseau, and gifts for AJ's family. Lata spied the tiffin carriers, lined up by height and decorated with matching pink bows. Molly was lying on the bed in a unicorn night-shirt.

'The lights outside are soooo tacky, AJ's grandmother has been hospitalised, the Germans are fighting with each other and' – Lata perched at the edge of the bed – 'there is no electricity on the ground floor. This electrician I got from the app was *useless*.' Molly buried her head in Lata's lap. 'Also, the cleaning company I had hired online did not turn up even though I paid them in advance. AJ's mother is full OCD. If she sees how filthy the ground floor is…'

Lata patted Molly's shoulders and said, 'Now listen to me. I know you've organised this whole wedding on the World Wide Web. But this is Calcutta. Some things have to be done the old way. Barun-da will get the *local* electrician.

The one who has been getting electric shocks from the mess of wires for generations and is the brother of the decorator who did the lights outside. They are not tacky. The house looks lovely. It announces, "We are all celebrating this union of our Bengali girl with a not-Marwari-but-some-such boy and we are chill." Nimki Didi will take charge of the cleaning. She can gather a crew in five seconds and I shall sponsor it. You can go to the beauty parlour tomorrow, as planned, ignore the Germans, and silently pray the grandmother doesn't pop off in the next two days. Even if she does, what are ventilators for? I can sponsor that too.'

Molly sat up and sighed. The role reversal, bringing them back to the original configuration, felt oddly satisfying to both.

'Now put on some clothes and come and say hi to Ronny.'

'Ronny-da's here?'

Molly's face lit up.

# 21

# Scone Das Biswas

On the days that his mother worked late, Josh Sen, custodian of the plum-headed parakeets Optimus Prime and Max, would convince his dad, distinguished professor of something very important but difficult to remember, to drive by the Kharkai and Subarnarekha rivers. Not that Vikramjit needed much convincing. He loved the Marine Drive (though he would have preferred a different name, one which did not occasion the patronising *oh yes, the other Marine Drive* nod-and-head-bob from Bombaywallahs).

Sometimes they would chat – updates about one's birds or the other's students were exchanged – but mostly, Josh would roll down the window (something his mother never allowed since the breeze interfered with her hair), stick his head out, and let the wind slap noisily against his cheeks. His father, who had grown up with dogs, delighted in his son's canine behaviour, folded up the sleeves of his Brooks Brothers shirts, and sang along to the radio. Eventually, they ended up at Brubeck, back in the city, and gorged on cakes. Tilo monitored Josh's 'refined sugar' intake during the week strictly, but father and son had perfected the art of operating on a strict what-Tilo-doesn't-know-can't-hurt-Tilo principle.

'Should we check in on Pixie and her folks?' Vik asked Josh that evening, after they had completed their usual run and turned towards the city again.

Josh took his time to reply. He could be reflective after his drawing class.

'Before or after we order the cake?' he asked finally.

'If we go before, we could take some cakes for them. If we go after, we could bring Pixie with us to Brubeck. And order the cake then. It all depends on how hungry you are now.'

'Not hungry. Miss gave us lots of cookies,' Josh replied. His drawing teacher was a flaky young Parsi artist, who lived in one of those stately if somewhat rambling colonial buildings and seemed to survive only on cookies and milk, which she set out before her students as she randomly showed them works of art projected on the living-room wall. Nudity was not censored. The kids adored Miss Patel.

'Don't mention the cookies to Mama, though. She might give Miss…'

'A lecture. I know. What happened to your healthy snack?'

Josh rummaged in his bag and extracted a little tiffin-box in posh blue chrome, and presented it to his father. Vik, who had his own chrome-blue box in his bag somewhere, long empty though, quickly wolfed down the cold quinoa cutlet with its side of home-made tomato relish. He could not stand quinoa and the coldness settled like an icy chrome-blue feeling in his stomach, with angry red lashings curling around, like memories of the tomato relish. 'Let's go over to their guest house then and see how Pixie is settling in?'

Josh handed his father his water bottle, also chrome blue.

'Is Pixie going to be invited to my birthday?' It was a loaded question though Josh sounded reasonable.

'I am sure,' Vik replied, handing the bottle back to his son and starting the car. 'In fact, Tilo has probably already invited them. Why?'

'She will go on and on about London. And my friends will find her lame.'

'Now now,' Vik said, accelerating the car.

'*And then we went St James's Park, and then we had tea with the queen,*' Josh mimicked Pixie's accent cruelly. His father was secretly impressed with its accuracy. 'Maybe she'll expect an Enid Blyton kind of high tea? With meringues and potted meat and ham and sardines and jam tarts.'

Vik narrowed his eyes and looked at his son.

'Josh Sen, is that what *you* want?'

'Whaaatt?' Josh said innocently.

Several well-appointed flats, airy and conveniently located, had been turned by the company into a group of serviced apartments, which offered greater privacy to long-term residents than the regular guest houses or hotels. A centralised hospitality desk offered luxuries such as room service and turn down (which, since she'd had to pick up after everyone in London, felt like an unbelievable luxury to Nisha), and the kitchen provided food which, while not exciting, was adequate.

One such apartment, off Kadma, was currently occupied by the Das Biswases, and its living room, with white walls, regulation sofas and severe landscapes, was caught in a terrific squall. Nisha was firm. The polka-dotted puppy who had been found under the mango tree must be returned to that spot. She had a toddler; she was not going to get another creature to look after; she was already on the verge of a nervous breakdown.

'But I am going to look after him myself, Mama, I promise, I promise,' Pixie wailed. 'And Lisa Didi can help me.' Lisa was the nanny. She lurked in the doorway and followed the war. She had fed some milk to the puppy and was on his side.

'Lisa Didi has her hands full. So do I. We will go back and return the puppy. I can't believe you smuggled him in when we expressly told you not to!'

Nisha's face was thunderous. Bappa hovered around the flat – unable to take a stand – and now decided to escape inside and call up admin to find out about the serviced apartment's policy on pets.

Pixie, equally firm, announced that if the puppy was going back to the mango tree, so was she. 'Lisa Didi, pack my bag,' Pixie called out.

Nisha couldn't decide what she should be madder about. The damn dog. Or her daughter ordering Lisa about so blithely.

'Pixie,' Nisha began ominously, when there were footsteps outside and the bell rang.

Bappa reappeared, phone glued to his ears, and breathed a sigh of relief after opening the door.

'Vikramjit-da, please come in, please come in. We have a bit of a situation here. In fact, you can help! Hello, Josh. Pixie will be happy to see you.'

The puppy, meanwhile, had hopped off Pixie's lap and wandered to the door.

'Woofwoof,' he said to Josh.

'Woofwoof,' replied Josh in return.

Pixie snatched him up.

'I didn't know you had a dog,' Josh said, as he came and sat down next to her.

'She doesn't,' Nisha said coldly. 'That dog's going.'

She forced herself to smile at Vik. 'Tea? Coffee? No Tilo?'

Having gauged the situation, Vik decided that it was better he sit. The puppy cast its soulful eyes on him. 'I wouldn't mind some tea,' he said. 'But only if it's no trouble.

Tilo is working late today. We were going to Brubeck and thought we'd take Pixie along if that's okay.'

'Tea is no trouble,' Nisha replied, and made her way to the kitchen.

'What's his name?' Josh whispered conspiratorially.

'Scone,' Pixie whispered back.

'What?' Josh narrowed his eyes exactly like his father.

'S-C-O-N-E,' spelt out Pixie, now no longer whispering. 'It's pronounced scon, like don, not scone, like cone.'

Josh looked doubtful.

Meanwhile, Scone Das Biswas had laid his little puppy head on Josh's knee. Despite his dislike for Pixie, Josh couldn't help but fall a little in love with the polka-dotted creature, who wasn't a patch on his birds of course, but was nonetheless a delightful thing to love. He stroked its velvety ears gently. Pixie did not say anything to that. Instead, she looked beseechingly at her father and his friend. Soon, fat tears rolled down her cheeks one by one.

It was around eleven-thirty that Nisha returned to their bedroom. She was freshly showered. (It was a habit she'd picked up in England and it drove her mother-in-law insane. 'Who takes a bath at night? It's like eating curd or bananas after sundown. A sure-fire invitation to a cold. But why should you listen to me?' But Bappa liked this ritual very much. The day's angsts sloughed off Nisha when she showered, and afterwards she wore a baggy, relaxed air about her limbs.) Though she'd dried her hair, a few curls were still damp and clung to her cheeks. 'Posto's asleep,' she said and sat at the dressing table, applying cream on her cheeks and neck.

Nisha smiled at Bappa in the mirror and a load lifted off his chest.

'So is your daughter and that Scone. He is ensconced – or should we say en-scone-d? – in her bed. Lisa is sitting on the carpet, looking at him adoringly. I hope she still pays attention to Posto!'

Nisha got under the duvet and folded her body against her husband's.

'So, your friend Vikramjit is quite the convincer. Should have gone into law!'

'He was a famous debater, baba,' Bappa replied, taking her hand in his. 'Long day, today,' he said.

Nisha's hair smelt all coconut-y and familiar. Bappa was half-aroused. It had been a while. Shifting continents with two kids was not good for one's sex life.

'How much do you think professors earn at that B-school?' Nisha interrupted.

'Sorry, what?' Bappa replied, a little annoyed at this new turn.

'Vikramjit and Tilottama – how much do you think they earn? Have you seen Tilo's saris? And Vikramjit wears only Brooks Brothers or Burberry!'

'Hmm,' said Bappa, 'I'd never really considered that.'

# 22

# The Angle

It was half-past eight. Outside, Calcuttans were walking about in their half-sleeve sweaters and woollen mufflers, now that it was officially winter. Inside the office, under the neutral glow of fluorescent lights, Aaduri Bagchi was looking over the copy of the next day's lead story, when she was interrupted.

The final once-over was something she did herself most days, almost obsessively, and the lack of typos or bloopers or fake news references this ensured had already begun to distinguish their content from a lot of digital stuff produced by their competitors. Somewhere in the middle of the piece – '#CookingGoals: We Divulge, Finally, the Definitive Recipe for Calcutta Biriyani, with Potatoes and Eggs, for the Daring Homecook' – Aaduri became conscious of a very faint whirring next to her.

It was Tiana Mitra, her newest employee.

Tiana had arrived in their office exactly ten days ago, armed with a degree in popular culture from an American university – which Aaduri did not care about – and a good grounding in grammar – which she most certainly did. Currently, Tiana was standing by her desk, almost vibrating in excitement, and giving off the distinct impression that she was about to explode as a result of some kind of a Eureka moment.

'Yes?' Aaduri asked, even though she wasn't very hopeful of Tiana's Eureka vibrations. She'd had to shoot down twelve ideas from the kid in the last hour.

'So, you know the actress Pragya Paramita Sen?' Tiana began, already bubbling over.

'Tiana,' said Aaduri patiently. (What kind of a ridiculous name was Tiana? What were her parents thinking, giving her a neither-here-nor-there name like that?) 'Sweetie, since we haven't seen her act yet, I am not sure we can call her an "actress". Or "actor", the gender-neutral term. As a journalist, you must learn to be exact. But yes, Pragya Paramita Sen, soon to make her debut in Ronny Banerjee's new film...'

'Has just started an Instagram account. It's about saris and books and paintings and cities – and the account is very very aesthetic. May I do a story on it? I can even get a quote from her social media consultant.'

'She has a social media consultant?'

'It's my friend, Mimi,' Tiana said. 'And the angle,' she added carefully, having been asked *but-what-on-earth-is-the-angle* on the twelve previous occasions by Aaduri, 'is that Facebook and Instagram are essentially different. Facebook is about your life in all its messiness or boringness or bourgeoiseness while Instagram is about aesthetics. Very few celebrities get this. They post the same old pictures of themselves on photo shoots or hanging out with their other celebrity friends on holiday or Pujo or whatever on Insta. But Pragya is actually doing aesthetics, thereby changing the game.'

Aaduri raised her eyebrows. 'Tiana Mitra, it is possible that you may have finally understood what an angle is. And it is also possible that you may have shot up in my estimation. Go write this piece. Be biting about the celebrities who don't get Insta. I want to read it first thing tomorrow morning. Let's run the first story on this before those blithering idiots who do that "Welcome to Instagram" or some such show on that Bengali YouTube channel. And – if you do everything properly – you'll get your first byline.'

Tiana gave a little whoop of joy.

'Hem-da!' she said joyfully, as she spotted Hem walking towards them. 'I just shot up in Ma'am's estimation.'

They did a high-five and Tiana sailed away in a cloud of bouncy bliss.

'Are you done?' Hem asked.

'No. Shush,' Aaduri said. 'I need to read two more pieces and sign off on them.'

Hem pulled up a chair and sat down behind her. He surreptitiously glanced at the clock that hung above their heads. 'You're putting pressure on me, Hem,' Aaduri complained. 'I hate that clock. And yes, I do have eyes behind my head.'

Hem only smiled.

And unseen to him, Aaduri betrayed the briefest of brief smiles too, a tiny inflection of the mouth that most normal people would see as an involuntary twitch, but in Aaduri's case it was, nonetheless, a smile.

Meanwhile, at Ghosh Mansion, the lights flickered mysteriously in Manjulika's quarters but never went out. Ronny, Lata, Molly and Manjulika were all sitting cross-legged on Lata's bed, at least three of them chattering nineteen-to-the-dozen.

Nimki had served them her famous jhaal-muri with tea, annoyed that no prior notice had been given for her to whip up a culinary extravaganza in honour of Ronny's return. (Nimki and Manjulika often discussed Ronny and what might have been, had Lata and Ronny not broken up and had Lata never met that dashing but innately unsuitable-in-the-long-run Aarjoe immediately after. They had also gone to the theatre to watch both his films on the Fridays they released.)

Nimki had given Ronny all the news about the now-retired household staff whom Ronny had befriended in the years he was a regular at Ghosh Mansion. Molly had stories of German work habits to share. Manjulika regaled them with accounts of the extreme politics in her school. And Ronny made them laugh with anecdotes of Shaarani Sen and her eccentric beauty regimen. No one mentioned Pragya. Not Manjulika, not Molly, not Ronny. Not even Nimki, who kept up with Tollywood gossip as though her life depended on that knowledge, brought up the beautiful Pragya Paramita, who was invariably photographed in diaphanous saris, or her impending debut in his new film.

The more this went on, the laughter interrupted by the crunch of green chillies that Ronny bit into with abandon, the scent of winter curling in through the skylights and settling into the damp patches of her childhood room that remained locked up for most of the year, the more distanced Lata felt from it all. She got up and slipped out of the room into the veranda on the left, which overlooked Dayanara's courtyard and, as an inexplicable anger flowed through her body, she fumed silently at the night.

What the hell were these women – her women – playing at? That in the magical circle they had created upon her bed they would simply spirit the last two decades away, rewind the story and rewrite its ending? Were they pretending that this was still 1999, and Ronny, the familiar Ronny who always carried his camera around, clicked their photos, and never took to heart Boro Jethu's bullying, that Ronny – now famous if not rich – would gift Lata Ghosh her happily ever after? And Molly? Why on earth was Molly a part of this? Uff, how disappointed was she in Molly. Her radical JU edge had been completely eaten away by that stupid AJ and the Germans.

Lata pulled her hair into a bun angrily, worked herself up some more, and returned to the room.

Everyone fell silent. 'Come join us, Munni,' Manjulika coaxed. The same tone she used years ago when she asked Lata to sing a song or recite a poem in front of some relative or the other and Lata would, like a stiff young foal, refuse to play along. And now, from the doorway, she could see Manjulika's face, the fine lines that had cast a net on her once-flawless skin, lit up in a hope that was, but of course, entirely misplaced. Lata refused to play along.

'Didn't you have dinner plans with Pragya?' Lata asked Ronny coldly.

❧

'So you've finally had time to come?' Nimki accosted Aaduri. 'There's a wedding happening, so much activity, but no sign of you! Who is this?'

'Nimki-di,' Aaduri said, 'meet Hem. He works with me. Hem, Nimki-di.'

Nimki looked at Hem appraisingly. Tall (ish). Fair (ish). Smiling.

'I know about Nimki-di,' Hem said. 'Lata told me she makes the best thekuas.'

Tall. Fair. Smiling. *Hindi-speaking.*

'I learnt how to make thekuas from this Bihari girl who used to live here,' Nimki gushed. 'Next time I'll make it for you.'

'Lata said you like Five Stars?' Hem slunk one out of his pocket and held it in front of Nimki.

The thrill of this Hindi-speaking, exotic animal trailing Aaduri adoringly would have been enough for Nimki's wholehearted approval, but the Five Star pushed her to a stratosphere of delight, where even the latest bit of family drama could be forgotten for a bit. She blushed, accepted the Five Star bashfully, and led the way down the corridor to Manjulika's tiny sitting room.

'I can't believe the depths to which you sink, Hem Shankar Tiwari. If this is the sort of bribery you are indulging in at Lata's, I wonder what you'll do if I take you to my parents'!'

'Is there any hope of that?' Hem asked.

'Of course not,' Aaduri replied. 'Now take off your shoes.'

'They've had a big fight,' Nimki whispered conspiratorially to Aaduri. 'Ronny-da was here.'

## 23

# The Dictionary of Obscure Sorrows

'Aaduri, that colour looks lovely on you,' Manjulika said in a bright voice, ushering them into her converted sitting room, 'And this must be…'

'Hem,' Aaduri supplied, 'Hem Shankar, actually.'

In Ghosh Mansion, a traditional boudoir adjoined the bedchambers. At least, that's what her husband had told her. And now that the years had rounded the edges of her many little upsets with him, she had begun to remember some of the trivia he would dispense liberally about the old house. The boudoir was formerly his darkroom (he was something of a photographer and fancied himself an artist) and after he passed away, Manjulika had stowed his equipment – in fact, she had given Ronny a few of his things – and furnished the little jewel box of a room with castaways from the rest of the house.

For instance, the pair of ivory-inlaid planter's chairs that Aaduri and Hem were now pulling out for themselves had been discarded by Boro Jethu and Jethi when Goopy got interested in elephant conservation. Manjulika had to only get the seats rewoven.

The once-removed Ghoshes who occupied the second storey in the left wing of the house had wanted to get rid of the mahogany divan and the carved pankha from the music room, but not permanently, only on a long lease. So Manjulika promised to hold them in trust even as she put them to use. (Precisely because they could be recalled at a day's notice, both Nimki and Manjulika had got violently attached to them.) She preferred to sit on the divan facing the door, and now Nimki stood behind her, discreetly straightening the cover which had been stitched from old silk saris.

Then there was the tiny two-seater sofa in Burma teak that had been rescued by Lata when auctioneers had carted much of the old furniture, books, paintings and ephemera – diaries, newspapers, postcards – away, after the restructuring of Ghosh Mansion – the formal paperwork dividing up the flats – and now, Lata's glasses and magazines, her favourite pair of polka-dotted socks and iPhone X were heaped on it. But no Lata.

Hem complimented everything liberally. The old Persian carpet that Manjulika's cousin had sent when their house in Ballygunj went into redevelopment, and that came out only in winter; the crocheted rug and the embroidered cushion covers, all bearing the stamp of long afternoons and lonely weekends; the wall of black-and-white photographs of Lata's childhood and youth (a project started by her husband and completed by Ronny). Hem complimented everything, walking up to see Lata and Aaduri in school plays and college picnics.

'Where's Lata-ji?' Hem asked eventually.

'When you call Luts that, it sounds like you are the host of a singing contest on TV, referring to Lata Mangeshkar,' Aaduri giggled.

'Lata-ji,' replied Manjulika, switching to her accented Hindi, 'is moping in her bedroom. She was rude to Ronny, scared off Molly, fought with me unnecessarily, and has now locked herself in.'

'You said some nasty things to her,' Nimki looked at Manjulika accusingly.

'That was afterwards,' Manjulika clarified.

'*Better you stay on in London. You've become cold in the bones like the goras you live with.* Are these things to tell your only daughter? Now if she doesn't come again you can cry alone, don't expect me to comfort you.'

'Don't get agitated,' Manjulika replied calmly. 'Get some tea for Hem at least. And check the mutton. If it's not soft enough, another whistle or two?'

'Don't teach me cooking,' said Nimki, and flounced off.

Lata unlatched her bedroom door and cracked it open an inch. When she saw Aaduri, she held it ajar briefly, locked it after her, and climbed back into bed wordlessly.

Aaduri went straight to the dressing table. 'Gaah!' she exclaimed, looking at her face critically in the mirror. 'I look ghastly.' She picked up an egg-shaped tub from the beautiful clutter of Lata's cosmetics and peered at the label. 'Hand cream?' She popped the lid and squelched a few large blobs onto her palms.

'Just a drop is enough,' Lata winced. 'You're wasting money, Aaduri.'

'*I* am wasting money?' Aaduri said, rubbing her hands together and perching at the edge of the bed. Experimentally, she sniffed her palms. 'The scent's not half bad, though,' she said.

'It's *Chanel*. Of course the scent's not half bad. I am not going to speak to Manjulika Ghosh, I'll have you

know, if that's what you're here to intercede for,' Lata told
Aaduri.

'I didn't for a second assume the scent of that hand cream
would be nice just because it's Chanel,' Aaduri replied. 'I
didn't like their No. 5 either, that much-feted perfume our
generation went crazy about. Manjulika, by the way, isn't
dying to speak to you. She is gabbing away with Hem. Who
seems to be humanity's gift to people's mothers.'

Aaduri stretched out her legs and propped herself up on
her elbows.

Glumly, Lata offered her a smidge of her Jaipuri razai.

'You know I was supposed to meet my co-liaison officer?
Bobby Bansal?'

'Yes,' said Aaduri. 'Oh, of course.'

'Bobby works with Ronny. Our Ronny Young-Bengali-
Gem. You knew that?'

'I know that Young-Bengali-Gem's assistant is a Bobby.
But I did not know that Bobby was linked to this wedding
in any way.'

'Well, anyway, he came with her – I am still not sure
why. My lens fell out, he gave me his handkerchief, we had
a weird moment.'

'It sounds like a Woody Allen film,' Aaduri commented.

'It was awkward – and then, Aadu, it just was not. I don't
know if there's a word for what we felt later – it was warm
and fuzzy and nostalgic, all in a good way. He despatched
that stupid Bobby to some meeting on her own – boy,
was she annoyed! – and we were alone. It became kind
of charged between us. We talked about all manner of
irrelevant things. Like, all banter, no substance. Of course,
he did ask in a roundabout way if I was still with Ari.'

'So he stalks you on Facebook!' Aaduri laughed.

'He confessed as much. And then he came here, Aadu. He said he wanted to meet Ma. And at the threshold of this house, all lit up with Molly's wedding lights, it became strange and confusing.' Lata sat up in agitation. 'He was waylaid by Boro Jethu, whom he indulged for a fair bit. Then he came up here, and Nimki and Molly and Ma just slobbered all over him – '

'So?' Aaduri said. 'Why on earth does that bother you? They've always loved him.'

'Because…' Lata replied shortly.

'Hmm,' said Aaduri, after waiting for a while to hear the rest of that sentence which never came. '*Because*. That's insightful.'

'I didn't fight with him. I just reminded him that he had dinner plans with Pragya Paramita Sen.'

'We might be publishing a story about Pragya Paramita Sen's Instagram account, by the way. Apparently, she is very cool.'

'Good for him,' said Lata. 'Famous filmmaker can marry Tollywood royalty. There's no need for that story to intersect with mine. I'm done with men. And that's the thing Manjulika Ghosh just does not want to accept! She lives in some fool's paradise and imagines that Ronny and I will magically get back together, and she will even get some stupid camera-carrying grandchild out of it. My father's reincarnation, I suppose.'

'Twenty years,' said Aaduri, walking up to the dresser and picking up her bag. 'Twenty years, and I can't believe we're still holed up here talking about Ronny Banerjee! There must be some strong karma.'

Lata looked up and into Aaduri's laughing eyes, 'Karma? Since when did Aaduri Bagchi start using terms like karma?'

'Here,' Aaduri said, her closed fist outstretched under Lata's nose. 'Your karma appears to be good, dear child.'

Lata tapped on it and Aaduri uncurled her fingers.

There, in the shell of her palm, was a single, perfectly rolled joint.

Several times en route, as the traffic waxed and waxed, Ronny thought he would call off the dinner and go home. But turning homeward meant an even longer time on the road, and so he stuck to the course. Between obsessively checking his notifications and obsessively thinking about what Lata Ghosh might have meant when she reminded him about his so-called dinner plans with Pragya, effectively asking him to leave. (It must be noted, though, he clarified to himself immediately, she did accompany him downstairs, wait for the cab with him, and in the split second before he got into the car, she did smile at him with that same heartbreaking candour lighting up her eyes. It twisted his insides, still.)

Around him throbbed the city, familiar in all its beauty and noise and disorder and lights, the sense of people pressed into each other on buses and roads and quietly moving towards their destinies. Ronny allowed his thoughts to drift. Boro Jethu's rheumy eyes; maybe he should watch *Le Jetée* again; Molly – Molly getting married; Bobby's meeting; Pragya's diction lessons; the meeting with his favourite composer this morning.

'Sir, your phone is ringing. Sir!'

At the cabbie's words, Ronny started.

It was Shaarani Sen. But Shaarani-di never called him!

# 24

# The One That Got Away

*9.05 p.m., somewhere in Calcutta, inside a cab:*

Shaarani Sen: Ronny baba.

Ronny: Good evening, Shaarani-di.

Shaarani Sen: I heard you are going to New Alipore for dinner?

Ronny: Yes, I am en route, actually.

Shaarani Sen: Good, then you can explain this to Pragya. It's a sensitive matter. I have given our conversation in Ranchi a lot of thought. Ronny, even though Abala Bose is a challenging role and I do like the idea of doing a memorable cameo alongside Bablu-da as Jagadish Bose, I don't think I can say yes to *Shomoy*.

Ronny: But why? I don't mind expanding the scope of the role even more…

Shaarani Sen: That's not the reason, Ronny. Don't be silly. But this film is Pragya's debut. From the time she was a little girl, my persona has overshadowed her life, her efforts. In school, on result day, her teachers would fawn over me – even though she'd done so well in her tests – and the other parents would neither come up to chat nor stop staring at us. A few parents were too clever by half. They sent their kids to strike up a friendship with Pragya simply because they wanted to come to our house and get pally with me. Naturally, these friendships would implode after a point. Why do you think she's always running to Mimi? Mimi was her only constant in childhood. Anything remarkable that she achieved on her own was ascribed to me and my contacts. Anything childish she did – once, she forgot her lines on stage when she was seven years old – was dissected with such cruelty. Why do you think I sent her to America to study? It was so expensive! But I had no option. I wanted her to find her feet and not be judged all the time. You see?

Ronny: I understand.

Shaarani Sen: So, if I am a part of her debut film, camco or whatever, you know what's going to happen. There is going to be a lot of unnecessary talk. Unfavourable comparisons. In general, it's not going to be good for Pragya.

Ronny: Pragya is the first one I spoke to about this, Shaarani-di. She's a big girl.

Shaarani Sen: I know, I know. She's a good child, forever wanting me, needing me, valorising me, even though I must confess I have not always been an ideal mother. Her father's death affected her a lot. And my way of dealing with it was different. I don't remember him as a perfect individual – but she does. Anyway. I am speaking too much. But you are part of the family now, Ronny. I can trust you.

Ronny: Of course.

Shaarani Sen: Pragya wants to prove all the time that she is not threatened by me. But I am her mother, Ronny, even though I might not always have been there for her when she needed me. I have to do the right thing. This must be

Pragya's film. Not mine, not even slightly. You should speak to Rina or somebody else…I can help you find someone suitable…

Ronny: It's okay, Shaarani-di. Let me figure this out.

Shaarani Sen: You know why I wanted her to work with you? Because you are a serious director. You follow the old-fashioned systems. You are making her work on her diction, getting her to read. I know you will have rigorous workshops with theatre persons involved, with historians and art directors. I wish I could have been a part of it. But no.

Ronny: Well then. I don't think there is anything I can say that'll change your mind.

Shaarani Sen: Go on, enjoy your dinner. Debu is making korma. I will be back next week. See you then.

Ronny: See you, Shaarani-di.

*11.30 p.m., Ghosh Mansion, Lata's room*

Manjulika: Can I come in?

Lata: You already have.

Manjulika: That boy is very nice. Ate luchi mangsho so happily. What's his name again? Sorry, I have become a bit strange with names.

Lata: Hem. Hem Shankar Tiwari.

Manjulika: Baba, Munni, your room is so cold. I didn't realise. It's because of those damp patches. We'd better get it repaired after the wedding.

Lata: You can share my blanket.

Manjulika: I am sorry, Munni. I know you have a certain dignity and I think...

Lata: It's not about dignity! You are all acting as though he is 'the one that got away'!

Manjulika: What is 'the one that got away'?

Lata: Oh, Ma.

Manjulika: I don't understand these post-Agatha Christie British phrases.

Lata: Then you should read some contemporary books. Bridget Jones, etc.

Manjulika: No thank you. I barely have enough time to keep up with contemporary Bengali fiction. And now at my age, I think I should start reading the Bhagvad Gita every day, Munni.

❧

*11.45 p.m., Hem's car, Park Street*

Aaduri: Tiana has sent me the article. I am, in fact, shocked at her alacrity.

Hem: You underestimate the young.

Aaduri: You overestimate the young. Anyway, I'll look at it later.

Hem: What *is* it with Ronny and Lata?

Aaduri: Uff. Don't make me go into it. Those two and their epic, never-ending nonsense. Ever since she's arrived in town, it feels like we are in *Romy and Michele's High School Reunion*. Fine, I'll tell you. Ronny fell for Lata pretty much at the orientation – 17 August 1997. They became friends the day she was christened Helen of Troy – 24 November

1997. Ronny liked to believe he was her best friend. But he wasn't. I was. Anyway. Then came her twentieth birthday.

Hem: And?

Aaduri: There's something about turning twenty.

Hem: Oh yes. The day I turned twenty, I promised that I would stop trying to be a poet. No, wait, the day I turned twenty-one. Or twenty? Don't laugh. At one time, in the college circuit of Uttar Pradesh, girls would record the recitations of Hem Ilahabadi at college functions, cry over the shers at home and write him letters in blood.

Aaduri: Blood?

Hem: Well, maybe red ink.

Aaduri: No wonder you and Lata get along so famously. She too received letters written in red ink.

Hem: Lata turned twenty and…

Aaduri: Sometime after, they became a couple. Third-year was that madly-in-love phase. Punctuated by stormy fights and break-ups that lasted five minutes. But there was something authentic about them. Then Lata went to IIM and Ronny went to ISI. I was away in Delhi myself at the time. Something happened, they broke up, I expected them to get back together, any day. But on the day of her campus placement, Lata met Aarjoe.

Hem: The husband?

Aaduri: The ex-husband, yes. It was a whirlwind, their courtship and the grand wedding in Ghosh Mansion. And after that Lata went with Aarjoe to the US.

Hem: And Ronny?

Aaduri: Ronny dropped out of ISI and went to Mumbai. Worked in advertising. Was very successful too.

Several serious relationships. But never married. Here we are. Thank you, Hem. I am getting too used to you driving me around.

Hem: I'll see you in the office tomorrow, then?

Aaduri: Unless…Never mind. Yes, tomorrow. Goodnight.

❧

*12.05 a.m., Manjulika's bedroom*

Manjulika: You are still watching TV? Turn it off right now. Is this why you stayed back tonight? To watch TV?

Nimki: Na na, I like to give my son and daughter-in-law some privacy. Who wants a mother-in-law hovering around all the time? I missed my serials today. First, Ronny-da came. Then you and Mamoni fought. Then Aaduri came. Now let me relax. You want a paan?

Manjulika: Fine, give me one. What happened to the girl who was kidnapped yesterday?

Nimki: Not yesterday. That was last week. She was saved by the hero. Now she is participating in a singing contest. But the dacoit sardar is there too, nobody knows why. Meanwhile, though he saved her, there was a misunderstanding between the hero and heroine. Here. I have added that sweet shupuri you like. Is Mamoni okay?

Manjulika: I think so.

Nimki: Tomorrow onwards, she and I are busy with Molly's wedding. She is incharge. I am second incharge.

Manjulika: It was nice to see Ronny. He's still the same.

Nimki: No airs. That's good. I am praying to Ma Kali that they sort out their fights once and for all.

Manjulika: Don't say such things, Nimki. Your Mamoni will bite off our heads. Apparently, mothers and aunts can't even wish happiness on their children because 'happiness' is an irrelevant concept. Have you heard of anything more ridiculous? It's my fault. Gave her too many books to read as a child, and she still lives in that world of books.

Nimki: I know where to say what. You are the one who is always blabbing. She has her pride, understand that. If Ma Kali doesn't listen and Ronny-da marries that what's-her-face girl, that actress, Mamoni should not feel too crushed.

Manjulika: You and your Mamoni, I am sorry to say, know nothing of love. What is all this pride? She must be willing to confront her own feelings, accept her mistakes, even make a fool of herself in love.

Nimki: Okay, now let me watch my serial in peace.

Manjulika: Who is *that*?

Nimki: That is the leader of the dacoits. He too has fallen for the girl. Now, let's wait and see what happens.

# PART FOUR

# 25

# The Thing with Childhood Love

Saratchandra Chattopadhyay, arguably the greatest exponent of relationships in literary Bengal, writes in *Devdas* that childhood love is, for all its intensity, ultimately cursed. It seldom leads to happily-ever-afters.

'But we are both over eighteen, Kakimoni,' Lata had replied softly, suddenly maudlin, even though she found the possibility rather remote that what they had – that perfect, precious, sunset-coloured thing – might be poisoned. She'd buried her nose in the pink pashmina shawl she had stolen that season from Manjulika's almirah.

When she lifted her head, she saw Kakimoni smiling. 'Whaaat?' she'd said, and Kakimoni shucked her chin. 'That pink is perfect for people newly in love,' she laughed. 'You *are* right, it doesn't apply to those who are not children.' But Kakimoni said that tartly, raising her eyes in the direction of the veranda where Ronny was bickering with Molly over the carrom board, much like a minor. 'We'll find out, won't we.' she said, 'whether you are children or adults!'

Kakimoni then heaved herself from the bed and went out to their little kitchen, carved out of a nook where a tertiary stairway had been boarded up – the Ghoshes had all divided up their kitchens by then – in order to make them scrambled egg sandwiches with cheese. And Lata dragged herself out of bed and curled up in one of the Bombay Fornicators kept outside on the veranda (neither she nor Ronny knew the term then), five of them in a line, and impatiently waited for Ronny to stop playing carrom and revise Economics with her. It's he who needs the revision more, she huffed. But the sight of him and Molly rapt in play also made for a pleasant picture. Once, unknown to Ronny, she had sneaked his camera out of his bag and taken pictures of them.

*Where are those pictures?* Lata now wondered. Hadn't Ronny framed one and given it to her?

When they'd broken up, she'd told Kakimoni bitterly, on a weekend she was home from business school, dark circles under her eyes, 'You were right. Childhood love is poisoned.'

'Not me,' Kakimoni had replied sadly, enveloping her in a hug, 'Sarat Babu.'

The Bombay Fornicators had vanished long ago.

Lata stood now where they used to be lined up and watched as the lights over the courtyard came on. It had been Ghosh Mansion all this while; now, in the blink of an eye, it was transformed from a decaying house in a decaying neighbourhood into an unfamiliar place, a new continent, one where happiness and success and glory were all a handspan away for the taking.

Ghosh Mansion had come alive in the last two days, once Lata had taken charge of the Molly-AJ wedding, along with the army Nimki had summoned from the massive contacts list on her phone. Given the paucity of time, the rooms on the ground floor were all locked up for the evening in lieu of being cleaned (Lata kept a roster of the keys and promised the various owners of the said rooms that it was a temporary matter). The corridor and the courtyard leading to the naachghar were scrubbed clean. 'Not even a speck of dust should be visible to the Marwaris,' Nimki was heard shouting every ten minutes or so. 'Molly's mother-in-law has OCD and we better live up to her standards of cleanliness. In any case, Molly doesn't know any housework. If they see dirty corridors here, they will always link the two. FOR THE REST OF HER LIFE.' Lata had also decided that since there was no time to get the walls repainted, a major red herring was required. She had cajoled the electrician to create a canopy of twinkling lights over the courtyard.

The effect, she now saw, feeling quite pleased with herself, was magical.

Molly stepped out of Kakimoni's bedroom in her engagement outfit and sighed at the lights. She wore a white chanderi full skirt trimmed beautifully with gold zari, paired with a postbox red choli. Much to her mother's unhappiness, she'd refused to wear anything but the plain gold choker that Manjulika and Lata had given her from Manjulika's own collection, and a pair of gold danglers that had been their great-grandmother's.

Lata looked critically at Molly, straightened her

tikli – the sole item from her parents' trousseau – and then gently kissed her cheek.

'I don't know what I'd have done without you,' Molly murmured into her hair.

'I'm glad I am here. And I hope you and AJ will come to London and stay with me, so I can dispense jamai aador and luchis like a grown-up Ghosh.'

Molly squeezed her hands. Boro Jethi's gold bracelet, studded with pearls and rubies, glittered. It had been a pair that, Lata knew, was given to Jethima, the eldest daughter-in-law, by their grandmother, and Jethima had given her one at her wedding, reserving the other for Molly. 'What about Goopy's bride?' Manjulika had said to Jethima then. 'Arre baba,' Jethima had replied conspiratorially, 'Goopy's wife will get a lot!'

'I miss Goopy,' Molly said. 'Though he would have made fun of everything, of course.'

'I was just thinking about him!' Lata exclaimed, 'Anyway, listen, Bobby's just texted me. They are about fifteen minutes away. I think you should go now and sit in the throne room. Guests have arrived. Where's the entourage?'

Almost as though they'd heard her, Molly's girlfriends, the old ones from school and college and the new ones from Berlin, all trooped out from her room, where they'd been getting ready. Their individual beauty enhanced by the collective glamour, the girls held themselves erect and frowned in concentration, speaking to each other in code. Lata did not miss a single detail of this pageantry: the wisps of hair slipping out of elaborate hairdos, the silken saris curving and catching at unaccustomed feet. They walked up to the balustrade awkwardly and then, finally finding their stride in their saris, followed Molly down the elaborate staircase, where the subjects of Victorian paintings in gilt frames looked down at them approvingly.

Lata took pictures on her phone, waving the girls away, exhorting them to mind their step. A few minutes later, as they crossed the courtyard, carefully, carefully, doddering on their high heels, saris and lehengas bunched up so that their calves were briefly visible, the light fell on their youthful faces and covered them with stardust.

From upstairs, in her pink-yellow tussar sari, Lata watched them and marvelled at the fierce brevity of childhood and youth.

Now it was here. Alive and flickering in the stack of Mills and Boon novels under her bed, clattering upon the carrom board, surfacing in the large bare cupboards in the storeroom which were perfect for stolen kisses, and the third-floor terrace which was perfect for horrible fights.

And now it was gone.

First came the ashirbad and then the ring ceremony. The not-Marwaris and Bengalis and Germans and assorted others all mingled happily, eating the delicious (if vegetarian) hors d'oeuvres and drinking gallons of Blue Lagoon.

As regards the food, Boro Jethu had firmly put his feet down. At the Oberoi, they could serve whatever mishmash modern cuisine they wanted to, but at home it would be old-fashioned comfort food. It was a gargantuan tragedy that the affair had to be made vegetarian. But no further dilution was to be tolerated. Yes, there would be piles of motorshutir kochuri with stuffed aloor dom and chholar dal with coconut bits. Yes, the old thakurs would whip up family secrets that would never-ever be revealed to the not-Marwaris. And yes, there would be five kinds of savoury fries, excluding mochaar chop, and five kinds of mishti, excluding doi. No chatter about calories would be entertained. No dahivada, golgappa or that sort of rubbish would be served, they were the Ghoshes after all. And there was no question of serving any kind of fancy salad with imported leaves, olive oil and vinegar – only the time-honoured slices of cucumber, tomato and onion laid decoratively on a plate, along with mustard and mayonnaise.

Lata had escaped the vice-grip of relatives, who had far too many questions than she could handle, and whose comments about how youthful her face *still* was and how expensive her sari looked were all lined with a certain malice. She now stood in a corner and exchanged notes about the next day with a surly Bobby (smoky-eyed and bewitching in a black chikankari anarkali-dress with mukaish work on it).

'Who's that?' Bobby asked, her interest piqued by a man who had walked up to Nimki and clasped her hands in his. He wore a beautifully tailored suit in charcoal grey. Lata found herself looking away.

# 26

# Protocol

As people milled about and ate and drank (Blue Lagoon only, but even so) and gushed over the young couple who were now sparkling on the makeshift stage in the naachghar, Boro Jethu found himself stranded in a corner of the glittering courtyard, listening to AJ's 93-year-old great-grandfather talk and talk, even as he unobtrusively used his tongue to tease out bits of cauliflower (from the shingaras) that had got stuck between his teeth. Should have been mutton, he sighed. Meanwhile, the chief reason for the vegetarian menu, the great-grandfather himself, hard of hearing and consequently given to monologues, was talking loudly about classical music – or wait, was it demonetisation?

As Boro Jethu wondered how to get a sentence in edgewise – 'Please come this way for dinner, it is time' – he spotted Aarjoe Mitra walking past. It couldn't be Aarjoe though, could it? Why on earth, what for? If there were any doubts about the face – years had passed and Boro Jethu's memory for faces was no longer what it was – the fine suit made of exquisite wool and the over-polished Oxfords belied his doubts. It was indeed Aarjoe Mitra, looking as dapper as ever – he had been surprised when Munni fell for that peacock – even though his hair now bore prominent silver streaks.

Boro Jethu frowned.

Who had invited Aarjoe?

Surely not Munni or Manjulika. However modern they might pretend to be, he was certain that neither of them would have gone that far.

Boro Jethu was also seized with a different concern now. What was the protocol for such a situation? An ex-jamai turning up – uninvited by most counts – at a family wedding? Ex-family, that is. Surely the Ghoshes were as ex to Aarjoe as he was to them?

Boro Jethu looked about himself, discomfited. Would we ask him to stay on for dinner? (Well, the dinner itself was a kind of punishment, come to think of it, so yes, we should.) Where was his wife when he needed her? Gadding about with someone, right next to the happy couple, no doubt, so that every photograph included her in that loud turquoise baluchari she should have stopped wearing two decades ago.

Boro Jethu grabbed a panjabi-clad shoulder in the vicinity – it turned out to be a nephew – and bossily introduced him to the Jaiswal patriarch. The monologue continued after that small interruption and Boro Jethu was able to excuse himself. Where was that Aarjoe?

What a grand wedding they had thrown Munni. The oldest daughter of their family, 'Rupey Lakshmi, guney Saraswati,' people had started saying after she went to IIM – as beautiful as Lakshmi, as talented as Saraswati. Fatherless, on top of that. Doing right by her had been vital to the family's character. ('I didn't know we had any,' his irreverent son Goopy had chuckled.) The ceremony had been flawless, executed by the uncles. Of course, that Manjulika had interfered in every decision – what flowers, what colour lights, what kind of fish fry, she'd had an opinion on everything. Despite that, the wedding had been memorable.

Boro Jethu tried to negotiate the crowds even as he attempted to locate the charcoal grey suit from the palette of bright colours that the evening had now devolved into – the pastel-pink shervanis, the beige tussars, the midnight-blue silks – and, inexplicably, as the waiters flashed past in white, and the crimson anarkalis of the groom's sisters twirled past his nose, Boro Jethu felt a kind of exhaustion surround him. He wished Goopy were here. He wished he could have sent Goopy to deal with the ex-jamai protocol. Instead of having to tell everyone loudly loudly that Goopy was now tenured at a fancy New York college, that Goopy was writing a novel, that Goopy was doing WONDERFULLY, he wished Goopy were here today so they could have had robust disagreements and flaming rows.

Boro Jethu stopped to catch his breath.

It suddenly felt so difficult, the act of filling his lungs with air and letting it all out, that most primal of all human impulses. The house was practically falling apart, all manner of real-estate crooks were circling above it like vultures, none of the young people were even remotely interested in staying in it, the whole city was becoming a giant briddhashram. Boro Jethu clutched the pillar.

'Dada, are you okay?' Manjulika asked gently. 'Borda? Should I get you a glass of water?'

Sudhiranjan Ghosh came to. He looked at his sister-in-law and sighed.

'Look at them,' he said.

Manjulika followed his eyes.

'Is that Aarjoe? What on earth is he doing here?'

Framed through the Etruscan pillars that surrounded the courtyard, with their fierce lion faces, Lata Ghosh and Aarjoe Chaudhary, deep in conversation, looked as handsome as they always had.

'If things had gone the way they *should* have, they would have had two teenaged children by now,' Boro Jethu sighed.

'But they would have still been unhappy, Dada,' Manjulika said softly. 'Come now, eat some kochuris before the oil becomes old.'

Boro Jethu allowed himself to be led away. 'We Ghoshes have always followed protocol,' he said, his voice thick. 'Even if he's come uninvited, we can't let him go hungry. Even if he's ex, he is a jamai after all.'

'I heard a little rumour that you might come,' Lata Ghosh told her former husband, the one she had agreed to marry on their fifth date together and whose looks had so perfectly complemented hers that even Ronny had told Aaduri, cryptically, after he'd met Aarjoe a few months after Lata met him, that they were indeed the lead pair. 'But I didn't really think you'd come. For one, you keep complaining about Calcutta on Facebook. For another, it's a bit too cool, no, even for you, to saunter into the wedding of an ex-sister-in-law, when none of the elders have invited you?'

But Lata said this smiling, and Aarjoe Mitra felt that familiar heat about his neck. The one thing that had remained unchanged through all the years of rancour was the sudden warmth that came from his memory of their very first meeting, when Lata had come in for the interview and he'd been instantly swept away. (Of course, the single memory, while visceral, had never been enough for the rest of their lives.)

'I was actually in Calcutta to wind up the old house. Now that Ma and Baba are gone, there's no reason to keep the place anymore. And...'

'I am so sorry,' Lata said.

(Aarjoe's mother, it must be noted, had been a Class A bitch. But his father had been a gentleman.)

'Since you were in town, almost serendipitously, I thought we should meet. There were a few important things to discuss, though now's not the time for that. Shall we go meet Molly?'

Aarjoe slipped a little Tiffany box out of his pocket.

'Ever the show-off,' Lata said archly. She led the way to the naachghar. 'I was sorry to hear about you and Maria.'

'Oh well,' Aarjoe said, changing the subject rapidly. 'Do you remember the house we nearly bought in Connecticut?'

'Of course,' Lata said. 'I sometimes wonder if the three-car garage was real or something I imagined afterwards. Now that I live in London, we are quite embarrassed about cars and garages.'

'My colleague – you remember Nick? – well, Nick bought that house eventually. And every time I visit, I think of the life you and I could have had there.'

Lata maintained a studied silence.

'Nick has three children, all brats of course. But we'd

have sent ours to a public school, right? So *they* wouldn't
have been brats…'

Lata stopped in her tracks.

'Why are you here, Aarjoe?' she asked, now facing him
squarely.

❦

Bobby Bansal, the other liaison officer of the Ghosh-Jaiswal
wedding, had one eye on her phone and the other on Lata
Ghosh and the handsome interloper, when her mother and
aunt – in matching chiffon sari – walked up to her, armed
with a selfie stick.

'C'mon now, stop looking at your phone and give us a
smile,' her aunt said.

Bobby obliged, pouting at her aunt's phone in the
manner she'd seen Pragya and Mimi do.

'I didn't know your Ronny-da was so close to the
Ghoshes,' her mother said, sipping her drink.

'Hai na?' her aunt, the groom's mother, chimed in. 'The
Boro Jethi told us abhi abhi. Nice lady. So friendly, not like
the husband. It seems your Ronny-da and this London Lata
had a big love story. Everybody thought they'd marry.'

Bobby looked surprised for a moment and then her face
became neutral again.

# 27

# Regrets

from: pixieandscone@gmail.com
to: lataghosh@gmail.com
date: 11 December 2017
subject: regrets

*Dear Lata (Pishi),*

*We got the card for your cousin's wedding and your letter (to me). The card had got lost because you had sent it to Baba's office and Baba's office is a maze and no one knows him yet and also because Baba's original office building is being broken down and he has been given a temporary glass cube until January. TBH, Mama–Baba have said that no one has any leave now especially because Baba's job is new and because my school is strict so they cannot take me to Calcutta for the wedding. On top, Posto has a cold. He ruins everything.*

*I was depressed because if we went to Calcutta for your cousin's wedding we would have met my Dadu too and so to cheer me up Baba opened this email account for me (Mama disapproves of it) to send our 'regrets'. But I don't want to send you regrets, I want to send you a magical unicorn that can be your pet. I think you should have a pet and unicorns make the best pets. At least you will come soon.*

*Do you think you can bring me some books from Calcutta? I am getting along by re-reading my old books and borrowing one or two from classmates (they are, overall, quite stupid, the classmates) but a few new books would be nice. Our stuff from*

*London has also not arrived yet so I don't even have my copy of* Ballet Shoes *to comfort me. Mama says our stuff has to remain in storage until the new old-house is ready and the new old-house is so dilapidated God knows how long it'll take to be ready for Human Habitation. (Don't tell Mama I said that about the house but ya it is very dilapidated).*

*TBH Jampot is stupid and I would have been devastated if it were not for Scone. But I will not tell you more on this subject on email and keep Scone as a surprise. (It's a big surprise.)*

*How are you? How is your Mama and Nimki. I want to meet Nimki. Does she make good nimkis? My Thammi makes amaaaayzing nimkis. Mama says too many nimkis are bad for my tummy but I don't agree. Josh had an Enid Blyton-themed birthday party which wasn't awful because the food was what the Famous Five eat: jam tarts, potatoes with butter and parsley, a salad with really crunchy lettuce, scones (nothing to do with Scone) with a kind of strawberry jam and cream, cold chicken sandwich, a type of cheesy pie, macaroons. There was a nice large cherry cake with sugar parrots on top. There was also ginger beer and some of Josh's stupid friends were squealing, 'Ooh, it's real beer, real beer.' Josh's parrots are nice. He continues to be quite idiotic.*

*Lots of love*
*Pixie*

❧

It was the day after Molly and AJ's sangeet. Lata's feet were aching from all that dancing on high heels. She hobbled away from the Uber now, even though she'd borrowed

Manjulika's flats before stepping out this morning. She'd had no energy to conceal the dark circles around her eyes, acquired from all the revelry that had gone on till the wee hours, and now she felt a teeny bit regretful about that. There was a protocol for dressing for one's ex, and everyone followed it more or less. (Even Aaduri, who couldn't care less about such things, had been known to get a pedicure and haircut before meeting the Professor.) She wished she could have slept in today, then spent the morning rubbing her feet with lavender oil and gossiping with Aaduri on the phone. It was that kind of a post-party day.

Disloyal though it might sound, the Jaiswals' sangeet had ended up being far more fun than the engagement-cum-ring-ceremony at Ghosh Mansion. For one, it was at a brand-new banquet hall with no sense of history. Naturally, there was no ancestral baggage overshadowing the joy. For another, after the general performances of the groom's and bride's coteries – the Germans gave good competition to AJ's cousins – and a cheerful, if unexceptionable (vegetarian) dinner, the uncles and aunts and parents and *their* parents had all left, and the real party began. (Bobby's brother had apparently sponsored this part of the evening, and the alcohol was not half bad.) Lata had really enjoyed last evening, sweetly accepting cocktail after cocktail from the dewy-eyed friends of AJ – all hatchlings – chiefly because none of her ex-es had turned up.

It was a good party.

'And the upshot of that,' Lata now muttered under her breath, 'this splitting headache.'

Then, there was the strangeness of this place – what *was* this place?

New Town, Rajarhat. Completely unfamiliar territory to her, the glass-fronted buildings catching the cold winter sun and casting giant shadows upon manicured lawns. And Aarjoe was nowhere in sight. He had said ten, hadn't he?

Lata stood patiently by the guard's cabin outside the gates of The Eiffel. How they'd laughed at the name all those years ago, when New Town in general and The Eiffel in particular, were mere blueprints and brochures, at best, clay models within spiffy glass boxes that architects had placed decorously in their offices. They'd embraced the pretentious name with good humour as they'd embraced many other things then, in the first flush of their happiness, which gilded the surfaces of things such that the banal became beautiful, the stupid, cute.

Now, standing right next to the exaggerated E spelt out in the hedges, Lata observed the retinue of maids, young and old, sari-wearing and jean-clad, swinging jaunty bags and flashing smartphones, make their way busily into the gated community, after getting their IDs checked by the security guards. Perhaps outside the Eiffel, the guards and the maids were friends or lovers or relatives; now, here, divided by the authority the uniform conferred, the security guards were agents of the State – or, really, the Eiffel's management – and they scanned the IDs the women proffered with eagle eyes.

Her red shawl aflame over her white kurta, her cheeks still pale from not having slept well last night, Lata began to wonder about the kinds of lives that were lived in these apartments, what the couples who lived here were like. Did they return home to freshly made beds, clean kitchen counters and fragrant laundry folded in cupboards? What would a couple's relationship be like if they returned home and neither had to start dinner or wait for the other to return so consensual takeout could be ordered?

A black limousine drove up. 'Sorry,' said Aarjoe, disembarking in a hurry, 'I am late.' He thrust a bunch of flowers at her face.

Lata frowned. The limo was signature Aarjoe – and, in her youth, she had found his flamboyance stylish. But the flowers? Where did those come from? (Also, how inconvenient to be clutching a bouquet at the entry to The Eiffel.) 'Shall we keep these in the car, then?' Aarjoe asked her, as though reading her mind, whisking the flowers back from her and handing them to the uniformed chauffeur, who nodded at Lata discreetly and glided away in the car.

'This way,' Aarjoe said.

The lobby was marbled in pale green. The lifts seemed straight out of a techno-thriller. And when they entered, the flat on the sixteenth floor they'd bought from a sketch in a brochure fifteen years ago with its all-glass western wall, engulfed them in such a dazzlement of gold light and blue skies that, for a moment, Lata was silenced. Aarjoe stood next to her, quiet too, though his eyes were not on the skies but on the garden below, to the left, a distant riot of colours, and the perfect, tear-shaped pool on the right where tiny humans swam lengths up and down.

'We had forgotten about The Eiffel, hadn't we?'

Lata nodded. She certainly had, that is, until Aarjoe had reminded her the other day.

'Though we'd divided up the other assets when we…'

'Divorced. Say it,' said Lata.

Aarjoe smiled sadly. 'This one slipped through the net.'

Net of grief it had been for her, though Lata kept that bit to herself.

'My CA reminded me earlier this year. He'd kept paying the EMI, of course, from my India portfolio. He collected the keys. I thought when we found a buyer, we could flog it off. You'd need to be here too. Then I met Molly and she told me you'd be in Calcutta…'

'Have you got a buyer?' Lata asked, wandering into what was presumably the dining space, and then through that, into one of the bedrooms.

Instead of answering her, Aarjoe said, 'Charulata Ghosh, do you ever wonder what might happen if we were to meet now, when life has taught us all these lessons, instead of in 2002? If we met for the first time at Molly's engagement-cum-ashirbad? Say, I was her Berlin boss and had been invited to the ceremonies like the others. And you, you were the beautiful sister of the bride, the renegade who had resisted the efforts of a hundred men at wooing her. Would it not have been different?'

# 28
# Bloody Men Are Like Bloody Buses

While Lata Ghosh was wandering about the flat that, in an alternate universe, she and Aarjoe Mitra might have filled with beautiful unnecessary things, alongside the flotsam and jetsam of coupledom, old tax receipts and inherited china, filmmaker Ronny Banerjee was holed up at home, in Salt Lake, attempting to cope with the several crises that had cropped up in his universe. Not *his* universe, to be accurate, the universe – multiverse? – housing Mondira and Srijon Shekhar and Trina and Ryan, his principals, who were probably feeling all stranded and breathless, now that so many black holes had emerged in their lives, within the final draft of Ronny's script.

The final script that still lived and breathed, unfortunately, only in Ronny's head.

It was half past ten in the morning. The meeting with the producers was at five. Despite the acidity, several cups of tea had been consumed already.

Scattered on Ronny's bed were drafts of the script, several notebooks, the little biography of J.C. Bose he was using for reference and which, invariably, made him very cranky – why on earth wasn't there a decent, mainstream biography of one of the greatest scientists in the world?! – and his well-thumbed volumes of Sunil Gangopadhyay's *Pratham Alo*, a novel that brought to luminous life the world of J.C. Bose and Tagore. Should Rabindranath have a cameo in the film now that Acharya was a protagonist?

Ronny sighed and looked at the time.

This thing was running away from him.

Like a lot of artists, Ronny had a complicated relationship with deadlines. They often brought the elusive muse scurrying to his window in their wake – and some of the most intractable plot problems had been solved by him at the eleventh hour, when the deadlines were truly upon him. But on a few occasions, as now, they chafed against his creative spirit and blocked him completely. He pushed and he pushed. Nothing.

By panicking, Bobby was making it worse.

Apparently, when he did not show up at the last meeting, Nikhil had been marginally offended. *Was Ronny becoming a flake?* Nikhil had asked Bobby. Privately, Ronny was certain. (Nikhil Maheshwari was his friend, for crying out loud!) But Bobby had reported it to him dramatically, widening her eyes to make her point. 'I really think you should take the next meeting seriously, Ronny-da,' she'd hissed.

This wedding business had made Bobby cross – Ronny imagined her relatives were badgering her endlessly about settling down, now that even AJ, the baby of the family, was married – and it made her hit the panic button on *Shomoy* harder than ever. She wanted Ronny to narrate the new script to Nikhil *this* evening. 'What?' he'd spluttered. 'If not the whole script, then, at the very least you should clearly demarcate the differences between the old script and the new,' she'd replied.

As though Ronny had it all figured out and simply needed to draw up two columns on a whiteboard: old script, new script.

Bobby would come by twelve, she'd said, to prep with him and decide upon specific answers to the questions Nikhil and his team would pose: *How many more days of shooting would it entail? How many more actors? Instead of Shaarani Sen, who? Iif it's not Shaarani Sen, how can we be sure this gambit will work? Bablu-da is a great actor but he's not a star!* And *most important, how significantly will all this impact the budget?*

God, Bobby would arrive soon, and within minutes her face would be lambent in disappointment. ('You promised me, Ronny-da, that I could enjoy AJ's ring ceremony and sangeet and not worry about the script, that you would be on the job!')

Were other filmmakers as terrified of their assistants' disapproval?

Absent-mindedly, Ronny moved his laptop, hot already, to the pillow next to him, and left the bed. He arched his back, half-heartedly gave a few lunges, dropped onto the mat and did the plank for two minutes. Then he walked vaguely around the room, going up to his desk in the converted study (it used to be a balcony) but not exactly expecting any epiphanies. The desk was a dump. He picked up an old timepiece from the mess, one that had stopped months ago, and glared for a while at the cube of clean wood that instantly appeared in the surrounding dust.

Circling back to his bed, Ronny picked up one of the oldest *Shomoy* notebooks – for each film, he had over twenty of these unlined notebooks – where he'd sketched the earliest scenes. As a devotee of Satyajit Ray, Ronny liked to follow Ray's techniques, even though most people thought he was going too far with the notebooks and the pictures. But there was something very therapeutic in the act of sketching his characters, Ronny felt. The protagonists and antagonists revealed intimate details about themselves when they came alive on the page.

As he leafed through the notebook, Ronny's mood improved, his breathing became even, he even asked for breakfast to be sent. Then, at some point, a half-bitten buttered toast in one hand, he realised that his Trina and his Mondira both looked far more like Charulata Ghosh than Pragya Paramita Sen. How had he not seen this before?

'We need more hits.' Hem Shankar Tiwari shook his head unhappily.

Hem and Aaduri were eating an early lunch at the small South Indian restaurant close to office and dissecting last evening's meeting with the boss and super-boss. The young daughter of the owner had just returned from Columbia with a degree in digital media, and the office was rife with rumours that she would soon take over the website's management. Apparently, coffeehouse.in was burning cash and needed five million hits *a month* asap. Like, by the end of the week, no pressure. After the meeting, they'd rushed to Molly's sangeet in response to Lata's messages, and had no time to go over the minutes. This afternoon, though, Aaduri had called for a team meeting.

'Calm down, Hem,' Aaduri replied, dunking her mini idli in coconut chutney. 'Management meetings are always like that. They keep asking for impossibles and you keep defending your turf. It's fine.'

'But we *do* need more hits. Look at the other sites we are competing with. They have at least one breakout story every week. One thing that goes giga. The old lady talking to Alexa in Bhojpuri? The dog who married the cat? The little girl stealing that pink umbrella from the supermarket and then returning it?'

'Yes, yes,' Aaduri said vaguely. She did not click on half the links Hem sent her.

'We totally need liquid content like that. That Pragya Sen Insta Goals-story did rather well. Do you think Tiana can shoot videos? You know how Kareena Kapoor's gym routine breaks the internet once in a while? Maybe we could get Tiana to grab a camera and make little videos of Pragya's fitness regime.'

'Pragya is not Kareena Kapoor, not by a very long shot, make that very very very long shot, let me remind you, Hem. I think we should redesignate you as video scout,' Aaduri said, looking around herself. 'After we return from Jamshedpur. And don't think for a second I don't know *why* you want all these ridiculous fitness videos. Not for the website.'

'Curator,' Hem clarified. 'Not scout. And please. Fitness boomerangs are the rage, that's all. I don't like Pragya's body type myself. I am much more of an old-fashioned Hindi belt type. I find Pragya too thin. Are you looking for your phone? It's charging in that corner.'

'Oh yes,' Aaduri remembered, motioning to the waiter to fetch it. 'Ever since I took this millennial job, I've become addicted to my phone.'

'Why are we going to Jamshedpur?' Hem asked.

But by then, Aaduri had her phone back in her hands and neglected to reply.

'Your friend Lata Ghosh,' she finally looked up at Hem, 'has sent me a poem. It's by Wendy Cope. Care to hear it, Hem Ilahabadi? It's sort of self-explanatory. Bloody men are like bloody buses — / You wait for about a year / As soon as one approaches your stop. / Two or three others appear.'

Hem started laughing.

'She is bloody bewitching, isn't she?' Aaduri smiled.

After paying off the bill, they started to descend the stairs and Aaduri recited, from memory, the second verse. After all, she'd introduced Lata to Wendy Cope.

'You look at them flashing their indicators, / Offering you a ride. / You're trying to read the destinations, / You haven't much time to decide.'

Outside the office, the street was as busy as ever.

Aaduri lit a cigarette and looked philosophically at the sun. By then, Hem had pulled out the poem via Google and, in his formal manner and the faint trace of accent that added a layer of charm to all his pronouncements, he read off his phone:

'If you make a mistake, there is no turning back.
Jump off, and you'll stand there and gaze
While the cars and the taxis and lorries go by
And the minutes, the hours, the days.'

# 29

# The Return of the Prodigal

*My dearest Pixie,*

*I was delighted to receive your email, with all your news. It would have been great to have you at Molly's wedding, but I do understand how busy Bappa and Nisha are in the new place, with the new job, and you, at your strict new school. But as you said, I am going to visit you soon enough and yes, of course, I shall get you a bunch of books that should see you through to the new year and hopefully longer.*

*Calcutta has kept me super busy. There was a lot of weddingy stuff to deal with, for one. Our old house needed quite a bit of work before we could host Molly's engagement. I have attached a few pictures here: the courtyard all dressed up, the bride in her controversial red-and-white outfit, and the lion pillars with the dancing lights. Then we had a sangeet yesterday which was quite fun too, lots of Bollywood dancing. The wedding, of course, is tomorrow. It's at a hotel, so there isn't very much for me to do but dress up and chitchat with people who come and go. I am secretly quite excited about helping open presents. Do you like opening presents? There is always one person at the wedding whose job is to make a list of who gives what (don't ask me why) and I inveigled myself into that role simply because I want to open the gifts with Molly and AJ.*

*Your letter to me, Pixie, was so honest and full of what you were feeling that it is only fair that I too pour (some) truth into mine. It's been a weird month for me. In the last week, a few people from the past, people I haven't met in years and years, have suddenly reappeared. Suppose ten years have passed, and you, Payal Pixie Das Biswas, have gone to London for a holiday, and you meet your old friends and teachers. You might wonder then, might you not, what your life would have been like had you not left London at all? That's how I have been feeling half the time. But it does not make any sense, this feeling. I have always believed that what happens in life is what was meant to happen anyway!*

*TBH, Josh's birthday party sounds like enormous fun. I always wanted an Enid Blyton-themed birthday party myself, but my mother hadn't heard of most kinds of Enid Blyton food. Like, she'd have made us chicken sandwiches. But that would be about it. And when I was growing up in the eighties, mothers (and aunts and grandmothers) organised birthdays, making everything from scratch, no ordering stuff from outside. Also, you couldn't buy peanut butter or tinned sardines in the market. So that was that.*

*I have a feeling that you will get on really well with my Mama and Nimki. (Both of whom are constantly badgering me about something or the other!) Yes, Nimki makes nice nimkis – though I don't know if they'll beat your grandmother's – but her fabulous prawn pakoras are the best in the world, and my mother bakes lovely chocolate cakes. Maybe I can bring some for you when I come to Jampot?*

*I have been writing this letter to you, sitting on a green bench in a little park in our neighbourhood. A beautiful white tabby is curled up next to me. I tried to make friends with her, but she seems grumpy. I think the grumpiness might be a front, though because she hasn't moved away so far and is allowing her tail to tickle my leg as I type this out on my phone. An old friend met me this morning and I asked him to drop me off here. I wanted to gather my thoughts in the sun and write to you (and to my friend Aaduri, whom you will meet soon in Jampot) before returning to my house, where guests will be arriving in droves all day today.*

*As a young girl, I would come to this park on winter afternoons and hang about while my cousin Goopy played cricket with his friends. Sometimes they let me play. Usually, I sat on the swing and read a book. When my friend Aaduri came to visit me at home, we would always play badminton and the shuttlecocks would fly far away, disrupting Goopy's cricket game or the impromptu gathering of birds. So, Aaduri and I spent more time hunting for shuttlecocks than actually playing!*

*I can see now that a whole team of crows has gathered up ahead, where the swing is, and are busily inspecting something. I have a feeling it might be a dead rat. So I am not venturing that side, even though there are clumps of my favourite pink-and-white flowers there, growing against the wall of the Community Club. (I say favourite because I cannot, for the life of me, remember their name! Little pink flowers on the vine? Your dad might know the name, ask him. If you pick the flowers and suck the stalks, you'll get a little shot of nectar. That's what we used to do before we went home in the evening.)*

*Give my love to your parents and Posto and Ram Singh and SCONE. Dying to know more about Scone.*

*Lots of love*

*Lata*

In a way, it was good that Aarjoe had appeared in that ridiculous limousine, thought Lata, as she walked towards Ghosh Mansion, clutching her flowers and swinging her bag like a girl. It meant the car couldn't come right up to the house and Aarjoe hadn't been able to invite himself inside, in an attempt to further ingratiate himself with Boro Jethu. Also, she had managed to gather her thoughts in peace, sitting in the park and writing an email to Pixie.

Her life had become a comedy of manners lately, hadn't it?

It was half past twelve. Aarjoe had been badgering her to have lunch with him, at some fancy place or other – Calcutta was full of these – but citing the wedding, she had begged off. She wasn't going to lie to herself. Despite what had happened, despite how the separation and the divorce had crushed her, she did not feel any bitterness on her tongue, not anymore. At one time, she had moved continents just to avoid seeing Aarjoe because the sight of him in those early days of heartbreak, him standing at the grocery store, getting gas, doing something as innocuous as that, opened up her wounds instantly. It took weeks for them to close again.

And now, here he was. Telling her sentimental things, inviting her for lunch, getting her flowers.

What was she feeling inside?

She had wanted to probe, to dig, to tease.

But there was only a blankness, a strange kind of calm, out of which arose a peculiar burst of girlish energy. All decidedly odd.

Lata walked into the lane, at the end of which stood Ghosh Mansion. Up ahead, she saw a yellow taxi stop at the gate. (Even Aarjoe's stupid limo would have squeezed in, she now supposed, had they taken the other route. But she was glad he hadn't pressed.)

A man got out of the cab, in a pair of blue jeans and a white sweatshirt, and effortlessly swung a suitcase out. As he paid the driver, Lata suddenly felt her pulse racing.

Was that him?

But he hadn't come to Calcutta in twelve years!

Lata streamed ahead, grateful again for the flats, the flowers shedding petals on the street behind her to leave a fragrant trail. She raised her voice. 'Goopy! Goopy, is that really you?'

The man looked up and flashed his lopsided grin.

'Munni, I never could induce you to call me Dada, could I?'

~

The news spread like wildfire in Ghosh Mansion. 'Munni has brought Goopy Dada home, Munni has brought Goopy Dada home.'

As the only son of the patriarch, Goopy was seen by the staff and the remaining few tenants as the true heir to Ghosh Mansion. His long absence from home had naturally engendered much muttering.

Lata had had nothing to do with Goopy's return. But she soaked in the credit nonetheless, as she led the way to Boro Jethu's quarters, stopping often to catch him up on specific news and point out the wedding lights and the rain damage. Raju, who was around to do wedding chores and eat the catered lunch, grabbed Goopy's suitcase; Nimki rushed to make tea.

Upstairs, though, it was all anti-climactic.

Boro Jethi had gone to the beauty parlour with Manjulika and Kakimoni. Boro Jethu had accompanied Kaku to the Oberoi for some last-moment menu adjustments. And Molly, Molly was still sleeping.

Raju kept the suitcase in Goopy's old bedroom and the cousins followed him inside. He opened the windows. They sat down on Goopy's carved single bed, facing the posters of his youth.

'You look lovely, Munni,' Goopy finally said.

It was only now that Lata felt her voice grow heavy. 'Did you come alone?' she asked him.

# 30

# The Cheetah

Goopy stared at the poster of Bob Dylan on the wall. Lata chewed her lips. Without intending to in the least, in the bare few minutes that had passed since Goopy's return to Ghosh Mansion, the cousins mimicked old patterns. From the window that Raju had thrown open, sunlight poured onto the white bedcover, a golden rectangle, interrupted, albeit elegantly, by the iron bars of the window. How Lata used to envy him his en suite, she remembered, as she stretched her toes into the patch of sun on the bed and allowed her feet to wiggle in its gentle warmth.

'No, actually, haven't come alone.' Goopy finally laid out the facts, in gentle boluses. 'Duma is here too. We landed this morning.'

'Where have you tucked him away?' Lata asked, raising her eyebrows and rounding her eyes.

Goopy turned to her and smiled his lopsided smile. 'I checked him into a hotel. I mean, we went to the hotel first, he checked in, I left. I suspect he is now stuffing his face with whatever's on the room service menu.'

'That's horrible, Goopy!'

'Calm down, Munni,' Goopy said. 'You may have spent a year or two in the West —'

'Fifteen,' Lata set the record straight, even though she could see that he was horsing around.

'And you may have befriended the token fey here and there, a diversity candidate or two —'

Lata now composed her features into her well-practised I-am-not-going-to-stoop-to-reply-to-your-accusation-that-I-work-hard-at-polishing-my-liberal-credentials-even-though-I-suspect-it-might-be-true face.

'But,' said Goopy, walking up to her and flicking her nose lightly, 'Charulata Ghosh, you have no idea of the protocol involved in bringing an "unsuitable" man home. At my age. From my end of the gender continuum. In Calcutta. Not that you've brought home any suitable ones either. Except Ronny, that is.'

'Never did you *once* tell me, in the ancient past when Ronny Banerjee was in and out of this house, like, all the time, that you thought, for a second, he was a *suitable* boy.' Lata stood up to hold open the door as Nimki entered with a tray: tea things, Manjulika's precious porcelain, the works.

'Is AJ a suitable boy?' Goopy asked her, seriously.

'I really think he is. Molly's chosen well.'

'I do think we Ghoshes need an encounter or two with "The Other". He is Marwari?'

'Jaiswals are technically not Marwaris, or so I have been told,' Lata clarified. 'But there is some dispute. Sane family, though.'

'Oh good. Since ours is off the rocker, sanity is desirable.'

Goopy lifted the lid of the chipped blue bowl as Nimki's tray floated into range. 'Marzipan bites! Nahoum's?' He picked a pink one and popped it into his mouth.

'Aaduri got them,' said Lata, taking over the tray and placing it on the bed.

'Na, *Hem* brought them,' Nimki corrected her. 'Uff, Boro Boudi! Not a single table is free,' she muttered. 'No place for the tray.'

It was true. Twelve years was a long time to allow the flat surfaces of an empty room to remain unoccupied. The bed, posters, guitars, cassettes, the tape deck: all there, of course, constituting the bare outlines of what was recognisably Goopy's room, but distributed into it were several kilos of objects that had leaked out from the rest of the house.

'Let *me* pour the tea, Mamoni,' Nimki offered. 'I know you both have to do everything in those places – London, America, wherever – but here…'

As Nimki waved her hands to indicate those far-off, possibly not-worth-the-fuss places, Goopy came and gave her a hug. 'Oh-ho, stop, now I'll slop tea on the bedcover!' she complained, her cheeks flushed with all the attention. 'It is the last one your grandmother crocheted, and her ghost will come and give me a tight slap if I stain it. Don't make a face, Munni. Ghosts do slap people. Don't stuff yourself. There's lunch.'

'Don't worry,' said Lata, helping herself to cheese biscuits. 'We'll have lunch after we come back. None of the others are getting home before three, it seems.'

'Going out again? Do what you want,' Nimki said, withdrawing. 'Just don't ruin that bedcover.'

'It's already become cold, Munni,' Goopy said, sipping the tea. 'No surprise, given the distance it has travelled. So where are we going?'

'To check out the room service menu, of course,' Lata replied.

'They cancelled.' Bobby looked up from her phone.

'What?' Ronny was putting finishing touches on the presentation that Bobby had put together last night – God know when she'd had the time – adding a sentence here, deleting a word or two there, appreciating the clarity of thought at one place, maddened by the lack of nuance in another.

'Nikhil's office has just sent an email. They can't meet us this evening.'

Ronny continued to tinker with the slide.

'They want to reschedule. Tomorrow's obviously out. How about later this week?'

Bobby had begun to furiously circle the bed, phone in hand, her yellow coat swishing. Like a tigress, Ronny thought drily.

'Let's wait for them to suggest an alternative date, Bobby.'

She now stopped moving and came and sat next to him annoyedly. 'Let me remind you, Ronny-da, the need is ours.'

'Calm down,' said Ronny, moving onto the next slide. 'I had an inkling this might happen. Go get the newspaper, the Chennai edition, it's in the drawing room. Baba reads it after me.'

'Can't you just tell me?'

'It'll take a minute.'

'Fiiiine,' said Bobby, 'I don't know why you can't just summarise it!' Her heels tap-tapped on the mosaic as she made her way out.

'Kenneth Atieno.' The tall man broke into a smile when he opened the door to Lata. 'But everyone calls me Duma.'

Tall, check. Muscles, check. Skin, the colour of seventy per cent dark hot chocolate, check.

Damn, her cousins were all getting their acts together, Lata thought, supremely jealous for an instant.

'You are an honorary Bengali already then,' she said, smiling, extending her hand towards Duma. 'All Bengalis have a *good name*. And a petname. My rude, almost uncivilised cousin who left you here while gallivanting home is called Goopy in these parts.'

'And you must be Munni.' Duma drew Lata inside warmly. 'Charulata. The family beauty. And brains.'

Lata laughed. 'La-taa now,' she enunciated, 'the dental t. What does Duma mean?'

'Cheetah,' he said, adding softly, 'I chose it myself.'

Goopy stayed suspiciously quiet through this exchange. At the first chance, he disappeared into the loo.

Lata followed Duma into the adjoining living area, all plush sofas and mood lights, where a cricket match was playing on television. 'Goopy surmised you'd be stuffing your face. But I can see your drug is different.'

Duma laughed – he had a delicious, easy laugh that animated his eyes – as he hunted around for the remote. 'Growing up in Kenya, a whole generation of us worshipped Tendulkar and, later, Sourav Ganguly. The first thing that pops into my head when I think of Calcutta is Eden Gardens.'

He found the remote and switched the television off.

'I suppose we can watch one at Eden after Molly's

wedding. I'm sure the IPL will be on,' Lata said. 'Or something else. Given how obsessed we are with cricket.'

'I'd like that,' said Duma, his eyes shining like a child's.

'Of course, *I* gave up on cricket when Hansie Cronje broke my heart. Little did I know then that *that's* what handsome men do. Except you, Duma, I hope,' Lata's eyes danced in mirth.

'Why have you been hiding her all these years?' Duma looked back and asked Goopy, who was now staring rapt at his phone with a grave face. There was no response. 'Come join us here,' Duma called again. 'Shall we order lunch, Munni?'

'No, no, we are all going to have lunch at home. I am here to escort you to Ghosh Mansion myself.'

'I still don't think it's a good idea,' said Goopy.

'Oh shut up, you,' said Lata good-naturedly. 'I am quite sure the Cheetah is up to facing a few Bengali aunts and uncles. No guns, only words. And lots of mutton curry and rice.'

'That settles it,' said Duma. 'I can even risk a bullet or two in the quest for the Indian goat-curry. With potatoes. Right?'

After ten minutes or so, Duma and Lata and the reluctant Goopy stepped out into Old Court House Street, into the glorious December afternoon in Calcutta, a city that pulls off winter like an old lady wears her prize jewels, elegantly, but with a touch of nostalgia. The sun was so mellow and the nip in the air so piquant, that it seemed as though the unlikely trio would stand there forever, by the Returned Letter Office, waiting for their cab, and the city would reabsorb them into her innards so they would be enveloped by safety and love and happiness and winter afternoons and cousinly warmth forever.

Then the cab came, they stepped in, and the doubts returned.

# 31

## Molly's Wedding Day

On Molly's wedding day, a somewhat curtailed gaaye holud was to be hosted in the morning by Boro Jethi and Manjulika, immediately after the ritual nandi mukh. The curtailing was because Molly needed to be in make-up by twelve-thirty latest – since the lagna was early evening – and a suite had been booked at the Oberoi. That barely left any time for a proper gaaye holud. Girls these days. What to do?

The nandi mukh was presided over jointly by Boro Jethu and Kaku. Standing guard behind Molly (who was, unbeknownst to the elders, nursing a bit of a hangover) was Lata, propping her up from time to time, tying her mukut, adjusting her sari. The ancestors being invoked formally by the pandit peered down at the bride in her traditional yellow sari, from their framed – and garlanded-for-the-occasion – photographs. Twice, Lata had to mediate a disagreement between Boro Jethu and Kaku about the titles of said ancestors. 'How does it matter if he was "Sir"?' Lata had to hiss. The videographer promised to edit those bits out.

Goopy and Duma had been joined that morning by Aaduri and Hem – who were planning to get to the office once the gaaye holud was over – as part of the welcome committee for the Jaiswals. Which meant they lurked by the porch and cracked jokes. Duma and Hem watched some wretched match on the phone, Goopy and Aaduri tried to catch up on twelve years' history at top speed. Eventually, despairing of any help from them, Lata shepherded everyone to Dayanara's courtyard herself, streaking from room to room.

The Jaiswal ladies finally appeared, dressed in fine cottons exactly like their Ghosh-Bose-Mitra counterparts, carrying the tawtto in beautifully decorated trays. (In fact, the liaison officers had helped interpret the rituals so well that instead of a real fish, which of course would be taboo to AJ's kin, the Jaiswals had cleverly commissioned a lifelike rohu fashioned of sandesh and coloured silver, and decorated that as a bride with the traditional red veil and a tin-foil nose ring.) The bride's family were wholly overwhelmed. There was ululation, conch music, and very civilised holud-smearing. 'Not my hair, please,' Molly was heard to beseech the women and they all seemed to be heeding her.

When, finally, the Germans reached, all starched dupattas and kurtas, Lata managed to slip out.

She decided to check if Molly's car had arrived. It was Goopy and Duma's job to accompany her – along with her outfit and jewellery – to the hotel. But the porch was deserted. There was no sign of the car or the men. Bobby Bansal was leaning against one of the columns, having a heated discussion on her phone. Lata didn't want to intrude. But neither did she want to go back in, right away. There was a nippy breeze this morning and in her white-and-red taant, she now felt a little cold. A sudden rush of goosebumps dotted her forearm.

'Hey,' said Bobby. 'Sorry about the shouting. There's always some work shit going on.'

Lata waved it away with a half-smile.

'I just wanted to let you know, I've invited Pragya Paramita Sen and her cousins too. It's a bit last moment.'

'There you are!'

Lata had not heard Aaduri walk up.

'Molly's looking for her Didibhai, Lata Ghosh.' Aaduri said. 'What's up with you?'

Lata looked at Aaduri, even though the words were addressed at Bobby really. 'Bobby was just telling me that Pragya Sen will be coming tonight with her entourage. In fact, Bobby, you should tell Aaduri all about it. She's the one who can organise the press at short notice, that sort of thing. I'll go check on Molly's car.'

'She seemed tetchy,' said Bobby, affecting innocence. Her hair, left open, billowed behind her like a halo, as another gust of wind came their way. 'Uff, Calcutta gets really cold in winter now,' said Aaduri. 'Actually, I was going to ask you why you seemed tetchy.'

Bobby sighed. 'Work stuff,' she said. 'I will be honest, Aaduri. A bit of publicity for Pragya wouldn't hurt.'

Having raided her closet and found nothing that suited her mood, Pragya Paramita Sen turned to her mother's. Shaarani Sen did not quite understand why Pragya was going to this wedding – a cousin of Bobby Bansal, basically no one – but she offered her daughter the new forest-green Benarasi with the gold border that had been gifted to her this Pujo by the New Jersey Bengali Society. It would be perfect with Pragya's gold choli and the emerald earrings that had been her grandmother's.

'Why can't I wear the pink-and-gold Benarasi?' Pragya pouted, squatting on her haunches and pulling out that stunning creation from the layers of muslin in which the sari was swathed. 'You never wear it yourself!'

'Because,' said Shaarani Sen, 'it's bad manners to wear something that might threaten the bride. As it is, you are a somebody, you will stand out. Wear it some other time.'

'Whennnn?' Pragya whined.

'At the premier of *Shomoy*?' Shaarani Sen smiled. 'Here, take the earrings.'

'Nobody wears that kind of a sari at a premier, Ma,' Pragya said, trying on the earrings in front of the dressing table where the mirror, like make-up rooms of the past, was surrounded by an orbit of light bulbs. Shaarani Sen's first husband had had it made, and though the marriage had not lasted, the Belgian glass and the Burma teak were still going strong. When Shaarani Sen had married Pragya's dad, she'd brought the dressing table with her.

'*Shomoy* is a period film, it would be quite appropriate,' Shaarani Sen said, carefully wrapping the sari in mulmul again and putting it back in its designated place. This one was almost an heirloom, and occupied pride of place in the closet, her sanctum sanctorum as it were.

'I think there is trouble with the producers,' Pragya told her mother. 'Ronny didn't say anything. But their big film this year – the one about the grand space odyssey with robots – that one has flopped badly. They were to have released it during the Christmas week. Then the astrologers preponed it, marketing was rushed, and it bombed. Mimi was telling me. She read the reviews on Twitter.'

'Are you worried?' Shaarani Sen looked up from the pyramid of red velvet boxes on the table, in one of which nestled the matching emerald bracelet. (If it wasn't in the locker, that is.) 'Should I speak to someone else?'

'Of course not,' Pragya replied, to her own reflection in the mirror. 'Will this work?'

Shaarani Sen looked at the so-familiar-that-it-appeared-almost-strange face of her child. It was a lifelong regret that Pragya had not inherited the natural arches of her eyebrows or the complex milk-and-saffron of her cheeks. 'You should wear your hair up tonight,' she told Pragya. 'The emeralds will glimmer against your cheeks. No necklace. Let's look for the bracelet for your right hand.'

'I hope I am papped,' said Pragya.

'What's papped?' asked Shaarani Sen.

Laughing, but not saying anything, Pragya began to methodically open the velvet boxes and look for the matching bracelet. She had her own reasons for attending the shindig.

'Why are we going to this wedding again?' Vikramjit Banerjee asked his wife as the car entered the outskirts of Calcutta and she roused herself from her nap.

'Do you want an apple?' Tilo asked.

It was late afternoon. The sun was weak, it was almost as though dusk was poised to make an appearance any moment. There was a wan, brittle air about the city. Vikramjit had not been in favour of moving back to India, and certainly not to eastern India. But these days, Calcutta, the city he'd grown up in, the city he couldn't wait to outgrow and leave, twisted his insides acutely. He missed his son suddenly.

'Because Lata invited us,' Tilo said, popping open a little tub of balm and applying it generously on her lips.

'Why did she?' asked Vikramjit, sullenly.

'Well, to be honest, she must have invited Bappa and family. And then she must have thought of us. After all, we have invited her to our college, it's an Indian Ivy League, on an all-expenses-paid trip.'

'But this is a wedding, it's different. Why are we going, Tilo?'

A flash of fury animated Tilo's features. 'Why do you always have to be contrarian, Vik? We come to Calcutta often enough to see your parents, anyway. I thought it might be nice to work in the wedding. And I do have that meeting at IIM-C tomorrow. What's wrong with going to a reception at the Oberoi and catching up with the group?'

Vik looked out of the window while his wife munched an apple. A group of boys and girls in school uniforms – blue trousers – white shirts, and white salwar kameezes with blue dupattas – cycled past them in abandon, laughing, chasing each other, their words getting mixed up in the wind. 'That's a group of friends,' Vik muttered to himself. 'A real group of friends.' But Tilo paid no attention.

# 32

## The Piri-Lifters

Golden light rained down from the chandeliers. The cutlery, perfectly aligned on the round tables below, caught the refracted rainbows. A soft shehnai played, as though from very far away. There was a profusion of pink flowers everywhere.

'Look at that waist,' sighed Kulkul. 'Same as what it was in her youth.'

'Naturally,' replied Kulkul's mother-in-law, Manjulika's cousin, Lata's Shumu Mashi, who had come to attend Molly's wedding from Nabadvip. 'That slim waist hasn't had to deal with childbirth, na. Motherhood ravages. Munni's body is unscathed, so naturally it is perfect.'

'Shhh,' said Tinku, Kulkul's husband, the youngest product of Shumu Mashi's multiple ravagements, sitting self-consciously erect at the table. Tinku's suit was jaunty, his collar was stiff, and the dry-cleaning chemicals had given him a rash that now bloomed underneath. 'Please don't say unseemly things, Ma,' he said tightly. 'Munni Didi has been extremely kind to us *always*.'

'Easy to be kind,' said Kulkul, now attempting to attract the attention of a waiter, who circumnavigated the next table and resolutely refused to look her way, 'when you live in London and America and come to Calcutta for five minutes in five years. Has she ever invited us to London? Okay, maybe not *us*. But when Mou went to Finland, why did she not invite her home?'

'Right, Finland and England are Ballygunge and Tollygunge,' Tinku said, his face impassive.

Having built the foundation of her married life on the assumption that her husband's irony was, in fact, agreement, Kulkul now turned her attention from Lata to her daughters, who were wandering about the banquet hall in their five-star-wedding finery, taking photographs on their phones. 'Aahaa re, they must be feeling hungry,' she mused. 'Where is all the five-star food?'

Lata Ghosh, who had accidentally-on-purpose overheard this conversation, now took her unravaged-by-motherhood waist, swathed in the tea-green Benarasi with its gold-leaf border – the sari she had not been able to resist buying despite its five-figure price – over to the banquet manager.

'Prasad,' Lata wagged her winger at him. 'What was our deal?'

The gold in Lata's earlobes winked. Prasad melted. 'I am trying, Madam, trying.'

'Trying is not enough. Please instruct your boys. While all the snacks should be rotated around the hall, the fish-fingers with mango-mayo relish and the galouti-pitas must be available *at all times* by the Bengali tables. The chaat-kits must be circulated *round the clock* at the Jaiswal tables. The guests are getting restive. Indian weddings are remembered by the food. It doesn't matter that you studied hotel management in Switzerland – ' Prasad had, in fact, studied at Taratala, but Lata's assumption made him puff up like a bullfrog – 'the food must make a mark. Go to that table – ' it was not difficult to pick out Kulkul's aubergine tanchoi in the crowd – '*yourself*. Ask them what they need.' Lata sweetened the instructions with well-timed smiles. Invigorated, Prasad rushed over to Kulkul.

'Where is my mother? Why isn't she keeping Shumu Mashi company?'

Lata sighed and helped herself to a fish-finger. It was seven-thirty, there was no sign of Aaduri who had promised to come early, and having been on her feet since the morning, she felt exhausted. At some point in the next five minutes, she knew she must go to the adjoining hall and check on the shubhodrishti arrangements. She didn't know who she should be more annoyed by. Aaduri? Who had sent a young chit called Tiana and a photographer in tow to 'cover' the wedding. Or Goopy? Who was avoiding the relatives and sitting with AJ and Kaku, devotedly following the rituals. She knew she should go and flutter about the Nabadvip relatives a bit – they were touchy and liable to feel insulted if proper attention was not paid – but she also did not know what to say if quizzed about her life goals.

Ugh.

Suddenly seized with an idea that might kill two birds with one stone, Lata briskly strode up to the gigantic flower arrangement at the centre of the banquet hall, where Kulkul's children were taking selfies.

'Girls,' exclaimed Lata, 'you look lovely!'

'Lata Pishi!' said Koli, the eldest. 'When did you come from London?'

'A month ago, sweetie,' Lata replied. 'I have just the job for you two now. Come with me.'

At sixteen and fourteen, Kulkul's daughters, in their matching pista-coloured anarkalis, round golden spectacles and newly-plucked eyebrows were adorable, all limbs and awkwardness. Lata marched them to the stage and stationed them on either side of Molly. 'Your job is to take the presents from Molly and pile them up carefully. Koli, since you are older, any jewellery or envelopes, you keep them carefully in this bag. Okay?' The girls nodded seriously. 'And smile,' said Molly, pulling the cheeks of the younger one. 'You're going to be in all the photographs!'

'How's AJ holding up, Didibhai?' Molly twinkled at Lata.

But before Lata could reply – AJ was doing wonderfully and his salmon-pink sherwani was apparently a hit with the Bongs – Koli poked her. 'Lata Pishi, is that Pragya Paramita Sen? Oh my god, oh my god, oh my god, I JUST DIED, it's Pippa, it's PIPPA, I have to Insta this right away!'

At the far end of the hall, Lata found a slim creature in a gorgeous green silk sari, wavering by the flowered arch, looking about herself uncertainly. She was followed by a minuscule entourage of two people, but there was no sign of Ronny. 'I'd better go and greet her,' said Lata. 'Don't abandon your spot in your enthusiasm, girls. I shall bring her here instead. The photographer will take pictures. But please *be cool*.'

As she walked up to young Pragya, who stood charmingly waifish by the gigantic door, and who, fortunately, hadn't been spotted by Kulkul yet – Lata wished she had refreshed her lipstick after chomping that fish finger. It was all great, just *great*. This chit of a girl would be spat out by the film industry after a movie or two. Obviously. She and Ronny would then marry. They'd have an adorable kid, one, given Ronny's age, but maybe even two or three. Ronny's filmmaking career would soar. Meanwhile, Lata would live and die alone in London and leave her property to Molly's half-Marwari kids. Great. Just great. Hang on, though, shouldn't she leave her property to a charity?

'Hello, hello, you must be Pragya,' said Lata, extending her hand. 'So lovely to meet. I am – '

'Charulata, I know,' said Pragya. 'You were with Ronny in college.'

'A hundred years ago,' said Lata. 'And you are…'

'Mimi's my cousin but she's also managing my social media these days,' Pragya explained. 'And this is Clay. He is an Indophile.'

'I believe Ms Bagchi is covering the wedding exclusively?' Mimi asked.

'Well, she has sent someone from her team. Come, let me introduce you to the bride, after that I shall hand you over to Bobby. She'll know all about the publicity stuff,' Lata said, with only the mildest note of sarcasm, and began to shepherd the group towards the stage.

These showbiz types, she thought to herself. Can't attend a wedding without publicity! Anyway. Apparently, she was the only old-fashioned one, getting annoyed at this. From Molly to Manjulika to Aaduri to Boro Jethu, everyone was excited about the exclusive wedding coverage. (Boro Jethu had tried to give Tiana a brief history of all weddings ever in the Ghosh clan and Lata had had to rescue her.)

'What time is Ronny going to get here?' Lata asked Pragya, maintaining a studied neutrality in her voice.

'He said around seven-thirty,' Pragya replied. 'But...'

'Oh yes,' smiled Lata. 'With Ronny that could mean eight-thirty or ten-thirty or seven-thirty next morning.'

Pragya laughed. It was a pleasant, tinkly sound. Lata tried to imagine Ronny listening to this tinkly, windchimey laugh all his life, before sex, after film festival screenings, at brunch. The bloody fool.

'Hello,' said Molly, coolly.

'You look lovely,' said Pragya. 'I feel embarrassed about coming empty-handed. But Ronny's bringing our present.'

But *of course* they would give a present together.

'Molly, it's time for the shubhodrishti.' Looking stunning in a cream and silver Dhakai jamdani, Manjulika appeared on stage from nowhere. 'There you are, Munni,' she said, ignoring Pragya. 'Let's proceed to the ante-chamber, now, shall we? The piri is ready.'

'But,' said Molly, 'but Mejo Jethi, I promised to wait...'

'There is no time, Molly, come on,' Manjulika rushed them on.

The girls trooped behind Manjulika and made their way to a little connecting room, from where Molly would be carried to the faux-chhadnatawla, which the Oberoi staff had painstakingly recreated from photographs. Molly sat down on her piri, Pragya made small talk, the Germans took photographs.

'Munni, will you come here a moment?' Manjulika asked.

Lata followed her mother back into the banquet hall. Kaki was standing there with an urgent expression.

'Who all will carry her?'

'Well, Goopy, of course,' said Lata. 'And Duma, naturally.'

'But if the Jaiswals ask...'

'Don't worry about that, Kakimoni,' said Lata. 'And Hem?'

'Oh, there you are!' Manjulika exclaimed, her voice shot with relief. 'I really thought you weren't going to come in time.'

'Of course I would,' replied Ronny. 'I told Molly I would be one of the piri-lifters. And Aaduri's young man is here too. Hem? I met them in the lift.'

# 33

# The Group

Tilottama Chaudhuri looked askance at her husband as he threw back his head and laughed. For a moment, the double chin that he had managed to acquire, despite her constant vigilance, disappeared. Her bitterness abated briefly.

Vik laughed again. Tilo looked away from the crowds – where she'd been looking for signs of Lata Ghosh – and returned to the proceedings in front.

The bride had been hoisted high up by the four piri-lifters, higher than the groom's shoulders and dangerously close to the chandeliers. Wait, Tilo narrowed her eyes. Was that Ronny Banerjee, sweating profusely as he balanced the piri? So he had no time to write out her keynote address, and his assistant had taken weeks – weeks! – to revert on travel details, but apparently he could gallivant about at random weddings. Tilo pursed her lips in annoyance. This was why Bengalis were always languishing. No professionalism. Also, could he be *that* famous if he was lifting piris at weddings still?

Tilo liked to maintain a roster in her head where everyone in her circle was assigned a place (after a detailed assessment of their overall assets, which included obvious things like net worth and location of property, but also things as diverse as where they'd grown up and how many followers they had on social media). The roster was closely monitored and updated. Any hint of a miscalculation and Tilo's mood curdled rapidly.

Thanks to Calcutta traffic, they had only just got in. Since the shubhodrishti was going on, they'd made their way straight to the action instead of looking for Lata. And even though Vik had been grumpy the whole time in the car, worrying about Josh (unnecessarily) and complaining about having to attend the wedding at all (also unnecessary), it now seemed the infectious nature of events had rubbed off onto him. Paradoxically, Tilo, whose idea it had been to come to the wedding, to dress up, meet people in their circle as well as new, interesting ones, rekindle some of that youthful sparkle inside, now felt an inexplicable sourness. Vik turned to smile at her and his hand gently paused at the small of her back.

The bride and groom were righted. A small cheer erupted from the friends and relatives gathered around the makeshift chhadnatawlaa. All said, Tilo told herself, at least they still looked good together. And here, at the Oberoi, among the Bomkais, ghicha silks, Benarasis and Chanderis, and the shockingly old-fashioned suits or sherwanis worn by most of the men, Tilo thought they looked quite distinguished in her simple blue tussar, paired with her real pearls, and Vik's navy suit and pocket square. They were certainly in the top one per cent here. The thought calmed her down a little. And raising herself on tiptoes – one of the reasons Tilo felt the need to assert herself everywhere was her diminutive stature – she finally managed to catch a glimpse of Lata Ghosh. There she was, standing next to Aaduri Bagchi, right behind Molly, throwing flowers at the couple.

Lata looked radiant. She was in a tea-green Benarasi that was heart-stoppingly beautiful. It was a rare sari. Tilo would have to ask her where she'd bought it. Who knows, maybe Lata Ghosh was one of those people who kept her recipes and sari sources close to her chest. Though she was only two years younger than Tilo, there was something strangely ageless about her. Tilo decided that she did not really like Lata. She turned her gaze to Aaduri. The ivory pallu of her black sari thrown casually around her shoulder, Aaduri leaned in and whispered something to Lata. Lata looked unconvinced. Cameras flashed. The bride and groom, having posed for pictures, went off to the mandap, where further (abbreviated) rituals awaited.

'Arre Vikramjit-da, Tilottama-di! How lovely to see you both.' Ronny was warm and effusive in his kurta and jeans. He wiped his brow with a handkerchief. 'Pragya, meet two of my most favourite seniors from college. Tilo-di broke academic records, Vik-da was a rockstar. Debate, quizzing, you name it. They are both professors now.'

Pragya Paramita Sen smiled at them. She looked as young as their students and thin as a pin. Attractive face. And those vintage emerald drops in her ears were definitely authentic. The doubts that might have assailed Tilo briefly about Ronny's place in her roster vaporised. Vik, however, immediately committed a major social faux pas and began to gush: how like her mother Pragya looked, how he was an ardent fan of Shaarani Sen, how the cinema club on campus would soon be screening a retrospective of her best films. Tilo would have to remind him to not embarrass her this way.

'And this is Goopy-da, Lata's cousin. He is a professor at Barnard.'

Tilo raised her eyebrows. She approved of Barnard. Barnard was very posh. See, this is why they'd come all the way from Jamshedpur. She smiled at Goopy and gently adjusted the Basra pearls in her ears. She now turned expectantly towards the African panting next to him. Ronny continued the introductions. 'And this is Duma. I just found out that he is part of this small start-up.'

Duma waved away his words and complimented Tilo's sari.

'Which start-up?' Tilo asked, staying on point.

'Epic,' Duma replied modestly.

'Oh. My. God.' said Tilo. 'I teach a case-study on Epic. How it became the most exciting OTT platform ever after failing at DVD rentals. Now – Duma, is it? – can I badger you for a bit?'

Duma smiled good-naturedly.

'Hello! So glad you could make it,' Lata had finally found the group. 'Vik, Tilo, this is Hem. Aaduri's colleague, Molly's favourite...'

'Hey!' said Ronny. 'That's me.'

'Well, *my* favourite then,' Lata finished. 'Ladies and gentlemen, Hem Shankar Tiwari.'

'Hello, Hem,' said Tilo, shaking his hand, even though her eyes were still fixed on Duma. 'You are joining us in Jamshedpur, right?'

'Ah, yes, of course. Thanks for including me in the invitation.'

Aaduri appeared next to Hem, gave Tilo and Vik a hug each and then announced, 'I think we should commandeer one of those tables. We are really in the way here.' Tilo nodded vehemently in agreement (she liked Aaduri), claimed Duma's elbow and led the way. She knew exactly which table she wanted. As expected, the group fell in line behind her.

Lata hung back and decided to look for Prasad and direct him to Tilo's table. She should probably go and check on the Sens and the Haldars whom she hadn't spoken to all evening, and hunt for the hospitable Bansals who had taken such good care of the Ghoshes at the sangeet to exchange some pleasantries. But then, feeling tired of it all, she changed direction mid-course, and slipped into the ante-chamber where Molly had waited before shubhodrishti. It was deserted. The scent of crushed flowers emanated from the single sofa in the corner. Lata stretched her legs and looked at her phone.

Oh, she had an email!

*Dear Lata,*

*What do you get when you cross a tortoise and a porcupine? A slowpoke!*

*TBH, Josh told me this joke. I have been spending far too much time with him because his parents are in Calcutta and he is going to live with us for two whole days. His jokes are the only good thing about him. Otherwise, he is quite annoying. He flip-flops around the house in his ugly yellow Crocs which is SO unfair because I can't wear my favourite sandals at home. He gets special treatment because he's a Guest. (I was calling him Ghost. Mama scolded me.)*

*I wish I could trade Josh for his birds. They are alone in his house with their Didi, and maybe they are lonely. Do you remember their names? Optimus Prime and Max. I bet THEY don't talk about Harry Potter CONSTANTLY.*

*I know I said it should be a surprise but I am attaching a picture of Scone because I can't wait. (Curling up with Scone is making the situation better.) I'm reading a book called* Gone with the Wind. *But I can only do it out loud when nobody's around. If Josh hears, he'll make fun of me. If my parents hear, they will confiscate the book. Scone keeps secrets well. I know you will love her because she is VERY sweet, even to the so-called Guest/Ghost.*

*Please come soon.*

*Lots of Love,*

*Pixie*

'If you're stealing away at a wedding to check your messages, then it can mean only one thing,' Ronny remarked.

Lata looked up and made a face. He was leaning against the doorway and promptly took this as an invitation to come and sit next to her. 'New friend?'

'My new friend,' said Lata, lightly brushing off a flower from Ronny's shoulder, 'I'll have you know, is even younger than *your* new friend.'

# 34
# The Ex

Molly's wedding, the Oberoi Grand, the end of an era. If this were not life but a film – not the kind of serious film Ronny Banerjee made, of course, but the sort of rom-com Lata watched on cold London nights when Bumble had been abandoned – then this would be the moment when a nostalgic melody from the past would cue in, and under the soft warm glow of the single chandelier in the ante-chamber, on that plush sofa scattered with flowers that Molly's garland had shed, Lata Ghosh and Ronny Banerjee would speak of the years gone by, of love and mistakes and second chances.

But this being life and not cinema, romantic music was replaced by the background hum of the banquet hall. The Ghoshes and Jaiswals mingling with the Bansals and Boses, chomping, laughing, comparing, balancing social vengeance with the bonhomie of new beginnings.

'Does your new friend bite?' Ronny asked.

'Does *yours*?'

Lata's voice had darkened with something. Not quite jealousy. But something like it, viscous, slick with shadows.

'No,' said Ronny, after a beat. 'She doesn't.'

'Mine doesn't either,' said Lata, smiling in relief. 'But, as it happens, my new friend has a new friend who might bite.'

'That sounds like a riddle,' said Ronny, impatient to get to the bottom of this business. 'Who *is* your new friend, Charulata Ghosh?'

'Why do *you* care, Shomiron Banerjee? I thought you would have had at least a decade and a half to recover from your insane jealousy.'

'I don't know what you are talking about. I am not the one who suffered from insane jealousy, even though I should have. Every single time I called on the landline, in your hostel at IIM-C, you were out. There was always group work, team projects, etc., etc, etc. And every time you came home, you just sat down in your room and studied like a bloody nerd. Why do you think Molly and I got so good at carrom in those months? Yet, if you remember correctly, jealousy was never my thing. It was yours.'

'Oh please!' exclaimed Lata, her voice, which had been velvet with irony all this while, now animated with angry sparks.

'Of course. Just because I spent all summer directing that play I wrote. Wait, what was it called?'

'*The Ex*,' Lata supplied, despite herself.

'*The Ex*! Right! I was so pleased with that title,' Ronny burst into laughter.

'And how apposite it turned out to be,' Lata smiled, her voice reverting to velvet.

'You were doing an internship that summer, Charu. *You* had no time. But you used to get *so* mad at me because I was obsessing over that stupid play. You know how tyrannical I get when I am in director mode.'

'You were spending far too much time with your leading lady, Ronny. Now, *her* name I can't seem to remember. But as we can see, the habit has stuck. Obviously, I was some sort of a clairvoyant.'

'That's utter nonsense. My previous leading ladies, in both my films, were happily married. And none of my other partners have had anything to do with the film world. Also, just a point of note, I never loved that Moyna Mondol from ISI. I didn't even *like* her that much. I was, if I remember correctly, madly in love with you, Ms Ghosh.'

'That's too many "loves" in one sentence, Mr Banerjee. I have lived in stiff upper lip England for far too long, where we don't bandy about that word. And, as it happens, I have parsed the fine differences of *love* and *like* and *in love* for decades. Anyway, let's not muck about in purono kashundi. The others must be waiting.'

Lata got up and adjusted the pleats of her sari unselfconsciously. Ronny did not get up.

'You are probably going to meet my new friend in Jamshedpur. She is Pixie, nine years old, Bappa's daughter.'

'Bappaditya from Statistics?'

'The one. Pixie has acquired a puppy called Scone.' Lata handed him her phone where a photograph of a cute polka-dotted puppy had just downloaded. Ronny looked at it blankly. 'Riddle solved? I'd better go and oversee stuff now. It's not too late for Boro Jethu to light a last-minute fire. I'll see you around.'

Ronny didn't get up or follow her out. After a moment or two, muscle memory asserted itself. It was his turn now to check his notifications.

There was nothing from the Maheshwaris. However, a slew of texts from Pragya. He typed, 'I'm coming in a minute,' but made no effort to move.

Of course he'd been insanely jealous when Lata had brandished that handsome Aarjoe she'd met at her campus placement – Who meets their future husband at a campus interview? How can it ever end well? – with his prospects and his cars and his fine suits. 'The only reason you're marrying him,' he'd told her in a black mood, when it was already too late, when Ghosh Mansion was already rigged up with lights and guests had begun to arrive, 'is because you are, at heart, a hypocrite. Just as your ancestors built this grand house in collusion with the British, you are going to collude with global capitalists. You have no respect for either knowledge or art. You are basically trading up, marrying an insufferable corporate type, a…a…stooge. You think I am a dabbler, like your father was. Dabbling in art. Maybe I am. But maybe I am not. Maybe I shall be a great filmmaker after all.'

'I do hope you become a great filmmaker, Ronny,' Lata had said simply, meaning every word.

'I hope you are happy,' Ronny had replied, barely tamping down his rage and not meaning it at all. He'd hoped she would be bitterly unhappy all her life.

By eleven, most of the guests had left, or were just taking their leave. None of the ladies had liked to burden their five-star fashion statements with sweaters and coats – after all, if you lived in Calcutta, you didn't really invest too much in beautiful warm clothes since winter was so brief – and so, half regretting that, they decided to leave early, before the night got too cold. In any case, tomorrow was a weekday.

The Ghosh elders, now congealed in a glut by the door, looked exhausted. Boro Jethu had his feet up. (One of the waiters had found him a footstool.) The Jaiswal patriarch had been bundled home a couple of hours ago, and AJ's parents were now thanking Bobby for her magic touch. Earlier, they had sought Lata out and thanked her too.

The bride and groom, surrounded by their friends and the few cousins close in age, were laughing over dinner. They would soon repair upstairs, where a little room had been booked for the after-party. They were calling it the bashor, of course. Lata and Goopy had excused themselves from this affair, they were too old for such things. They would return to Ghosh Mansion where, tomorrow, a final lunch had been organised, after the vidai. The Bongs had got their bashor and kalratri, the Jaiswals had got their sangeet and vidai. And Boro Jethu had had the last laugh. Tomorrow's lunch, after the Jaiswals left with Molly, would have both mutton and fish.

At the other end of the banquet hall, Tilo's table was going strong. Tilo's mood had rapidly improved after she'd found out that Goopy and Duma could be great contacts for the future, and now she sat between them regally. Ronny, from his seat next to Pragya, gossiped endlessly with

Duma about the world of films and shows – a conversation that flourished like an underwater stream just below the expansive saga spun by Tilo. Lata was finally eating her dinner though she'd lost her appetite long ago. She silently observed Aaduri finishing off Hem's rabri.

'Hope you have Harry Belafonte ready, Lata?' Vik asked, spotting a lull in his wife's rhetoric and managing to edge a question in. 'Molly and AJ seem to be leaving…'

Lata looked genuinely mystified.

'Oh hahahaha, I got it, I got it,' Hem said ebulliently. He turned to Lata and explained, 'Charulata-ji, thanks to you and Aaduri, I am now an expert in chao questions. The answer is Jamaica Farewell. Or jamai ka farewell.'

Everyone laughed. Once again, Lata wondered at the tinkly, wind-chimey sounds that emerged from Pragya's reed-like form. How could Ronny bear it? And why was she still here? Hadn't she been in a rush to leave?

'Now, here's one for you lot,' Hem said. 'What were the Ghosh relatives and friends singing on the day of Molly's sangeet?'

'Meat na-a-a-a-a mila re man ka…' sang Ronny, tunefully. Pragya shot him a besotted look.

At that exact moment, Lata looked at Aaduri. Aaduri looked at Lata. And suddenly, the ridiculousness of it all hit her. She began to laugh, and one by one, everyone joined in. This little life, thought Lata. Sometimes you cry in a cab and sometimes you laugh around a white table laden with good food while the shehnai plays in the background. And sometimes it's the other way round.

# 35

## The Cousins

If Lata had imagined that after the hurly-burly of Molly weds AJ, she could return to her childhood bed with her childhood books and spend the rest of her holiday – which, thankfully, did not seem all that endless any more – left to her own devices, sending wedding pictures to her London friends, counting the battles lost and won, and preparing for the glassy routine of life in England, she couldn't have been more wrong. Even though the bride and groom were off on their honeymoon and the canopy of twinkling lights had been dismantled and dust had begun to crowd the corridors again, the senior occupants of Ghosh Mansion remained in grand spirits after the wedding, much like children who've returned from a birthday party on an acute sugar high and insist on running around in circles, simply refusing to go to bed. The elders at Ghosh Mansion *just* wouldn't cool down.

By day and by night, Boro Jethi and Kakimoni cooked up (competing) storms to educate Duma about the nuances of the Bengali kitchen. Always more of an about-town person, Manjulika dashed about, Lata in tow, returning gold to the bank locker, helping Molly's Germans shop for their step-parents and friends, carrying wedding sweets and gossip to the very elderly or housebound relatives who had missed the wedding. She even dragged the cousins to her feminist book club in Hedua on Sunday, announcing to Goopy and Duma en route that the group had several 'LGBTQ-plus persons'. (She always remembered the 'plus'). Lata had looked away stoically while Goopy and Duma rolled in laughter for the rest of the journey.

In the days leading up to Molly's wedding, the Ghoshes had been eating their catered lunches together in the covered courtyard at the back. And now, after decades of separate kitchens and severe differences, they seemed a little reluctant to give this practice up even after the caterers had packed up and left. The formal dining room downstairs where, all those years ago, Boro Jethu had made his cruel comments – unwittingly galvanising Lata and Ronny's romance – was called into action for sit-down meals every day. Even though it meant the old servants went crazy with logistics, utensils were carried up and down many flights of stairs several times a day and then counted and taken back (everyone was very possessive about their own ladles and bowls), they did not complain. After all, what was the point of having such a large dining table if the young and the old *never* sat down and ate their meals together? Also, the house had been bereft for far too long.

Finally, on the fifth day of such relentless activity, Lata came down with a temperature.

After lunch, which she had been consequently excused from, Goopy and Duma crept up to her bedroom and found her under two blankets, listening to an audiobook. The boys climbed in and soon she was flanked by them on either side. It felt comforting.

'So this is your strategy for avoiding the *Hum Saath Saath Hain* meals?' Goopy remarked. 'Calling in sick?'

'What is Um Sa Sa Um?' Duma asked.

'I *am* sick,' Lata said hoarsely. 'My insides are all melty, my brain is short-circuiting stuff.'

Duma felt her forehead. 'She has a fever,' he confirmed.

Goopy waved his expertise away, checked her forehead himself and said, 'It's nothing! She just wants to mope about Ronny.'

Lata rolled her eyes. 'Your comment is so 1998, Goopy. I know it feels like we are teenagers trapped in this hellhole all over again, at the mercy of our adults but, in case you haven't noticed, you have grey hair, I have grey hair (under the honey-brown shade that my colourist favours) and Ronny has grey hair.' She now turned her gaze on Duma. '*Hum Saath Saath Hain* is a cult Bollywood film about these super-rich people who, despite playing happy families for ninety per cent of its nine hundred hours, manage to exile the stepbrother briefly. It's one of Goopy's all-time favourite films. I am surprised you haven't seen it on Epic.'

'I liked your Ronny,' said Duma. 'I want to watch *his* films. But I do not approve of his arm candy.'

Tiana Mitra's story on 'Wedding Goals Set by Molly and AJ', accompanied by photographs of Pragya Paramita Sen in her green silk and vintage emeralds ('borrowed from Ma!'), and of Ronny in his charming piri-lifting act had been oohed and aahed at, on the internet. They were calling her a style icon. Duma and Goopy's little story had made a nice strand too. Even the print edition had picked up a few of the photographs, Lata lurking in the backdrop in one, looking out of focus. It was intensely annoying. The only good that came of it was that Nimki and Manjulika had stopped talking about Ronny altogether.

'Don't blame him,' Goopy was quick to interrupt. 'Our girl broke his heart.'

'No!' said Lata, sitting up.

'And your cousin calls himself a feminist,' said Goopy, patting her shoulder commiseratingly. 'Oh, by the way, we may see him this evening, your Ronny.'

Before Lata could ask why, what-for, Manjulika entered with a tray, Boro Jethu and Jethi trailing her.

'Munni, drink up!' she said, handing Lata a tumbler of a vile-looking cinnamon-scented concoction. Goopy got up and found chairs for his parents. Manjulika sat at the foot of the bed on a cane mora.

'Ugh,' burbled Lata, taking a sip.

'I think you might have to cancel Jamshedpur, Munni,' Manjulika announced happily.

'Of course not,' said Lata. 'Pixie will be *devastated*.'

Manjulika pursed her lips. 'I don't care if Pixie is devastated. What is this sudden fascination with other people's children? If you are sick, you simply cannot travel alone.'

'I have an idea,' said Goopy, tentatively. 'Why don't *we* go with her? It'll be a nice break for us too. I haven't been to Jamshedpur since the football match in 1995, and we shall keep an eye on Munni.'

The mothers looked unhappy. 'But you *just* came,' Boro Jethi mumbled to Goopy, 'And there is all the bank work you promised to help with. What about taking Baba to the doctor?'

'Ah, let them go, let them go,' said Boro Jethu magnanimously. 'Let the young people spend some time together. Munni, you need to start taking antibiotics right away, though.'

'Antibiotics are awful, Baba,' began Goopy, but Lata raised her eyebrows. Goopy stopped in his tracks. They'd secured a small victory. They shouldn't risk it with an unnecessary argument on antibiotics. Manjulika and Boro Jethi looked mutinous but it appeared that Sudhiranjan Ghosh might yet carry the day.

'I'll text Tilo and tell her,' Lata said, crawling back under the blanket. 'Though it means you'll probably have to invite her to Barnard someday, Goopy.'

'I *really* think you should start calling me Dada now,' Goopy finished.

❧

Around five o'clock, as a few errant grey clouds appeared, giving a nice noir filter to the day, Ronny Banerjee began to walk down from Jadavpur University – where he'd given a lecture to the film studies MA class – towards the police station, from where he'd turn left to South City Mall. The weather was pleasantly bracing, and Ronny had time on his hands.

As he'd waited for Nikhil Maheshwari to call these last few days, or if not Nikhil, someone from his office to call – if not him, at least Bobby – a chilly thought eventually insinuated itself in his brain: this was not going to happen. At least not now, not this way. The moment had passed.

Nikhil was a keen businessman. (Entrepreneur, Ronny amended, since the word 'businessman', with its ring of socialist judgment, was one that new India had dispensed with.) Nikhil was a canny entrepreneur. The huge losses they'd suffered recently in the Telugu market – what Ronny called 'the other Tollywood' – the two back-to-back big-budget flops, were a result of Nikhil's elder brother's rashness. Everyone had heard Navin declaim, 'Go big or go home!' sometime or other. And now that he had, in a manner of speaking, gone home – or, in this case, gone to London where he had a flat in Hampstead, to lick his wounds – the tremors of his unfortunate decisions were likely to be felt across the company. Chiefly, here, in Calcutta, in Nikhil's fiefdom. And somehow, though Bobby had tried to maintain a taut front, Nikhil must have sensed Ronny's mixed feelings about *Shomoy*. That would be enough for him to pull the plug. If the director was not madly in love with his own script, Nikhil had said on occasion, it was unlikely the audiences would.

A grey veil fell upon the sun. The kiosks began to light up.

Despite what he now knew in his gut, Ronny no longer felt any of the intermittent panic of the last few months, the attendant anxiety and acidity, the constant loop of self-doubt-soaring-high-self-doubt. Ronny felt calm, Ronny felt fine, Ronny, as a matter of fact, felt young. He hummed. He stopped to take photos in the interesting light. And while, for the last several weeks, he had absolutely dreaded this book launch (Why on earth had he agreed to launch this novel? He would have to actually read it!) he now looked forward to meeting the writer. He looked forward to the upcoming trip, even though he had no idea what he would say in his keynote address. And he looked forward to spending time with Lata.

# PART FIVE

# 36

## New Arrangements

'If cities had superpowers,' Aaduri Bagchi mused aloud to
Hem Shankar Tiwari on Sunday morning, while they were
reading newspapers in bed, 'what do you think Calcutta's
would be?'

'You mean,' Hem replied thoughtfully, 'what Calcutta's
superpower *should* be? Hmm, let me think.'

He folded away the Classifieds section into a precise
rectangle. His hair was mussed, his morning stubble had
left a faint trace of shadow on his fair skin. Aaduri observed
how his brows were beetled together, his features wholly
absorbed in her question. This was one of his qualities she
found most endearing: Hem was willing to engage seriously
with even the most eccentric of her notions – of course,
it annoyed her too, this relentless generosity – but mostly
it felt charming. But after the Professor, with whom she'd
had to play the generous listener part, having to respond
constantly to his literary stances, which were plentiful
and often obtuse, Aaduri felt quite pleased with the new
arrangement. That's what she was calling it. The new
arrangement.

Lata had, of course, scoffed. *Arrangement-
shmarrangement*, she'd said, her fevered voice sounding

quite hoarse on the phone. 'I knew it was only a matter of time.'

'How about self-cleaning?' Hem asked finally. 'Too boring? Self-*restoring* then?'

Here's what led to this moment.

Short version: they'd been watching superhero films last evening on Epic. First the *Battle of New York* and then the *Battle of Sokovia* – and the mounds of rubble the Avengers habitually left in their wake – led to Hem's postulate. Self-restoring cities. Whether alien attack or plain old Father Time, the city would bounce back. Hmm.

Long version: Aaduri wanted to binge-watch *Agents of S.H.I.E.L.D* (apparently to run a series of articles on comic-book science) and since Hem didn't know S.H.I.E.L.D. from A.D.A.M., Aaduri was initiating him into MCU, one film at a time. Not that they had much time, between their still-colicky baby – the website which guzzled 'liquid content' and immediately demanded more – and the terms of the new 'arrangement' that had emerged between them, which had not been given a label yet, which, if Aaduri had her way, would never ever be given a label.

Longer version: Sometime around Molly's ashirbad-cum-ring ceremony, Aaduri and Hem had found themselves settling into a pattern. Hem would pick her up in the mornings en route to Ghosh Mansion – or the office, depending – they'd grab a coffee and a croissant, later they'd run into each other several hundred times in the newsroom, then, as evening fell, they'd go to Lata's – or to one of the functions thereof – and finally, at night, he'd drop her back home. At some point, he began to come up for a nightcap. Aaduri's orderly house, everything in its designated place, seemed an oasis of calm compared to his old-fashioned rooming house, what was called a 'mess' in Calcutta.

The conversation never stopped.

One night, Aaduri told Hem about the Professor. Afterwards, Hem spent several hours manically Googling him. Hem read out his poetry to her – handwritten in a fat Allahabad Bank diary from the year 1999 – and she was unexpectedly moved by it, by the quiet revolution in his verses, the sense of youth passing too slowly and then too quickly, by the images of Allahabad that bled into his lines – city by the intersection of three rivers – and by the nuance of his vocabulary. The night of Molly's sangeet, he stayed over for the first time.

Since then, they'd discovered unknown continents in themselves and each other.

Sometimes these days, Aaduri tried to remember what life had been like before this one week and found herself blanking out. Yes, there used to be time for things like grocery shopping and ironing and cleaning the refrigerator and returning calls and responding to WhatsApp messages from Tiana late at night. But even the specifics of those seemed fuzzy. How *had* she lived in the past?

She felt a tiny bit horrible at how soon she was thinking such things, how quickly the Professor's shadow had begun to recede, and how quickly spring had begun to infect her immune system. She tried to edit herself whenever such thoughts sprung up like defiant shoots of green. 'Calm down, you ridiculous creature,' she wanted to tell her heart. But her heart had no patience.

'If a city could *restore* itself, then it would never age,' Aaduri said reflectively.

'Ghosh Mansion would – well – remain Ghosh Mansion, grand, untouched by time,' added Hem.

'But,' they both began together, then stopped.

'But without decay, how would we appreciate youth?' said Hem finally.

'Without destruction, how would we appreciate love?' Aaduri smiled.

The doorbell rang.

'Oh, is Lata here already?' Hem jumped up from the bed. 'I'd better shower and get dressed. Have you finished packing?'

But it was only the maid, Nalini.

Around ten, Lata arrived in a cerise jumper and a pair of dark glasses. Apparently her eyes were red from the mysterious sickness. Nalini had breakfast on the table and Aaduri and Hem were both ready and waiting, slightly edgy from facing Lata, the first witness to the new arrangement.

'So are Duma and Goopy taking the train?' Aaduri asked, after the initial oh-you-guys-look-so-adorable and Aaduri-stop-looking-cranky-when-you're-secretly-elated and Lata-ji-it-is-all-because-of-you-s had been dispensed with. They slathered peanut butter on their toast. (At Aaduri's, for breakfast you always had peanut butter, jelly and Nutella, and masala tea and cheese omelettes. Lata, who was passive-aggressively figure-conscious in the manner of many beautiful women, critiqued the menu every time, told Aaduri to grow up, and then proceeded to eat heartily.)

'Oh no, they are going with Ronny later today. Jethi had some work at the bank this morning. They met Ronny at some book launch a couple of days ago, and he invited them to tag along.'

'I hope you realise that he wanted *you* to tag along,' Aaduri smiled.

'Oh, look at you, Ms Bagchi, all mellowed by *luuurve*,' Lata smirked. 'Nothing like that. Bobby is organising this trip. We all know her views on me. Also, I couldn't pass up the opportunity to hear Hem's poetry.'

Hem started. Lata gave him a playful little shove with her elbow. Aaduri called for tea.

'Why does Bobby hate you, Luts?' Aaduri said, 'Is it a territorial thing? Or is it genuine – like she's worried you'll upset his life, become this big bad influence on him, and like Nadira Naipaul, throw out all the old friends from his life?'

Lata waved away her words airily – she couldn't care less about Ronny Banerjee's entourage, she wanted to say – but her eyes twinkled and the amount of Nutella she smeared on her toast suggested that she was in a remarkably chipper mood. This trip might be more fun than she'd anticipated, Aaduri admitted to herself, as she picked up another – well, the last – toast and slathered peanut butter on it.

'When will Lata get here, Mama?' Pixie asked her mother for the ninety-ninth time that hour. Nisha sniffed.

It wasn't that Nisha did not like Lata – she did – but her daughter's adoration for Lata made her a little grumpy. Here she was, plodding behind Pixie all the time, planning and plotting with Bappa to give her a well-rounded life, all the advantages of their upper-middle-class life, with nannies and drivers and tennis and what-not, but also the right values, the sort of middle-class upbringing that she and Bappa themselves had had, and persevering with her full-time mom role even though Tilo seemed to sneer at that choice. And here was her daughter, besotted with Lata Ghosh.

She checked her phone. 'No updates, Pix,' she replied wearily. 'I've told them to call once they're close.'

The guest house had been spit-polished in anticipation of Lata's arrival. Food had been ordered for a fancy tea-party from Brubeck. Lisa, the nanny, was stuffing Posto into an attractive red romper as he waved his fat arms about merrily. Pixie herself had chosen her clothes carefully: a white dress with ruffles they'd bought from Mini Boden just before returning to India, paired with a pink cashmere sweater that had sparkles on the front placket. The entire outfit was worth more than Lisa's monthly salary, thought Nisha crossly, though, of course, the annoyance was somewhat misplaced since she and Bappa had themselves bought it for Pixie.

It was another hour before Lata finally arrived at their doorstep. She found Pixie fast asleep on the sofa, in her perfectly aristocratic outfit, exhausted from all the waiting. It was Scone who rushed out to welcome the party. And as per his mistress's instructions, after perfunctory barks at Aaduri and Hem, he threw himself upon Lata Ghosh and covered her hands and face with a hundred welcome licks.

# 37

# The Fine Art of Failure for Beginners

Tilottama Chaudhuri, the dean, was intensely proud of the gardens on campus. A battery of gardeners might have done the actual job of planting and weeding and scrabbling about in the mud, and the landscapers she had flown in to Jamshedpur from Bangalore 'to consult' might have imagined the perfect squares of red and yellow and white and pink, but the flowers – much like all else in school – were ultimately answerable to Tilo.

Upon her arrival from the States, Tilo had decided that the campus needed 'a talking point'. After reading somewhere that Michelle Obama had commissioned a kitchen garden when she first moved into the White House (it goes without saying that Tilo considered herself the Barack in their marriage), she'd snappily decided upon flowers by the auditorium and herbs behind the tennis courts. Each time there were visiting dignitaries on campus, saplings were planted, photos were clicked, and later, said dignitaries were sent pictures of said sapling, underpinning their long relationship with the business school in extravagantly ecological terms. Even Vik had had to admit there was a touch of genius about this strategy. (Once, a particularly voluble CEO's sapling had died. It was discreetly replaced by the gardeners and photos continued to be sent twice a year.)

On the day the Festival of Ideas was due to open, Tilo stood skittishly by the narcissi, a little after ten, waiting for

Ronny Banerjee, her keynote speaker. He had arrived safely late last evening – she was grateful to Goopy for having kept her posted – and ought to have made an appearance by now. She had deputed a student to trail Ronny but Ronny had sent the student off this morning, with assurances that he would find his way on his own.

Fortunately, Lata and the rest of the party were here already. Having duly admired the gardens – Josh had led a campus tour, reciting the peculiarities and provenances of each flower and vegetable – they were now milling about, drinking cappuccinos, chatting with the students, the other guests, as well as the crème de la crème of Jamshedpur who had come since the keynote session was open to the public. Thanks to Epic recommendations, Ronny's films were quite popular outside Bengal.

'There you are!' Tilo cried out in relief when one of the campus cars drove up and Ronny was glimpsed behind the tinted window.

'I was actually walking down from the guest house, it's such a lovely day, but then I found myself whisked into this SUV,' he laughed, after the driver had rushed out and opened his door. 'It's nice to see you, Tilo-di, charming campus, and the air…there is something sweet about the air in Jharkhand.'

Tilo said sternly, 'I was panicking. Your assistant didn't send me the final title of your presentation. We usually publish it in the day's newspaper. Anyway, it appears that we have a full house. Vik's film society has been screening your films and documentaries to create a buzz. Come, let's hurry up.'

Caught up in the gale force of her movements, Ronny quickly fell in step beside Tilo.

'I have your introduction ready, Ronny. But please tell me what the title of your talk is.'

'Ah that,' said Ronny reflectively. 'Let's call it "The Fine Art of Failure for Beginners".'

Aghast, Tilo stopped in her tracks. She should never have listened to Vik's suggestion and invited Ronny as the chief guest, National Award Golden Lion be damned! This was clearly going to be a disaster.

Lata Ghosh sat in the audience, in the second row to be precise, in a pearly cashmere cape that now seemed all wrong. She should have worn a sari. Lata was flanked by Pixie (she'd insisted on attending the keynote address even though it meant she'd had to miss school) and Aaduri, who was, as usual, dispensing messages to Tiana furiously. The students had handed Lata a bag that morning, with a notebook, a lanyard and details of the programme. Pixie had commandeered the bag while Lata vaguely fingered the programme on her lap. The keynote was to be followed by a mid-morning tea break.

The hall was full. People had spilled out to the aisles and many stood at the back, in little clusters. There was a sense of expectation, the students chattered, and every now and then a single voice rose over the general din to make an exceptionally banal statement. Lata looked about herself nervously. So many people had come to hear him speak? *Her* Ronny? (Well, that was technically very far from the truth,

Lata knew. Even if she couldn't bring herself to say *Pragya's* Ronny, he certainly wasn't hers.) There was something gratifying about the crowds, of course. But Lata found her throat closing up in terror. 'I hope he's actually prepared a speech,' she squeaked tensely. Aaduri looked up from her phone and said, 'It's very unlikely.'

The lights dimmed.

A soft hush descended as Tilo strode onto the stage in her ivory muslin jamdani sari with tigers woven along the border. She welcomed everyone in her clipped diction, even though Lata thought she detected a cold undertone to it all, and efficiently lit the ceremonial lamp herself. 'Hmm, that's interesting,' observed Aaduri. 'Usually they get the chief guest to do the lamp lighting, no?'

Pixie poked Lata. 'Was Ronny Uncle your boyfriend?' Lata widened her eyes slightly, then nodded in the affirmative. 'A very very very long time ago.'

'Now I shall invite Shomiron Banerjee to the podium,' Tilo was saying. 'He needs no introduction.'

'He's handsome,' Pixie said. 'May I have your phone? I want to take pictures.'

'Ronny tells me his talk is titled "The Fine Art of Failure for Beginners". I cannot wait to be enlightened,' Tilo finished her piece frostily.

Lata handed her phone to Pixie.

Ronny walked into the cone of light that fell somewhat theatrically upon the now-darkened stage, clutching a sheaf of papers. The papers, however, remained idle upon the podium for the rest of the hour, because Ronny decided to speak unaided. He opened with a joke, commented on the irony of his subject to India's most 'successful' students, decanted sentimental mentions of campus life, and, finally, towards the end of his unconventional introduction, directed a warm stream of gratitude towards Tilo and her dedicated team who, by inviting a filmmaker to speak, had put the arts firmly at the centre of the conversation.

By now, the audience was eating out of the palm of his hand.

Lata relaxed in her seat. The voice and the words were familiar and unfamiliar at once, mesmerising in their effect. Anecdote upon anecdote unfolded as Ronny tracked the story of his artistic journey with honesty and humour and an emphasis on the failures that were invariably overwritten by the victories. Parallelly, in Lata's head, the story of *her* life in those years unspooled. The NYC years, the Connecticut unravelling, the divorce, Mumbai with Joy, the management consultant years, Twitter and Ari, the terrible online dates.

Eventually Ronny came to the crux of his argument. '*If* you want to become a filmmaker – why only a filmmaker, any kind of artist, a writer, a painter, a musician – then don't do it to be rich or successful. You are MBA students. You know far better than me how to harness wealth, how to be successful, how to strategise and maximise, how to double and treble portfolios. You have all come here after attaining success in several difficult exams. There is no advice that I can give you. I can simply tell you the unvarnished truth. Attempt a life in art *only* if you are ready to fail again and again. And I don't mean simply in the sense of modalities, that you may not find a publisher or a producer or a patron at once, but of course there's that too. I mean the deeper failures that drive growth. Every time I begin a new project, I am all at sea again. How to tell the story best? How to write characters whom you will *like* – not just love, but *like*? I flounder and grasp at straws until, bit by bit, a shape begins to appear. And then, even before I can feel happy for five seconds, it vanishes.'

The audience laughed appreciatively.

Ronny went on to speak about the script of *Shomoy*, which had seemed quite perfect to him a year ago and which he was now overhauling almost in entirety.

Lata exhaled gently.

Pixie leaned her head into Lata's softly cashmered arm.

Ronny's words had cast a spell upon them both.

'Ultimately,' he said, 'contrarian though it sounds, the truth is that to pursue a life in art, you must learn to fall a little in love with the idea of failure. As long as you are unafraid to fail, you will feel the creative energy swirling through your body. Embrace it. It's harrowing, excruciating, The Worst. It's also the most glorious feeling on earth. After love, that is. But then, like art, love too is audacious. One fails at it only to return to its door, again and again, humbled and made new. Thank you.'

There must have been applause. But Lata did not hear it.

# 38

# Nemesis

'And who might this be?' Sir asked, removing his bifocals and squinting, as though contemplating an exotic rabbit that had suddenly appeared on his desk by a remarkable sleight of hand.

As it happened, Tiana Mitra, sporting a pink headband with tiny bunny ears, had slunk in quietly while Sir, dapper in his three-piece suit, had his eyes on the giant flat-screen TV mounted on the wall. Consequently, she had been forced to take the only empty chair available, the one right under Sir's nose. The television screen was as incongruous in the editor's wood-panelled, book-lined, computer-free, colonial-era room as twenty-three-year-old Tiana, fresh-faced and eager-beavery in her white jumpsuit was, among the gathered group of hacks who were all forty and above and wore expressions of utter world weariness.

'This, Sir, is Aaduri's newest hire,' Sumona Munshi, the films editor quickly explained. 'She's representing our – ' she searched for the right words – 'our *online self* today, since Aaduri and Hem are both away.'

'Oh, I see,' said Sir, looking distracted at the mention of Hem. Hem was his right hand. Hem was his Boswell. Hem rarely took leave. Without Hem, Kamaleshwar Dattachaudhuri felt quite lost. 'This one will help us go bacterial?'

Tiana stifled a giggle.

'Viral,' said Sumona with a straight face.

KD looked mystified for a few seconds.

'*Go viral*, that's the phrase, Sir,' Moidul, the bureau chief, took upon himself the mantle of explication.

'Right, go viral, hmm. I can't sleep at night, what with journalism dying a slow and painful death the world over, and here we're supposed to embrace viruses. But we will not go gentle into the good night, we will rage, rage against the dying of the light. Do you know the source, young lady?'

Sir's voice had suddenly lost its rambly quality and focused, pointedly, on the rabbit in front.

'Dylan Thomas,' Tiana replied, after a beat.

The rest of the room breathed a collective sigh of relief.

'Well done, young lady,' Sir continued. 'So, how do you plan to take us to the viral age?'

Tiana relaxed and said good humouredly, 'I have some ideas.'

The gathered hacks laughed. The ice was broken. The sports editor took over, followed by Sumona, and Tiana was not called upon to speak again.

Later that day, Sumona found Tiana texting by the coffee machine. She stopped to congratulate her. 'Full marks on the Dylan Thomas answer!'

Tiana looked at her blankly. 'Oh that,' she finally replied, after the morning had swum back into her consciousness. 'It was Siri.'

Sumona sighed. Millennials were so fascinating, all sass and Siri. She peered into Tiana's phone. 'What's that?'

'Snapchat,' Tiana said importantly. 'I am working one of my sources.'

While Tiana was trying to set up a confidential meeting with a source who could be useful in her quest to go bacterial – she'd been utterly charmed by Sir and was now going to use 'bacterial' herself – her boss Aaduri Bagchi was sitting in the sun, in the sylvan surroundings of the Beldih Club in Jamshedpur, sunning her toes and trying to provoke her best friend, Lata Ghosh, into speaking what was on her mind, now that tongues had been potentially loosened by the several Cosmopolitans they had downed with lunch. But Lata was staying mum. Since the sun was in her eye, she had covered part of her face with the beige cashmere scarf that had been wound around her neck in the morning, and her cheeks were pink and flushed. She looked even more beautiful than usual, Aaduri noted, as she leaned back in the chair and maintained an air of perfect stillness.

Bappa had thrown a lunch in Ronny's honour at the Blue Ginger restaurant and after the food and gossip had been consumed in courses, the party had now spilled out onto the emerald lawns. 'The fact is the Chinese are out-producing the next four steel-producers, it's crazy,' a tall man in chalkstripe trousers was addressing his words to a motley bunch of younger colleagues, Bappa included. At lunch, he had sat across from Aaduri and informed her that he was an amateur marathoner. Behind Lata, one of the other speakers, a woman in an indigo sari, was holding forth on the subject of her talk the next day. 'You do realise, right, that whether in the future your company sells soap or tea or steel, it has to be a technology company?' The recipient of her pearls of wisdom was a courtly Sikh gentleman, the head of something, Aaduri had been told but was now forgetting, who wore an appropriately interested expression.

'I cannot stand such corporate talk,' Aaduri said snippily.

'Well, I find it more interesting than political talk,' Lata murmured.

'Political conversation is egalitarian, Luts, everyone in India has a view, unlike some nonsense about steel or tech. Where's lover-boy?' Aaduri responded.

Lata refused to rise to the bait. Ronny was somewhere inside still, no doubt being fawned over by the very people who had composed his epitaphs when they had heard he'd quit his advertising gig to make documentaries and stay at his parents' in Calcutta. Bappa's other guests, his new colleagues, were all huddled in groups of their own, indulging in detailed shop talk. Lata recognised them from her own friends and colleagues in London and avoided them carefully, even though they smiled at her with acute politesse.

'I miss Pixie,' Lata said finally. (Half an hour ago Pixie had been extracted from the melee by Nisha and taken home, kicking and screaming, for a nap.) Aaduri, who had little patience with kids and littler patience with Lata's other friends, merely grimaced.

'Hello girls!' Duma appeared in their range of vision, resplendent in his white kurta and pink Nehru jacket.

'Munni,' he said, pulling up a chair next to her. 'You know how there are people in America who propose to their partners at the Superbowl? I used to wonder what that felt like. Now you can tell me.'

Aaduri snorted with laughter and nearly fell off her chair.

'Oh shut up,' Lata said.

'No, really. What *did* it feel like?'

'I really don't know what you are yammering on about. Yes, he's my ex, and yes, he gave a speech where he mentioned love in a passing comparison to art…'

'And yes, after that he came and sat next to me at lunch in a terribly coupley fashion and stole chunks of mutton from my plate,' Aaduri added.

'And yes, Goopy and I as your appointed guardians here are expecting to be seriously spoken to this evening by the young man in question. Filmmaking is not exactly a stable job but apparently the father has a government pension, the mother still works, and he is an only son.'

Lata got up in mock anger and turned towards the restaurant. (Actually, she was really thirsty and needed a glass of water.)

'Stay, stay, Lata Ghosh,' Aaduri called out, but Lata gracefully offered the middle finger in the air.

Up ahead was Ronny Banerjee, star of the day, smiling gently as he loped towards her. 'You left your purse behind, Charu,' he said, handing Lata her bag.

The truth was that for as long as Tiana Mitra was in college in Phoenix, Arizona, she and Mimi Dasgupta couldn't stand each other. But as it can happen sometimes with frenemies, when their paths crossed in Calcutta recently, they found that the memories of their college years had been broken down and reconfigured in their heads by the radiance of nostalgia. It resulted in a strange kind of kinship. Well, maybe kinship was pushing it a bit. But a new kind of alliance had developed, one that was mutually beneficial. Tiana got her first byline – and Aaduri's approbation – with the story about Pragya's Instagram account, something that Mimi had drawn her attention to in the first place, and in turn, after that story, Pragya realised just how valuable Mimi's inputs were to her social media posture. Soon, they became each other's 'source'.

After planning around their schedules for days – Tiana had work, *ugghhh*, while Mimi had gym, pilates, kickboxing, film screenings and store openings alongside Pragya – they'd finally managed to meet up that evening for a drink in a hip new pub that Mimi had chosen after careful deliberation.

'I'm going to have to run, though,' Tiana said, moments after they'd mwah-mwahed in the air, squealed appropriately and complimented each other. (Tiana said she couldn't *believe* how thin Mimi was looking – Mimi confirmed it was the weed – and Mimi said Tiana must tell her which website she had ordered her furry white jumpsuit from, like, immediately, it was *that* nice). 'My boss is travelling, and I am basically holding down the fort,' Tiana added in explanation.

'Isn't your boss that Aaduri lady?' Mimi asked, vaguely waving at the waiter. 'Our nemesis Lata's BFF?'

'Is Lata our nemesis?' Tiana asked, contemplatively. 'But I liked her so much. Even though I was just a reporter at her cousin's wedding, she treated me like a guest, fed me, introduced me to her family, etc., etc., etc.'

'You don't know anything, Tee,' Mimi said darkly, now turning her attention to a waiter who had appeared with a carafe of water and two glasses. 'Scotch for me, please.' The waiter turned to Tiana. 'Diet Coke,' Tiana said apologetically. 'I really will have to go back to work.'

There was a momentary pause in the conversation as both girls looked at their phones simultaneously.

'So why's she our nemesis?' Tiana prodded, having cleared her notifications.

'Because I think she's super jealous of Pragya and is making a play for Ronny. Apparently, he is her the-one-that-got-away, I think. Or so she imagines.'

Tiana reflected upon this. 'I thought you *wanted* Ronny and Pragya to break up?'

'Well, not *now*,' Mimi conceded. 'Let that damn film happen first. Also, she will be broken-hearted. She loves him, the poor fool. She is pining away because he is in Jamshedpur giving some keynote speech.'

The liquor arrived with a platter of assorted kebabs.

'Mimi,' Tiana said cautiously, 'Lata is in Jamshedpur too. Aaduri shared a selfie on Insta this afternoon.'

Mimi drew herself to her full height – which, to be honest, wasn't too threatening, because she was tiny.

'And…' Tiana took out her earphones. 'I think you need to hear the last bit of his speech.'

The two huddled together and listened carefully over the loud music, sharing Tiana's earphones.

Afterwards, Mimi thumped her empty glass on the table, asked for another and said, 'It's war.'

'*Totally*,' Tiana agreed vehemently, terribly cheered at the bacterial possibilities of this particular war. 'Ronny is Kashmir.'

'We are India and they are Pakistan,' Mimi said. 'Your Aaduri and Lata.'

'To be fair, Lata's claims are older,' Tiana said, gingerly chewing a breadstick. 'Shouldn't *she* be India then?'

'Why not, why not,' Mimi agreed sagely, and despite the grim portents of war and its consequences for the three subjects in its crosshairs, the girls began to giggle unstoppably.

# 39
## A Requiem for Max

Late afternoon at the club in Jamshedpur, a conspiracy of blues. The languorous azure of the skies, the glittering cyan of the pool, the pale sapphire of Lata's dress. Even the white marigolds that swayed in the breeze seemed to give off a faint blue haze as the day ripened into its finest bit: the half hour before twilight descended.

Lata Ghosh and Ronny Banerjee were sitting by the pool, not saying very much to each other. But the silence that sat between them was familiar, gentle. (If separation could be personified in chronological terms, theirs was a beautiful if somewhat self-absorbed teen.) It was almost as though after the exchange at the Oberoi on the night of Molly's reception, the bitterness had been expunged, the purono kashundi had been put back upon the old shelf in the unused kitchen. Now, like two people on the brink of a new friendship, they were curious and tentative and oddly interested in the other. He was solicitous and gallant; she, funny and charming.

'When is your talk?' Ronny asked, as though suddenly reminded that it could not be all play all day, of course.

'Tomorrow morning.'

'I've always wanted to know what management consultants actually do.'

'Oh, they work very long and very hard at being frauds. That's basically the summation.'

Ronny laughed.

'But the money is good,' Lata added. 'You get used to it.' Softly, she spoke again, referring obliquely to what Ronny had said earlier in the day. 'I wish I had known about all the times you were worried…about stuff…I could have helped…'

'Are you saying you take in strays at your London home?'

'I haven't so far. But I wouldn't mind supporting a struggling artist or two. I'd feel important, boast about my magnanimity to the shallow corporate stooges I work with. That's how you think of the lot of us, don't you?'

Lata's tone was jocular, but Ronny felt a little uncertain. Had he gone too far with his snide remarks against the corporates? I mean, they were funding this talk, this lunch, this film.

'Ari was big on charity. I used to get *so* annoyed at how he would never pitch in to help his sister, a painter, an extraordinarily talented one at that, if quite batty, but he would contribute to all kinds of fancy charities. Buy tables at galas, paying hundreds of pounds every other week. I would use you to make a general statement.'

'It's good to hear about your noble intentions,' said Ronny, 'since in all probability I have no producers for *Shomoy*.'

Lata looked up at him in surprise.

'I thought it was all sewn up?' she said.

'It was. Before I decided to rewrite the script and include J.C. Bose!'

Behind them, by the flower beds, a sudden conference of mynahs commenced.

Lata tapped him on the shoulder and indicated that they should get up.

'Tell me all about it on our way to Tilottama's. She may scold us if we are late. She has arranged for us to rest in her house.'

'Why do we have to rest in her house? Why can't we just go back to the guest house?' Ronny grumbled.

'Because,' said Lata.

And that was that.

Vik and Tilo lived in a bungalow tucked away at one end of the campus. Lata knew her way about because last evening Bappa had brought her over for an elaborate dinner, en famille, during which, in a bid to avoid the many men – all serious academics, very full of opinions about the nation and the world – who had quickly begun to take more than a passing interest in her, she'd fled to Josh's room and spent her time with the two kids and the birds. Far more interesting company. (Josh had fussed over Max, who was rather quiet, while Pixie kept up a constant stream of chatter.)

Lata and Ronny pushed the wrought-iron gate open and walked in. The front door was ajar. Inside, in the gloom, Pixie was sitting silently on the sofa, wearing a mournful face. Scone was curled up at her feet. Vik and Tilo were sitting on the sofa opposite Pixie, looking uncharacteristically forlorn, while Aaduri sat on a divan at the far end of the room, earphones plugged in, busy on a call. 'Oh, thank God you are here, there's been a terrible tragedy,' cried Pixie, running to Lata and throwing her arms around Lata's waist.

Vik and Tilo got up to greet them. Sombrely, Vik said, 'Come, come, sit.'

'What's going on?' Ronny asked, divesting himself of his bag.

'It's Max,' said Tilo.

'Josh's parakeet,' Vik explained to Ronny. 'He passed away this morning when Josh was in school. We were all busy on campus, as you know. Josh discovered that Max was cold and gone only after he returned from school, and in fact, neither of us was even home. He's devastated.'

'Where is Josh?' Lata asked.

'He's refusing to open his door. He is sobbing inside. Of course, we could always go round the veranda and enter from the other side...' Tilo said. 'I have the keys to that door.'

'I think he should be left alone to mourn,' Ronny said softly.

'That's true,' Vik murmured.

'Sorry about this,' Tilo replied. 'Best laid plans and all that...'

'I think I know what may help,' Pixie said. She picked Scone up and looked beseechingly at Lata. (Yesterday Josh had begged Bappa for Scone's company. Lata had helped with the negotiations.) Now Lata followed Pixie down the corridor, to where she knew Josh's room was.

Pixie knocked.

'Go away,' Josh's voice came out, all muffled and sobby.

'I am going away,' said Pixie. 'Just leaving Scone here at the door. He wants to see you.'

After a minute, the door opened and Josh came out, his face wet with tears. Pixie handed Scone to him and Scone immediately began to lick Josh's face.

Pixie followed them in and Lata walked back to the drawing room and informed the adults that a breakthrough had been effected.

Ten minutes later, as they sipped tea in funereal silence, Josh and Pixie appeared. Josh was carrying Scone, and Pixie had a shoebox in her hand. She placed the box reverentially upon the coffee table. 'It's Max's mortal remains,' she said. Josh refused to look at either of his parents and addressed Lata. 'Will you help us organise a funeral?'

Lata nodded.

'Joshie,' Tilo said, putting an arm around his shoulder, 'are you okay?'

Josh ignored her.

'Let me dig a grave for Max,' Vik said, throwing open the door. 'Beneath the night jasmine tree in the corner. Josh? Then flowers will fall on it every evening.' Josh nodded sullenly. Vik was followed out by Pixie, Josh and Scone, in that order, and Lata and Ronny decided to join them outside.

Tilo sat back on the sofa and they could hear her in the background: 'He'd been telling me for a couple of days that Max needed the vet. I was just so busy!'

'It's not your fault, Tilo-di,' Aaduri said, finally done with her phone call.

('It's totally your fault, Tilo-di,' Ronny whispered to Lata, as they stepped out into the lawns.)

Outside, the trees and flowers in Tilo's immaculate garden had caught the fire of the sunset. Optimus Prime, who had been left in his vintage aviary while Josh sobbed over Max's lifeless body in his bedroom, sat dolefully on Josh's shoulder. Scone had been transferred back to Pixie's lap. In deference to Optimus Prime's grief, he desisted from yapping.

'Ronny Uncle,' said Pixie, 'would you mind recording the funeral ceremony? Josh might want to watch it later.'

'Sure,' said Ronny. 'But my phone is out of juice. Maybe I can borrow Lata's.'

'No, no, I have a playlist on Lata's phone. Need that for the music. Let me get Aaduri's phone. Hers is also an iPhone X.'

Pixie bounded inside.

Meanwhile, Josh came up to Lata. 'Will you design the ceremony with Pixie? I am too sad to think about these things. But it should be proper, very formal.' He now plucked Optimus from his shoulder and held him tenderly to his chest. 'Poor Optimus, I can't imagine how she will take the death of her mate. She might try to kill herself. I will have to keep an eye on her.'

'Here,' said Pixie, panting as she handed Aaduri's phone to Ronny. 'Shall we decide upon the script? Where will you be positioned?'

Though her feet were killing her, and his head hurt, Lata and Ronny returned to the guest house oddly invigorated. Did death do that? Even if it was the death of a bird? After the funeral, the atmosphere at Tilo's had improved considerably. Pixie and Josh were allowed to watch Epic uninterrupted to forget their grief and, at some point, Tilo was marginally forgiven by Josh. (At least he was answering her questions.) The conversation remained tepid enough for Ronny and Lata to make good their escape by eight-thirty, after a quick dinner, and they left while the rest of the party lingered over their drinks.

'A quick rum-and-coke?' Ronny asked her as they got to his room first. 'Like old times.'

Lata paused and smiled and touched his shoulder. 'Not tonight,' she said. 'I better get my thoughts in order for tomorrow's lecture. You've set the bar pretty high, Mr Banerjee.'

'Then, Ms Ghosh,' Ronny said, taking her hands in his, warm like the soft breast of a bird. 'How about tomorrow morning I commandeer one of Tilo's SUVs, keep the engine running, and whisk you away after your session to the Dalma Wildlife Sanctuary? We could hang out with the elephants?'

'I'll think about it, Mr Banerjee,' Lata said, turning away from him.

'Wait a second. Give me your number, Ms Ghosh!'

'Tomorrow,' said Lata. 'We'll see.'

# 40

## Before and After

Back in her room at the guest house, a couple of floors above Ronny's, Lata stood by her suitcase, laying out her clothes for the next day on the sofa. It was an exercise that always calmed her nerves. Not that she *needed* any calming down per se, she told herself, she was a just a tad psyched, that was all.

She focussed on the colours. Did they work?

A beige leheriya sari she'd bought many years ago in Jaipur and left in Calcutta for Manjulika to dry clean and stow away, and a red Raw Mango blouse, with its stylish Peter Pan collar. She extracted a pair of dull gold skinny heels that she wore only with her saris and placed them on the floor. Upon the dresser next to the sofa, she kept her minimal accessories: a vintage red barrette with faux rubies she'd bought from a car boot sale in Bath, a sort of secret lucky charm, and a tub of her favourite postbox red lipstick.

Lata stepped back to admire the colour palette. The buzz she'd been feeling all evening became less acute.

Afterwards, she hopped into the shower – her blow-dried-in-Kadma hair stuffed into a shower cap that housekeeping had thoughtfully provided – and changed into her nightclothes: soft, well-worn cottons smelling of Nirma washing powder overlaid with her regular London detergent. She rubbed peppermint balm on the soles of her feet, and *carefully* – she didn't want anything oily near her hair – she went back to the bathroom and lathered her hands clean. All the while humming distractedly.

*Jolene, Jolene, Jolene…Joleeeeene…*

It had been a weird day. And so long, so filled with disparate things – Ronny's keynote, the liquid lunch of merciless teasing, the bird funeral, the invitation to Dalma Wildlife Sanctuary that sounded far too much like a date – that it almost felt as though they had been in Jamshedpur a whole week and not just a day and a half.

Ma would be pleased at this latest development, she thought tartly, not that anyone was going to tell anyone.

Lata had, as it happened, called Manjulika's cell from Tilo's house earlier in the evening but found it switched off. There was nothing surprising about that. Manjulika often forgot to charge her phone – or charge the power bank which Lata had got her – and mostly it was Nimki who provided the updates. But Nimki had gone to attend a great-grandniece's annaprashan in the village and would only be back tomorrow night. Hoping to get lucky, Lata dialled the landline. No luck.

Wait, wasn't today Ma's (feminist) book club day?

On book club days, sometimes she stayed back to get dinner with her feminist friends.

Lata climbed under the quilt and propped open the laptop to go over her presentation for tomorrow. Always a conscientious preparer, she had put together a series of slides that shared her chief learnings from the fifteen-odd years of being a management consultant. She'd planned a narrative arc that traced her own journey, part-anecdote, part-insider knowledge, but now suddenly, as she re-read them, the slides seemed too dry, too factual, too verbose.

And really, a PPT? Wasn't that too rehearsed?

Lata sighed. She hated making last-moment changes. But in the light of her realisations (and the clear and present need to impress a certain someone who might be in the audience tomorrow), she really should make the whole affair a little more interactive. How about if she divided the entire class into groups, and let's say every group was assigned the name of a well-regarded consulting company, and given a real-life case? How about that?

Excited by this whimsy, Lata began to rework her entire presentation. The more she thought of tomorrow's group as a consortium of young management consultants she needed to break in, rather than students she had to address in a classroom, the more fun the exercise became.

Maybe it was a good thing, after all – being impulsive, scratching things out at the last minute, pushing the bar, tearing hair? Maybe the Ronny model was not so bad, after all?

Around half past eleven, she was finally done.

Checking her notifications, she found that though her mother hadn't called her back, Aaduri had called several times, and then, presumably not having got her, left a slew of messages.

*So Hem has come up with a brilliant strategy for my talk. I am going to get these MBAs to give me ideas to get more hits on the website. Isn't that cool? Crowdsourcing! I mean I am going to rant about declining journalistic standards in the age of clickbaiting for 5 minutes but then get them to give free ideas. Good?*

How very management consultant of you, Aadu, Lata thought, scrolling down.

*I see my talk is at the same time as yours, which is annoying because I wanted to come listen.*

Clearly, there's no need, Lata thought.

*Anyway, after that, I am going with Hem to Ranchi to meet his brother's family. I know, I know. You want to come along?*

Umm. No. I have plans.

*Anyway, I don't know if I should get suspicious that you are not picking up the phone. If you are getting back with Ronny and doing stuff you are not supposed to, make sure I am the first to know. (Although we cannot let my assistant Tiana find out. She would go right ahead and publish some nasty stuff that will get a hundred thousand hits and maybe even get her a promotion! She is serious, that kid. I didn't think millennials had that kind of hunger but clearly I am way too prejudiced.)*

Illumination!

*Okay, fine, you are obviously too busy to check your messages. Goodnight. See you tomorrow. I hope you'll come to Ranchi. I don't know how I agreed to all this family visit kind of stuff but apparently I did and there's no backtracking. xoxo*

Tap, tap.

Tap, tap.

'I know you don't want to create a ruckus, Duma, but I *do* think we need to knock louder,' Goopy whispered.

Duma banged the door a decibel harder.

'Munni!' Goopy called out. 'Wake up, Munni!'

There was a muffled sound on the other side. Footsteps padded towards them uncertainly and then ceased. 'Munni, it's us,' Goopy said, his voice ringing out clear like a bell. Duma winced.

The door opened.

Looking more confused than annoyed, Lata peeped out. 'What's up?' she asked her cousin sleepily. 'What time is it? What's going on?'

In the split second that separates the before and after in our lives, their sombre faces and half-mast eyes faced hers, in the little pool of blue that the night light had cast in the corridor. Lata's words dried up and a kind of alertness prickled through her body. Her eyes became hyper-observant, things began to leap out at her: Duma's pink Nehru jacket, the mud-crusted shoes Goopy wore, the flower arrangement on the console table, the paisley pattern of the wallpaper.

Somewhere far away, a motorbike whizzed past.

'What has happened, Dada?'

Her voice was an odd combination of softness and steel.

'Munni,' Goopy said finally, 'we have to leave for Calcutta right away. Tilo has arranged for a vehicle. You must get dressed right now.'

Ronny Banerjee ended up oversleeping.

It was a glorious day outside, all windy and golden, Tilo's flowers showily performing a morning raga for the visiting dignitaries. Around eleven, Ronny, cursing himself roundly and sporting a nick from having shaved in a hurry, left the guest house in search of Lecture Theatre-201 in the New Academic Block. Across the lawns and up and down various flights of stairs – he was too impatient to wait for the elevators – he asked for directions and resolutely looked for the room, refusing to get into conversations with people who had heard him speak the day before and had questions for him.

Finally, 201.

A group of students was milling around.

'Is this where the management consulting thing is happening?'

A girl with a mass of curly hair and a large nose ring replied. 'Sorry, sir, unfortunately that session was cancelled.'

'Cancelled?! But why?'

'No idea,' Curly Hair's friend, a bald guy in a white linen suit and a yellow tie with owls on it, replied. 'We'd been looking forward to it too. Sad it was cancelled. By the way, I enjoyed your talk yesterday. I am writing a script. It's based on a mindblowing idea. I am already beta-testing the concept and looking to pitch it to a consortium of investors who are visiting our campus next month. If you don't mind, can I show it to you?'

Ronny looked at him blankly. Mumbling, 'Sure, sure, why not,' and not meaning a word of it, he walked away.

Tilo. Tilo would know what was going on.

'Ronny!' Tilo said happily, as he entered her expansive offices. 'I was just about to call you! Look who's here!'

Ronny's eyes widened in confusion as Mimi hopped towards him in a preposterous hot pink hoodie. 'Surprise!' she squealed.

Though his view was blocked by Mimi's bouncing form, behind her he could hear a gentle tinkly laughter. Rony blanched.

# 41

# Cat

'Did you clear the cat story?' Hem asked.

'What cat story?' asked Aaduri glumly.

It was afternoon. Aaduri was sprawled on the sofa in Hem's brother's house, Hem's niece and nephew, fifteen and ten, flanking her body proprietorially. They'd begun to colonise her almost as soon as they'd set sight upon her yesterday – it was entirely instinctive and, to Hem, who knew Aaduri's dislike for kids, almost fatal. But Aaduri seemed far more accepting of the arch, book-reading Naina with her perennially raised eyebrows, and the clear-eyed, phone-stealing Robin, than she had been of, say, Josh and Pixie, who, unbeknownst to Lata, she'd pronounced to be brats.

The last two days had gone by in a blur. There'd been so much catching up to do. Hem was visiting the folks in Ranchi after several years, for the first time with a lady-friend. Hem's brother and sister-in-law took leave from work to spend time with them and, much to Hem's relief, everyone had got along with everyone else. So, it was only this morning that Aaduri had learnt the grim news from Calcutta. Since then, she'd sunk into deep gloom, while the children took it upon themselves to cocoon her. Hem, equally devastated by it all, felt a little left out.

'What cat story?' Aaduri asked again, somewhat roused now, stretching her hand out for her phone. Robin instantly pulled his one-moment-please face. His sister extended her long slim arm across the leather seat, grabbed the phone wordlessly and handed it to Aaduri, before returning to her vampire book. 'Your friend Ronny got a cat with his girlfriend and your protégé Tiana did a story on it, and that story is now apparently getting thousands of hits. You haven't checked the work group?'

'What?' said Aaduri, sitting up in surprise. 'Ronny and Pragya got a cat? When? Where? I thought Ronny was in Jamshedpur and Pragya was launching some jewellery store in Calcutta. No?'

'According to Tiana's sketchy little piece, Pragya came to Jamshedpur spontaneously to raise money for a kitty shelter – and surprise Ronny on their anniversary. The whole kitty shelter thing was instigated via Instagram. Pragya rescued a little black kitten that, apparently, she and Ronny will now co-parent.'

'Hang on,' said Naina. 'You guys *know* Pippa Sen? The actress? I saw the video of the kitten she adopted. It's *adorable*. Black. And they put a red bow around her neck.'

'She's not an *actress*,' Aaduri said. 'She hasn't *acted* in anything yet. *Pippa Sen!*'

Naina explained patiently, 'But to be a social media influencer, you don't actually have to be good at anything specific. Wait, let me show you the cat post, one second.'

Aaduri looked at Hem dolefully. 'Sumona must have cleared the cat story. I think we need to get back to Calcutta before Lata does something drastic and/or Tiana steals my job. I mean, look, I am happy about the hits. But it's just so ridiculous!'

'Wait, who's *this*?' Naina said.

Aaduri looked sideways at her phone in Naina's hands. 'That's my best friend, Lata. You see, these two kids, children of our friends, had a funeral for a parakeet in Jamshedpur, which Ronny Banerjee – the filmmaker, your Pippa's love interest? – shot on my phone. I'd clean forgotten about it.'

'Bird funeral!' Robin jumped up, 'Let me see, let me see.'

Hem loomed over them and, together, all four began to watch the video of the bird funeral.

In Tilo's garden, with its symmetrical rose beds, the last dregs of sunlight cast a haunting sort of light upon the little grave. Lata kneeled at its edge, holding the box in which Max's lifeless body lay in state. On one side of her, Josh – Optimus Prime perched on his shoulder – shed silent tears. On her other side, Scone mewled gently in Pixie's lap. Ronny Banerjee, wielding the phone-camera, clearly knew his job.

'Dear Max,' said Lata, simply, affectionately, her right arm around Josh and her voice free of artifice. 'Today is not a day that we mourn you. No. Today is a day we celebrate your brief but beautiful life.' Josh nodded. Lata continued, 'Even before you were known, Max, you were dearly missed. How many of us have had that privilege? Optimus Prime pined for you night and day, losing her feathers, suffering the pain of your absence, until you arrived one fine day, in a flash of green.' Josh smiled wanly. Lata continued, as Josh and Pixie leaned in towards her, 'Dear Max, know that this is but a brief parting. According to the laws of karma, those who are loved are never lost in death. There are only interim separations. Now that you are free, we hope you will find the choicest fruits and nuts to nibble upon, as you wait for us on the other side or return to us in other forms.'

Josh gave a little sob. Ronny's hand wobbled a bit. Pixie took a few steps forward, a black shawl draped around her shoulders in a cloak-like fashion, and lowered Max's bier ceremonially into the grave. Scone barked. Josh threw fistfuls of earth. After a last lingering shot of Lata's face, the camera artfully followed Optimus Prime as he flapped his wings and circled over Max's grave.

It was barely two minutes long, unedited footage, but Aaduri, no great lover of animals or kids by the way, found herself tearing up.

'Now *that*, Chachu,' said Naina, burying her nose into Hem's arm, 'is the sort of stuff that breaks the internet. Why can't you share *that* video on your website? My friends will go crazy about it. Everyone will go crazy about it. All you have to say is, "This Bird Funeral Video Will Make You Cry".'

'No, no,' Robin interjected. 'You should say, "If This Bird Funeral Video Doesn't Make You Cry, You Are a Psychopath." *That* should be the headline.'

'I should hire you two!' Aaduri laughed.

'How much will you pay?' Robin asked seriously.

❧

'It's Alzheimer's. Isn't it?' Manjulika Ghosh said to her daughter. 'Don't sugar-coat it, Munni.'

'Ma,' said Lata tiredly, 'let's not jump the gun.'

She tucked Manjulika in – mother and daughter were both grateful to be out of the hospital with its sterile pink walls and back in Manjulika's bedroom – and then Lata sat down next to her, holding her hand. Manjulika was feeling like herself now, she was bickering with Nimki about the salt in the dal and cracking jokes with Duma. And so, Lata found it almost impossible to wrap her head around the events of that night, even though Manjulika had reconstructed it so perfectly for the neurologist.

At nine-thirty she left the book club meeting, as usual, her head buzzing with ideas that she wanted to discuss with Munni, once Munni returned. After five minutes, she felt a little cold and paused to take her cardigan out from her bag and put it on. After that, when she looked up, she just couldn't make sense of where she was. The shops had shut down and the road was emptier than usual. And just like that, it was as though the coordinates had completely vanished from her head. She couldn't figure out the way home. She *knew* she had to go home. But she just couldn't remember where home was or where she stood in relation to it. But oddly, she knew the place was known to her, she recognised the signs and the trees. The harder she tried to find her way, the more lost she seemed to get. No, she clarified to all the doctors who interviewed her, nothing like this had ever happened before. Yes, she often forgot where her phone and her charger were, and several times she had found herself teaching the wrong class in school. But she had never lost herself on a familiar route before this. It was the first time.

In the wee hours of the morning, Lata, Duma and Kaku had found her sitting on a bench by the Ganga, very cold, but perfectly composed. 'Now that you've found me, we may as well see the sunrise,' had been her first words. Goopy and Boro Jethu were at the police station, AJ's father and uncle were trawling hospital wards. The rickshaw-pullers who slept in the courtyard had fanned out across the north, alerting their network and sharing a photo of Manjulika on WhatsApp.

Afterwards, a whole battery of tests were conducted and Dr Basu, the head of neurology and Boro Jethi's cousin, had insisted on keeping her overnight, under observation.

'I know the early symptoms of Alzheimer's, Munni,' said Manjulika stoically. 'The sense of spatial geography is the first thing to go.'

'Just because you discussed *Still Alice* in your stupid book club doesn't mean you know everything,' snapped Lata.

'Ah, don't be mad,' Manjulika mollified her daughter.

'I'm not mad at all, Ma,' Lata replied, stroking her mother's hand, immediately softened by guilt.

'Was Ronny there in Jamshedpur?' Manjulika asked.

'Yes, he gave a good speech,' Lata said shortly. 'Then he got a cat with Pragya. The cat is now the subject of internet discussions.'

'Munni,' Manjulika said urgently, abandoning the subject of Ronny and the cat. (Cat?!) 'I have to tell you *everything* important before I forget. But you are so busy, when will we talk?'

'Will you stop with the doomsday talk already! It's probably stress or something. Really. Dr Basu has told me we need to wait for the results.'

'And Munni,' Manjulika said, as though she hadn't heard a word Lata said, 'will you take me to London with you when you go back? I want to do all the things I always said were too expensive or too silly or too dramatic…'

'You mean you will finally watch *The Mousetrap* at West End? Shop for tea at Fortnum's? Eat caviar on blinis for breakfast?'

'Also, champagne tea at the Ritz,' Manjulika finished.

'Don't think you are going to London without me,' commented Nimki, entering the room with Manjulika's dinner tray. 'I have Aadhar now, I will get a passport also. Why are you crying, Mamoni? Ma Kali is watching over us. Don't cry, come now, wipe your eyes.'

# 42

# Going Bacterial

The bird funeral video was posted on Aaduri's website on Tuesday morning. It was a quiet, plain Jane, bhaat-daal-alubhaja type of day, the sort of Tuesday when you decide you will clear out your desk at work because things are so dull. No major politician or minor celebrity had said anything trend-worthy and no wardrobe malfunction or sexist comment had stirred the opinionated into social media frenzy. Impossible though it might sound, it appeared as though the internet had paused to catch its breath, stretch its arms and do a spot of shavasana, while it languidly awaited the next flap of the proverbial butterfly wings to instigate a new round of churning in its imperium. Only, in this case, it was not a butterfly but a parakeet, and besides, the parakeet was dead.

At half past eleven, @SimplyAaduri sent out a tweet tagging filmmaker @RonnyBanerjee, who had 3,00,000 followers on Twitter, sharing the #ARequiemForMax video, immediately after which their website's handle – managed by Tiana – reposted the video with a whole range of relevant hashtags. A few minutes later, Bobby Bansal – whom Aaduri had sounded out – also reposted the video from Ronny's handle (which she was now managing since Ronny, highly disgruntled by the cat story that, he said, was riddled with errors, had gone offline and was unavailable for comment), with just the words: 'A Requiem for Max.' Fortuitously, that very minute, somewhere in Mumbai, filmmaker Imran Ali, current enfant terrible of Bollywood and childhood resident of Jamshedpur, who had been on jury duty with Ronny in Sharjah and was a fan of Ronny's Twitter TL in particular, picked up his phone to tweet. The first thing he saw was Ronny's requiem and, having seen it thrice to analyse the deft composition, he tweeted it out with the caption, 'the dark and the light come together in a beloved pet's funeral #requiemformax #jamshedpur #throwbacktomychildhood'.

At twelve-forty-five, when Aaduri returned to her desk from a meeting with Sir, she found Tiana wriggling agitatedly on her purple rug. 'Guess what guess what guess what!' Tiana shrieked. Aaduri refused to indulge her and calmly picked up her purse. 'I have to go out for a bit, Tiana. So if there's something you have to tell me...'

'It's going really and truly bacterial,' Tiana exclaimed.

Aaduri flinched – she hated this 'bacterial' usage which their entire office had adopted. 'Malini Bhutt shared it!

*Malini Bhutt!* Any minute now, YouTube will place it in their #trending section. Pinky Kapoor-Kumar has posted it on Instagram with the caption 'How to Talk to Children about Death'. So, naturally, *all* the mommy-blogger types who follow her are going nuts about it. Ronny's fans are circulating it also, of course, so Tollywood is buzzing. That I knew anyway. But it's possibly going pan-Indian. Which is BIG. And, you know, everyone is wild about your friend, Lata. People are going crazy asking, *Who's that woman? Who's that woman? Is she someone? Is she a star?* Should I, like, tag her or something? Is she on Twitter? She must at least be on Facebook?'

'No, no, don't do anything of the sort, Tiana. She's going through a very difficult time personally.' A shadow crossed Tiana's face. Aaduri continued, 'She gave me permission to share the video *only* if we kept her out of the loop. Of course, she hadn't the foggiest that it might go viral.' Aaduri allowed herself a smile. 'She's not a very plugged in person. She's a reader of books. You should see her house in London: it's like a library, stashed to the brim with books. You remember the time Dhanush's song went viral? I'd called her and she was complaining about something and I said, *Why this Kolaveri, di?* She stayed silent for a full minute and said, "What the hell are you saying, Aadu, have you gone mad?" She didn't get the reference at all. Her mother, on the other hand, is super plugged in.' Aaduri smiled as she thought of Manjulika's Instagram account, where she posted pictures of typical North Calcutta buildings every day, and Manjulika's Facebook messages, frequent and long, that were all written in Bengali, with proper salutations and sign-offs.

In a small voice, Tiana asked, 'Why did you say she's going through a difficult time?'

Aaduri gave her a hard look. 'Family stuff,' she said finally. 'I am actually going to meet her for a bit. You can hold fort?'

'Yes,' Tiana said. 'Of course. Legally, we are all clear, right? Now that it's going everywhere...'

'Oh yes, the video was shot using my phone camera, the people whose garden it is, the parents of the kids, they all agreed to it being shared on the website. And Ronny is missing, but his assistant cleared it. Not that I expect him to care. He's quite generous with his art, that way. Like Dayanita Singh. You know, the photographer? She will take a picture of you on *your* phone if you ask. I was totally bowled over by that. Anyway, I have to run. Tiana, I don't know why I am talking so much, must be the stress. I shall forward the consent emails to you in case Legal asks for them. But, basically, it was shot on my equipment – so we needn't worry.'

'Okay, great,' said Tiana. She waited around uncertainly for a few more seconds as though she wanted to say something. But since Aaduri – who had a faint idea what it might be about – did not offer any helpful prompts, she melted away.

Half an hour later when Aaduri walked into Flurys, Lata was already seated in the far corner, sipping a cup of tea. They'd left home together this morning – Aaduri had gone straight to Ghosh Mansion from the airport upon her return from Ranchi and had stayed over for a couple of days to be with Manjulika, who was astonishingly cheerful, and Lata, who was crying in the bathroom every couple of hours and not able to sleep at night. Aaduri had gone to the office, to publish the video, while Lata had trekked down to the hospital for a detailed discussion with the neurologist. They'd decided to meet for lunch.

'And?' Aaduri raised her eyebrows, walking up to Lata who was looking out of the window, at the magazine-seller outside.

'I ordered us lunch,' Lata said, motioning to the waiter for another cup. The dark circles beneath her eyes were now baggy. 'The usual, Tuna Melt.'

Aaduri pulled out a chair, divested herself of her bags and shawl, and settled in.

'Did the test results come in?' she probed, even though she knew that had the news been good, Lata would have got straight to that.

'They did,' Lata replied, pouring out tea for Aaduri in the tiny spare cup the waiter brought them. 'There is definite degeneration in the parietal lobes. Though there are apparently different ways to interpret that.'

Aaduri sighed. Lata continued, 'I have spoken to my boss. I mean, I haven't given him the full picture, but I am going to need a more flexible schedule. Nimki's passport should come in soon. Then, of course, there's that long wait for the visa. But as soon as the paperwork is done, I want them to come to London. Someone I know – one of Ari's friends actually – is a consultant at Maudsley Hospital in

South London. I've spoken to him already. He is going to do a thorough examination once Ma gets there. Not that I doubt Dr Basu's assessment, and he is not jumping the gun or anything. He is not even ready to use the A-word yet.'

'Hmm,' Aaduri nodded. Dr Basu, Boro Jethi's cousin and Aaduri's father's bridge friend at the club, was a great doctor, if a little cut-and-dried.

'But what I am going to do over the next few days is speak to everyone close to her, her book club friends, the other teachers at school, and Nimki and my aunts and uncles, and try and capture details about her lapses so the doctors can have a fuller picture. Reconstruct the past few months. Did *you* notice anything, Aadu?'

'Well,' said Aaduri thoughtfully. 'You know how she sends these letter-type missives to me on Facebook Messenger, since you refuse to download it. Sometimes she'd send me the same thing three or four times: *Aaduri watch this play. Oh, Aadu, there's this play in Academy of Fine Arts on Sunday. Oh, Aaduri, there is this play that I think you might like.* I did note it, in passing. But then, you know how *my* mother says the same thing a hundred times. Wash your hair, wash your hair, wash your hair, until I do it. Mothers repeat things. But naturally there *was* something off. It was almost as though she was sending each message as the first. Should I have told you?'

'Aadu, I stayed with her for a whole month and realised nothing. She forgot where she kept the locker keys after the wedding and I thought it was perfectly normal. She always forgets to charge her phone. But I forget these things all the time too! Anyway, I have to assemble all this data before I go.'

'Sounds like a wise plan,' Aaduri said. 'And I am sure there are effective new drugs? Clinical trials you might be able to get her on?'

'Goopy is going on and on about clinical trials. He and Duma are being very American about this. *We can find a way. We shall sort this out.*'

Their Tuna Melts arrived.

'So, if you go now to set all this up, do you want me to accompany Mashi and Nimki to London later? Because it wouldn't be right for them to go on their own.'

'That's what I thought, Aadu,' Lata said, looking relieved. 'Do you think you can get away for a few days?'

'I was going to ask you myself, Lata Ghosh. You think I haven't heard about the champagne tea plans at the Ritz?!'

The girls – though, of course, the passersby who saw them through the window or the waiters who brought them their glasses of water or the people who brushed past their chairs saw them as women, not girls, mature women who were in charge of things – the girls smiled sadly at each other.

'I think we should tell Ronny,' Aaduri said. 'He loves Manjulika Ghosh, Luts.'

'Aadu,' Lata said softly. 'We are *never* going to have this conversation again.'

# PART SIX

# 43

# Mrinalini

Three months later. London in April. The spirit of spring in the air.

Tourists, who were arriving in droves from all parts of the world and cluttering up the tube stations with their eager laughter and bald enthusiasm, and altogether getting on the nerves of the regular commuters with their overcaffeinated frenzy, were still muffled up. But Londoners themselves had begun to strip down. Spring colours – pinks and peaches and robin-breast blues and the return of cyan this season – were out in full force and hemlines were dramatically rising, now that the sun was out till half-eight in the evenings. The flower-sellers had crowded their window displays with bluebells and crocuses and daffodils and tulips and 'Spring! Spring!' they all seemed to be crying out from every corner, much like the teenagers holding hands in the streets and the mothers pushing their pink-cheeked babies in strollers in the parks.

Spring was here.

Unseeing of all this excessive beauty and jollity, Lata Ghosh hurried out of the cab – the cabbie had, in fact, jumped down and run across to open her door, something London cabbies never did, by the way, though by then she was halfway to the church already. It was twenty minutes past eight in the morning, and Lata was in a rush. She clattered down the stone stairs to the basement, the Jimmy Choos pounding on the stone, until she came to that spot by the vestry where – like every other time – she paused to catch her breath. Her heart dropped.

The same ice-cold sensation every time.

Lata took a deep breath and barrelled past the piles of new hymn books that still smelt of drying ink, and the old tables cluttered with things people had donated for a sale. She reached the back parlour. It was a cosy space. Buttery walls, mismatched chairs, a table laden with tea things and a thermos of coffee, chocolate biscuits set out on chipped plates, wildflowers in large jars. Lata had met Lauren, the South Korean lady who led the programme, at an outreach session at Maudsley, and Lauren had convinced her to come to the support group. And soon after, Lauren had met Manjulika too, pointing out to Lata that Manjulika's reaction to her disease, her plan to do all the things on her bucket list, was quite exceptional. Denial and depression were the more regular responses. And so, a couple of weeks ago, Lauren had invited Manjulika to come in and speak to everyone. The caregivers, the volunteers and many doctors attended. A few patients too. In her summery Kota sari and a string of pearls, with a single white rose in her hair, Manjulika Ghosh had been a hit.

Now, pausing by the door, Lata quickly scanned the group. Lauren stood at the head of the group. She was tiny, with jet black hair running down to her waist. While her bright cerise skirt and her many jingly bracelets gave her a young and airy vibe, she was, in fact, deceptively firm. Lata quietly made her way to one of the empty chairs and discreetly waved to her.

'Hey, Lata,' Lauren called out.

'Hey, Lata,' everyone else chorused.

There were about eight members gathered this morning – on some days there were only two or three, and once Lata had counted twenty-one heads – and these were all people who had dear ones suffering from Alzheimer's. Today, only one grey-haired lady at the back looked familiar to Lata. But there was nothing surprising about that. People had difficult schedules and what with their caregiving responsibilities, they tried to drop in as and when they could. This was an open group, and anyone could come in. Lauren was here at eight, five days a week. A middle-aged lady in hijab, whom Lata had never seen before, was wiping her eyes and a young man, presumably her son, was patting her shoulder gently. Lauren pointed to Lata, gesturing to her to speak up.

'Hi,' Lata began shyly. 'I am Lata. My mother was diagnosed with Alzheimer's three months ago and I am one of her chief caregivers. We spent the last few months doing all the things she had ever wanted to do with me but had always thought too expensive or too frivolous or too unhealthy. It's as though we gave ourselves a holiday to escape from the diagnosis which we knew was coming. But there *is* no escape, and now we both realise that we have to eventually go home, to the place Ma is most familiar with, our city Calcutta, for her to grow old in. She's always lived in Calcutta. But I haven't lived there in fifteen years. We don't have to go immediately. But by the end of the year. And that means I have no option but to face all my own...' Lata's voice became shaky.

'Fears?' The man sitting next to her prompted quietly.

'Exactly,' Lata said. 'Thank you. My own *fears*. You know, I might be thirty-nine but, in my head, I still think – thought – of myself as a young person, the one with the rights. The right to fly high and discover strange things and go live in Lagos for a year if I wanted to and...'

And then she said the words that were the hardest for her to utter aloud, but here, in the anonymity of this group, she found she could: 'And think about myself. Love. Children. Holidays. Beautiful things. And yet, now I cannot be that person any longer, the uncertain person still looking for things that might please her, *save* her. *I* must be the one in charge. Not just that, I must be *stoic* about it. But it's so hard. I keep thinking, *why me, why me, why me.*'

Everyone nodded. Everyone assembled in that room – much like everyone else walking the streets outside and everyone walking all the streets of all the world – had felt that precise thing at some point. In the case of those assembled in the room, they'd felt the banging sensation of the *why me why me why me* maybe earlier that same day.

'I can't sleep at night for more than forty minutes at a time, and during the day I can't sleep at all! I haven't had a full night's sleep since the diagnosis. I am always exhausted, always groggy. But my GP doesn't want to prescribe sleeping pills. She wants me to *meditate*.' Lata's voice took a high mocking tone. 'And that just makes me angrier!'

Once again, everyone nodded. Their assent worked like

an instant stressbuster. Feeling lighter, Lata said thank you and sat down.

After everyone had spoken and the meeting was formally adjourned, people milled around drinking coffee and chatting with each other. Lauren herself was busily inspecting the new posters that had been designed by one of the members who was a graphic designer. The man who had sat next to her, a South Asian, introduced himself. 'Lata, I am Pankaj,' he said. 'I admire your honesty.'

Lata smiled. 'Hi Pankaj,' she said, shaking his hand.

'All this while I kept thinking you look really familiar.'

'I get that a lot,' Lata said, trying to brush the words away.

'Weren't you in that bird funeral video? The one that went viral? A requiem for Max?'

'Ah, yes,' Lata said, deciding not to lie to someone at the support group meeting – after all, everyone operated on trust here. 'Guilty as charged.'

'It was very charming, very wise, there was something about it that spoke to everyone who saw it,' Pankaj smiled. 'My father had just been diagnosed and I was very depressed. A friend sent it to me, and I remember I was quite moved. Who were those kids?'

'Oh, the children of friends. Though now, to be honest, the kids are more my friends than the parents. Is that odd? The little girl, Pixie, she writes me the funniest, most hilarious emails, almost every day.'

'How nice,' said Pankaj. 'I have a nephew who emails me. Though his emails are very brief: *Can you please send me the new Nintendo? Thanks.* Do you come here often?'

'Oh, maybe two or three times a week. On my way to work.'

'Whereabouts is work?'

'Canary Wharf,' Lata replied, now looking to catch Lauren's eye. She'd have a quick word – Lauren had wanted Lata's help in raising funds for a new chapter of the support group – but Lauren was deep in conversation with the lady in hijab.

'You don't say! I am over at One Churchill Place.'

It meant he worked at Barclays.

'And where are you?'

'Bank Street,' Lata said vaguely. 'How's your dad now?'

'Well, he is in the Cotswolds. With my sister and her family. I was wondering, Lata, may we get lunch sometime? Outside of this? There's this wonderful new restaurant that's opened just next to my office. Unless there's some place you'd prefer.'

Pankaj was nice-looking enough – wavy hair, clean brown eyes, a good physique, expensive Italian brogues.

Lata sighed.

'I am so sorry, but there are rules about these things, Pankaj,' she said evasively. 'It's not done apparently. *This* is where we must meet. Sorry!'

'Ah, no problem,' nodded Pankaj. 'It was nice to meet you, Lata. And I am sure we'll run into each other again.'

'See you,' Lata said, and deciding on the spot that the chat with Lauren would have to wait, she waved goodbye to Pankaj, and without waiting to chat more – 'Shall we split a cab to CW?' – she climbed up the stone staircase and stepped out into the sun. Roddy, her boss, had called a meeting at eleven, and in the tube she needed to quickly scan through some stuff and come up with a token idea or two. Walking briskly towards the station, she squinted at her To Do list on the phone. Oh, right. She'd have to stop at a cashpoint and withdraw some money. Their colleague Louise had just had a baby – at 42! – and they were collecting money for a gift. At one point, the task of buying a little dress or a silver charm bracelet would have fallen to her, everyone knew how she picked the most perfect presents, but now her colleagues were treating her with kid gloves. No extra responsibilities, no gossip by the coffee machine, no forwarded jokes. Sometimes Lata hoped they'd just treat her normally so she could forget that she no longer belonged in her old life.

'Watch where you're going, lady!' a young man shouted, as he swerved his bicycle away from her. Lata had absent-mindedly drifted into the wrong lane and, it appeared, not heard the cyclist's bell. 'That phone will kill you, you know,' the cyclist called back.

Lata put away her phone guiltily.

It was going to be a lovely day, the sun was out, and all Lata could think about was whether the new medicine would work.

The light wore the soft, used-up quality that made early evening in summer so luminous, when Lata stepped out of the office a little earlier than she had planned to. She'd promised herself she'd catch up on work tonight, after dinner, instead of slipping under the covers and reading a mindless magazine. The good weather had lasted through the day, and now, waving to a group of colleagues who were going to the pub, Lata remembered her To Do list again. She thought of the cyclist from the morning and stood under the awning of the next building – the security guard doffed his cap at her. She would need to visit the shops to get the things she had been ordered to bring.

First, the Bengalideshi store for the rice and dal and panchphoron. Then, Marks and Spencer's, where she dithered for a while by the aisle and finally allowed herself a pack of mint chocolate digestives – her absolute favourite kind – even though she was on a diet. Then she called a cab. While in the cab, she replied to Pixie's email.

Just as she was alighting, a light rain began to fall. Children squealed and dogs romped and mothers tried to herd them all back in. Lata smiled at a neighbour and patted a succession of blonde heads that could have been child or dog.

Outside the house, shielding herself from the rain with upturned palms, she rang the bell twice – what a joy it was to have someone open the door for her, to not have to let herself into a cold and empty house – but it was a while before the door opened.

'Hello,' said the man who opened the door, in a bright voice.

Lata took one look at his face – that intimately known face – and felt her blood rise thunderously to her brain. Her cheeks were aflame. *How dare he?*

She pushed past him, drops of rain clinging to her light pink cardigan like little shards of glass, and carried her bags down the hall to enter the parlour to the right. 'Where's Ma?' she asked, crossly.

'Upstairs. I got them some of the latest Bengali films on a hard drive,' Ronny replied, closing the door and following her into the hall.

'Oh please, our Bengali film needs are well met by the OTTs.'

'Shondesh needs?'

'Don't be facetious. In any case, what are *you* doing here? Isn't it cruel to have left that cute cat of yours behind in Calcutta? What sort of a co-parent are you?'

Lata crash-banged her way into the kitchen and poured herself a glass of water. A large amount slopped onto the counter. She looked for towels to soak it up and found none. When she returned, she found Ronny sitting calmly on her favourite sofa.

'I never agreed to *co*-parent that cat. You should take this matter up with Aaduri. What can I do if her website maintains no journalistic standards whatsoever?'

'Please. Her website got the whole world and their cousin interested in you. It even got your runaway producer back!' Lata said stoutly in Aaduri's defence. 'That damn bird funeral video. Not all of us want to be in the limelight, Ronny. I can't go to an Alzheimer's caregiver support group without someone bringing it up!'

At the A-word, both paused.

'You should have told me,' Ronny said.

'Why? So you could swoop back into my life to save me? With your legendary reliability and your excessive fame, leaving your cat and co-parent behind?' Lata flopped down on the sofa, not exactly next to him.

'Oh God, will you stop with that! You know Pragya and I parted ways almost immediately after our return from Jamshedpur. She "read" the truth in our bird funeral video, Charu, which, strangely enough, Tiana forwarded to her the day it was published. She saw it forty-one times apparently – according to Mimi – and claimed the way I had captured your face on camera said everything about my feelings for you. And look, even though Nikhil *was* interested, I told him I needed a real break to rework the script from scratch, I certainly couldn't shoot it in time for a Pujo release. I told him I needed to spend some months in England to research J.C. Bose's Cambridge days. Bobby, as you know, is a genius in these matters. She managed the negotiations single-handedly. Pragya will now debut in an out-and-out commercial film for Nikhil's company. She *may* act in *Shomoy*, that will all depend, but since it's no longer her debut, Shaarani Sen may make her comeback as Abala Bose. Manjulika is thrilled about this bit, by the way. All this wrangling took a while. You refused to answer my emails or calls. I tried to call you from so many random numbers – but you don't ever pick up your phone!'

'Terribly sorry, Ronny, but I was trying to process my mother's situation and hold down a job I don't love but don't hate either, which I may soon have to quit.'

'I know, I know,' Ronny said soothingly. 'After I sorted through all the paperwork, I found a fellowship to pay for my flight – Duma helped, actually, don't tell him I told you that – and found a home for the cat and decided to take you up on your offer.'

'What offer?' Lata said, stretching her legs out and turning her back on Ronny, sort of.

'You said you'd like to take in an impoverished artist-stray? Didn't you have some elaborate point about charity to prove?'

Lata looked fractious.

'I *could* let you stay on as a charity case, I suppose,' she said eventually.

'And in lieu of your generosity I would like to take over some responsibilities. I shall gladly escort Manjulika Ghosh to West End, the Ritz, her doctor's appointments, swimming lessons, the park, Buckingham Palace, wherever. I can do the grocery, too. Run other errands. Dry clean your clothes. Carry your lunch to office in a dabba.'

Her legs now stretched out on the sofa, Lata closed her eyes and took a deep breath. She felt his soft, fragrant breath upon her forehead. His smell was citrussy, like an old-fashioned aftershave, and smoky, like home. As a single tear errantly rolled down the side of her cheek, past her earlobe, she felt him gently wipe it away.

'Where's the cat?' she asked him afterwards, not opening her eyes but turning on her side, so that his hand became her pillow.

'Pragya decided she didn't want to even look at her after we parted ways. So she's with my parents, in Calcutta,' Ronny replied. 'They've named her Mrinalini. But her daak naam is Mini.'

'Mini,' said Lata, trying out the name like one tests the flavour of a new kind of chocolate. 'Mini the cat. Do you think Mini will like me?' she asked.

'More than anyone else in the word,' he replied.

Later, when Nimki came down to ask if Ronny was hungry, she found them fast asleep on the sofa, curled up against each other. She crept soundlessly back upstairs.

# Acknowledgements

Having been a great admirer of serialised fiction, both in Bengali and in English, it was an honour for me to attempt one of my own in the pages of *The Telegraph*, a newspaper I grew up reading. And for this I must thank the entire *Telegraph* family – those who publish the daily and those who read it, for letting such an experiment flourish for over a year, that too in the age of ever-shrinking print space.

Particular gratitude is due to Sumit Das Gupta, editor extraordinaire, the one who first envisioned a serial novel in English for the pages of t2; Samhita Chakraborty, who, undeterred by my many idiosyncratic tendencies, urged me to try my hand at turning my little chapter about a certain Charulata Ghosh into a novel, and who then, at some point, crossed over onto its pages; Reshmi Sengupta, the editor who truly shepherded *The Romantics of College Street* – often, with wonderful suggestions for plot points – and Smita Roy Chowdhury, the editor who saw it into its golden sunset. Suman Choudhury illustrated each chapter with such heart that, even now, when I think of the characters, I see them as he did. And, finally, no words will ever be enough for Abhijit Mitra, who handled the *Romantics* for 42 weeks and bore with fortitude the brunt of my chronic struggle with deadlines. He offered sage advice not just to the large and often wavering cast of characters but also to me and, most vitally, never balked when I repeatedly failed to tell him how many more weeks Lata Ghosh was planning to stay on in Calcutta.

Every Sunday brought me letters and suggestions from readers, and that added to the fun of the project. I want to especially thank Gaurav Das for providing Ronny's Lucknow question in Flurys.

If there's one thing every writer secretly wants, it is to be taught in a classroom. Thank you, Aditi Sriram, for assigning *The Romantics* to the (frankly brilliant) students in your 'Craft of Writing' class at Ashoka University, while it was being serialised. No one has ever paid me a better compliment. It even made me write the remaining chapters more responsibly. Hat tip to my former students at Ashoka who patiently, lovingly, only a little exasperatedly, explained to me what memes were, and then gave me honest feedback upon my amateur attempts. No points for guessing that like Ronny Banerjee, my memes had barely a level-and-a-half to them. Yes, I'm looking at you, children of woke: Teesta Rawal, Pratiti, Surabhi Sanghi, Anant Shah and Amlan Bibhudatta. Also, many *many* thanks are due to Himadri Agarwal for deep research on the Marwari/not-Marwari conundrum of the Jaiswal–Ghosh wedding – she called up relatives in the middle of the night, people, and thus ensured I did not get lynched.

I am grateful to the entire team at Westland, not only for making the book feel at home, but also the writer. I got so lucky when V.K. Karthika decided to adopt me all those years ago, and I am lucky that she continues to lavish her signature love on my books. One day I shall write a book worthy of her. (And I promise, by then I shall also stick to the deadlines I agree to.) Thank you, Priya Kuriyan for the gorgeous covers (for being my friend and partner-in-crime and favourite artist). Thank you, Vishwajyoti Ghosh for always indulging my (very irrelevant) inputs on matters of design. Thank you, Shrutika Mathur for reading the many drafts so carefully and for indulging all my last-minute change requests.

For providing a haven to my scattered selves, much loving gratitude is due to my own circle of women: my friend from school, Sharmishtha Mukherjee; my friend from college, Esha Sil; my friend from university, Amanthi Perera; my friend from millennialia, Gurmehar Kaur; my friend from Write and Beyond, Kiranjeet Chaturvedi; my friend from the vague women's club we co-founded, Gitanjali Chatterjee; my friend from the subcontinent, Aneela Babar; my friend from Flurys sessions, Neelini Sarkar; my friend from another life, Rupa Thapa.

This is also the moment to formally acknowledge the manifold contributions of my fortuitously un-vague and highly brilliant research assistant, Payal Nagpal, who helped me keep my sanity while the book was being serialised, managed the Facebook page on my behalf, and, most incredibly, transcribed an entire chapter which she recorded while I read it out to her on a terrible phone connection from a remote mountain outpost in Arunachal Pradesh with no internet. Ms Nagpal, in many ways, saved the book.

And while speaking of saving stuff, my friend, the writer and surgeon Ambarish Satwik, not only saves people

I love – he really saves them – but also offers pro bono consultancy to my fictional characters. When Manjulika Ghosh displayed symptoms of Alzheimer's, Ambarish recommended I speak to specialists, the fabulous Drs Rajeev Ranjan and Ritu Verma, and they helped me understand the ways in which the disease works and the way to live with it.

My favourite filmmaker Srijit Mukherji, despite his hectic schedule, found time to mentor his fan Ronny Banerjee and advised him on fixing the script of *Shomoy* – though, naturally, like all mentees worth their salt, Ronny ended up doing his own thing. Also, many thanks are due to my friend Sambit Dattachaudhuri, who not only lent his name to 'Sir', but also provided a lot of cinematic references for Boro Jethu's benefit.

Some real-life inspirations: Madhabi Haldar is very Nimki-ish. The parakeets, Optimus Prime and Max, were borrowed from my nephew Saksham Jha (don't worry though, the real-life Max did not die but simply flew away), and some of Pixie's style and sass were borrowed from my niece, his sister Meenakshi. It is because I miss them so much that the action moved to Jamshedpur at all. Meanwhile, I shall tensely await my older niece Priyanka Mukherjee's feedback (her first love, these days, is Anuja Chauhan.)

The chief reason to thank Nilanjan and Manidipa Roy, Sukumar Jha and Susnato Roy – other than all their selfless love and sacrifices and stuff – is that they read the serialised novel in *The Telegraph* every Sunday morning, along with all the nine million people they discuss things with on the phone, but they never brought up plot-issues with me.

The rest of the family and all my friends followed suit, though one person – who shall remain unnamed – demanded a puppy for Pixie and then extracted it.

Indrayudh Banerjee, Arunava Sinha, Manaspratim Mitra, Abhishek Chatterjee, Chandrashekhar Bhattacharyya, Amit Upadhyaya and Rishi Pratim Mukherjee must be thanked for being the invisible but steadfast piri-lifters in my life. There is no way I'd have finished this book without Decode, Vasant Vihar. Jeevan Singh Aujla, Aniket Singh and Priya Rana are the heroes of my life; their affection and guidance made this terrible student of fitness a (marginally) fitter – and therefore (marginally) less-prone-to-meltdowns – person. Thank you. I am coming back tomorrow, no excuses.

All my love and then some for Nayantara Chatterjee, whose quiet kindness inspires me daily, and the Charulata-esque Priya Basu, who, in addition to answering endless London questions, re-affirmed my belief in happily ever-afters.

The final thank you is due to Presidency College, Calcutta, for giving me Saurav Jha, the reason I still write love stories.